I0784759

Banner of Death

Cynthia Hickey

The Sheriff of Misty Hollow, Book 5

ISBN-13:9781968792206

To Stormi: The girl who gave me the idea of the red blanket.

Prologue

His knees pressed to his chest as he curled into the corner of the closet. The red blanket smelled like warm laundry and crayons. It muffled the screaming outside—the slamming doors, the shattering glass, his mother crying, his father shouting. He rocked, rubbing the frayed edge of the fabric against his cheek, whispering the numbers he knows. One, two, three, four…

The blanket had been his grandmother's gift last Christmas, soft wool dyed the color of winter berries. She'd wrapped him in it that snowy morning, her papery hands smoothing it around his small shoulders as she whispered, "This will keep you safe, little one. When the world gets scary, you wrap yourself up tight." He'd carried it everywhere since—to the breakfast table, to the couch for Saturday cartoons, to bed each night, where it transformed his mattress into a ship sailing through dreams.

Now it's his fortress, his sanctuary in the narrow space between winter coats and his mother's old dresses. The closet smelled of mothballs and forgotten perfume, but the blanket carried better scents, fabric softener, and the waxy smell of his coloring box, where he'd accidentally left a red crayon that melted slightly in the summer heat. The color had stained one corner, but he'd grown to love that imperfection, tracing the waxy patch with his finger when sleep wouldn't come.

Five, six, seven, eight…

The numbers were his lifeline, each digit a stepping stone across the chaos beyond the closet door. His teacher, Mrs. Patterson, taught him to count when he felt overwhelmed. "Numbers don't lie, young man," she'd said with her kind smile. "They don't shout or break things. They just are." So, he counted, his breath dampening the wool as he pulled it tighter around his face.

The fighting started after dinner, as it always did when his father came home with that particular heaviness in his step, that sour smell clinging to his clothes. The boy had been coloring at the kitchen table, a picture of a house with smoke curling from the chimney, a yellow sun, a family of stick figures holding hands in the yard. His mother had been washing dishes, humming softly under her breath, the way she did when she was trying to make everything feel normal.

Then the front door slammed. His father's voice, thick and slurred: "What's this mess? Can't keep a simple house clean?" The crash of the coloring box hitting the floor, crayons scattering like broken promises across the linoleum. His mother's quiet voice, trying to soothe: "Danny, please. Our son is right here."

But he wasn't there anymore. At the first raised voice, he'd grabbed his blanket and run, muscle memory guiding him to this sanctuary he'd discovered months ago. Here, wrapped in red wool, he could disappear. Here, the world shrank to the size of his small body and the rhythm of his counting.

Nine, ten, eleven, twelve…

Through the thin closet door, he hears his mother's sobs, high and desperate. Then the sound of something heavy hitting the wall, maybe the ceramic vase his grandmother had given them, the one painted with tiny blue flowers. His mother loved that vase, kept it on the kitchen windowsill, filled with dandelions Tommy picked for her. Now it's probably in pieces, joining the landscape of broken things that litter their home after these nights.

His father's voice boomed again, words too slurred and angry to understand, but the venom in them reached the boy's ears even there. He pressed his face deeper into the blanket's softness, counting faster now, the numbers tumbling over each other in his whispered litany. Twenty-one, twenty-two, twenty-three…

The blanket remembered better times. It remembered Saturday mornings when his mother would make pancakes and they'd eat them together on the couch, Tommy wrapped in its warmth while cartoons played on the television. It remembered the afternoon his mother read him stories, her voice gentle and musical as she turned pages of picture books about brave knights and gentle dragons. It remembered the night he had a fever, and she sat beside his bed all night, stroking his hair and humming lullabies while the blanket kept him warm.

A thud. Footsteps. Heavy, uneven, getting closer.

The boy's counting falters. His small hands clutched

the blanket tighter, knuckles white with desperation. The footsteps stopped outside the closet door. He held his breath, making himself as small as possible in the corner, willing himself to disappear entirely into the red wool.

The door ripped open, light stabbing the darkness. His father's silhouette filled the doorway, eyes wild, belt in one hand, beer in the other.

"Get out of there, you little freak! Why can't you be more like your brother?"

The harsh light burned the boy's eyes after the closet's darkness. His father swayed slightly, the smell of alcohol rolling off him in waves. The child could see his mother behind him in the hallway, her lip bleeding, her dress torn at the shoulder. She reached toward him, her face a mask of terror and helplessness.

The boy flinched. But when his father snatched the blanket, he screamed.

"No! Please."

The wool tore slightly as his father's fingers dug into it, pulling it away from the boy's desperate grip. It was more than fabric being stolen. It was safety, comfort, the last piece of his grandmother's love, the only thing that made the world bearable.

But the man only laughed and dragged the blanket out by its edge. Out into the living room, where furniture lay overturned and glass sparkled on the carpet. Out through the front door. Onto the porch, where neighbors might see but never intervene.

And lights a match.

The flame caught immediately, greedy and bright against the darkness. The red turned black in the dancing fire, wool curling and melting, the scent of burning memories filled the night air. The boy watched from the doorway, his mother's hands on his shoulders, as his sanctuary became smoke and ash.

The fire consumed not just fabric but something more profound—the last of his childhood faith that someone could keep him safe, that love could build walls strong enough to hold back the darkness. As the final threads blackened and fell, something inside the boy went silent and cold. Forever.

In the orange glow of the dying flames, the child stopped counting.

Chapter One

Mist coiled low over Misty Lake when Donnie and Carla Rose, a middle-aged couple, strolled down the path that circled the lake as they did most mornings. The sun started to rise, a dim orange disc behind a veil of clouds that hung heavy with the promise of rain. Ancient pines stretched toward the sky like silent sentinels, their bark scarred by decades of weather and wildlife. The only sound was the occasional splash of a fish breaking the water's surface and the steady crunch of the couple's boots on the trail, worn smooth by countless hikers over the years.

Their morning ritual had begun three years ago, after Carla's doctor recommended daily exercise to help manage her blood pressure. What started as a medical necessity had become their sacred time together, sixty minutes when the world belonged only to them, when Donnie could forget about the failing hardware store and Carla could escape the endless parade of customers at the diner. They'd mapped every root, every fallen log, every bend in the path that wound through the state park.

"Someone left their fire burning." Carla pointed to the

smoldering embers, her voice tight with disapproval. Singed red fabric lay scattered near the coals, the edges blackened and curled. She'd grown up camping with her father, a park ranger who'd drilled fire safety into her bones. Unattended campfires were cardinal sins in her book.

Her husband stepped closer to the tent, his nose wrinkling at something metallic drifting from the orange nylon structure. The smell reminded him of the slaughterhouse outside town, where his uncle had worked summers during high school. Sweet. Coppery. Wrong. "There's blood," he whispered, moving closer to his wife.

"Go see." She gave him a push, her nurse's training overriding her growing unease. "Someone might be hurt."

Heart hammering against his ribs, he nodded and took a step closer to the tent. The campsite looked normal enough, a cooler beside a camp chair, hiking boots lined up neatly by the tent flap, a coffee pot still sitting on the grate over the dead fire. But that smell grew stronger with each step. "Hello? Anyone here?" His voice cracked on the words. He unzipped the tent flap with trembling fingers.

The stench of decay hit him like a sledgehammer to the gut. Flies buzzed in a lazy, obscene cloud. Inside lay a man and a woman on sleeping bags saturated with their blood, the fabric so soaked it squelched under the weight of the bodies. Both had puncture wounds at the base of their skulls, precise and deep, as if someone had driven an ice pick through bone and brain with surgical precision. The woman's hand still clutched a paperback romance novel, its pages splattered with crimson.

Donnie staggered back and vomited into the leaves, his

breakfast of eggs and toast painting the forest floor. Despite his choking warning, Carla glanced into the tent and screamed—a sound that sent birds exploding from the trees and echoed across the still water of the lake.

~

Forty-five minutes later, Sheriff Shea Callahan and Deputy Trevor Bolton arrived on the scene, their patrol cars kicking up dust on the narrow access road. Yellow crime scene tape fluttered around the campsite like party streamers at a macabre celebration. The area crawled with CSI techs from the state bureau, their white coveralls stark against the green forest. The flash of a camera strobed from inside the tent, documenting horrors that would haunt the photographer's dreams.

Shea ducked under the tape, her trained gaze taking in every detail. She'd seen her share of violence in her years of law enforcement, but something about this scene made her skin crawl. The red fabric burned in the fire pit caught her attention first—partially melted synthetic material that had once been bright crimson. Near the tent, a scarlet camping flag flapped in the morning breeze, pristine and new. She noted the words ironed onto the flag in block letters: Camping Arkansas. "What's with all the red?"

Trevor consulted his notes. "That flag is a lot newer than the fabric burned in the fire. This one has the names of other campsites listed—Devil's Den, Buffalo River, Hot Springs. All Arkansas state parks."

"That's odd." Shea crouched beside the fire pit, studying the partially melted remains. The burned fabric looked older, more weathered than the flag. Different material entirely.

Trevor took a shaky breath, still fighting his gag reflex. "I think the newer flag was planted after the kill. Why burn the first one but leave this one untouched?"

"That's what we're here to find out." Shea shuddered, though the morning was already growing warm, heavy with humidity from the approaching storm. The way the newer flag had been planted in the soft earth reminded her of a marker near a gravesite—deliberate and ceremonial. "Come, Heidi." She called her German Shepherd away from the crime scene, where the dog had been sniffing around the perimeter with intense interest. "You need to stay in the truck this time."

With a disappointed whine, the dog trotted back to the patrol vehicle and pressed her nose against the window, dark eyes following her partner's every move. Heidi had been with Shea for three years, trained in narcotics and search and rescue, but even the seasoned K-9 seemed unsettled by the scene.

Shea entered the tent with Trevor, breathing through her mouth to minimize the assault on her senses. The victims looked peaceful despite their violent end. The woman appeared to be in her early twenties, blonde hair splayed across a blood-soaked pillow, her face relaxed as if she were sleeping. The man looked slightly older, maybe twenty-five, his arm draped protectively over his companion even in death. "I'll rattle off details while you take notes."

Trevor pulled a small pad from his pocket, his handwriting already shaky from adrenaline. "I'm ready."

Doing her best to maintain professional detachment despite the brutality in front of her, she began her examination. "Victims appear to be in their mid-twenties. Deep puncture wound at the base of each skull, entry point approximately two inches below the occipital bone. No defensive injuries visible on hands or arms. Death appears to have been instantaneous. No signs of struggle within the tent." She turned her head toward the tent opening to take a breath of cleaner air.

"Two wallets and cell phones are positioned neatly beside the sleeping bags. IDs show Rebecca Martinez, twenty-two, and David Kim, twenty-four, both from Little Rock. A couple of empty Budweiser bottles on the tent floor, positioned as if they'd been drinking casually before sleep. No sign of car keys anywhere in the tent. Based on the lack of defensive wounds and the positioning of personal items, I don't think this was a robbery. Let's move outside and examine the perimeter." She picked up a cell phone and handed it to Trevor. "Have forensics see if they can find anything."

Trevor followed her into the blessed fresh air, gulping oxygen like a drowning man. The contrast between the horror inside the tent and the peaceful forest seemed surreal as birds sang in the canopy above while technicians photographed carnage below.

Shea hunkered down next to boot prints pressed into the soft earth near the campsite. The impressions were clear in the morning dew. Two different tread patterns, one significantly larger than the other. "Two of those prints match the couple who found the bodies." Trevor jerked his head toward where Donnie and Carla Rose stood near the road, their arms wrapped around each other for comfort. "Said they were on their morning hike when they came upon this nightmare."

"The third set is our killer." Shea studied the impressions carefully. Size eleven or twelve boot, with a distinctive wear pattern on the left heel. "Look at the depth. Those who made these were moving slowly and deliberately. Not running or hurried."

Near a downed log about twenty feet from the tent, Shea found a dark smear on the bark. "Blood spatter. Looks like the killer wiped off his weapon here after the attack." She made a note for the forensics team. "This gives us a partial timeline—kills the couple in their sleep, exits the tent, cleans his weapon, then takes time to burn something in their fire and plant that flag. Very methodical. He wasn't worried about being seen." Which is why some people preferred primitive camping over the more crowded sites with water and electricity.

The witnesses still trembled near the road; Carla's face streaked with tears and Donnie's complexion the color of old newspaper. Shea approached them gently. Trauma like this would stick with them forever, and she didn't want to make it worse. "I know this has been terrible for both of you. Can you walk me through exactly what happened this morning?"

Donnie cleared his throat several times before speaking, his voice hoarse from vomiting. "We walk this trail every morning at six-thirty. Same routine for three years. When we rounded the bend and saw the campsite, the flag caught our attention first. That bright red color, you know? And the fact that their campfire was still smoking. This campground has strict rules about extinguishing fires before sleeping."

"Did you touch anything at the scene? Move anything?" Shea kept her voice gentle but professional.

The man shook his head emphatically. "Soon as I saw...what was in that tent, I called 911 on Carla's cell phone. We waited over here by our car until your people arrived. Didn't go near the campsite again."

"You did exactly right. We'll need formal statements from both of you, but that can wait until you've had some time to process this." Shea's attention drifted back to the crime scene as two body bags were loaded into the coroner's van. "Can you think of anything else unusual you noticed? Any sounds last night, vehicles on the access road?"

Carla spoke for the first time, her voice barely above a whisper. "We live about two miles from here. Didn't hear anything unusual, but our house faces away from the park. Sometimes we hear cars on weekend nights—kids partying or late campers arriving."

A slight breeze picked up, fluttering the red flag once...twice...and then folding it in half like a silent bow. The whole scene felt choreographed, theatrical in a way that made Shea's skin crawl. This wasn't random violence, it was a performance. "I want to know where that flag can be purchased. Check camping stores, sporting goods places, online retailers. Hopefully, there's a receipt in one of the victim's wallets that might give us a lead."

"On it." Trevor headed back toward the tent, pulling on latex gloves.

"This feels like the start of something," Shea muttered, watching the flag ripple in the wind. She'd learned to trust her instincts, and every nerve in her body screamed that this wasn't a one-time killing. The ritualistic elements, the burned fabric, the planted flag, the precise nature of the wounds, all suggested someone who'd been planning this for a long time.

~

It's quiet now. The kind of quiet that lives beneath birdsong and breeze, deeper than sound, heavier than silence. The kind where nothing has happened yet, but something terrible waits in the wings like an actor preparing for his entrance.

He crouched in the underbrush fifty yards from a different campsite, still as a weathered stone, and watched through a lattice of pine boughs. His breathing moved slowly in and out of his nostrils—controlled, paced, meditative. Like the sound his mother used to make when she tried not to cry too loud, when she pressed her face into her pillow after the hitting stopped and thought no one could hear her broken sobs.

His mother hadn't known he'd been listening from the hallway, pressed against the wall in his dinosaur pajamas, counting her tears.

Neither did this girl know she was being watched.

She camped alone in a lime green tent that clashed violently with the earth tones of the forest and drew attention like a neon sign. The color offended him. Too bright, too cheerful, too oblivious to the darkness that moved through these woods. She hummed while setting up her portable camping grill, an off-key tune that matched whatever played through the earbuds connected to her phone. Every few minutes, she'd glance at the device, checking for cell reception that would be hard to get this deep in the forest.

He catalogued her every movement with the patience of a predator. Mid-twenties, shoulder-length brown hair pulled back in a messy ponytail, hiking boots that looked fresh from the store. A weekend warrior, soft from city living, trusting in the safety of designated camping areas and park ranger patrols. She'd driven a silver Honda CR-V with Texas plates and a bumper sticker for some college he'd never heard of.

His eyes widened as she draped a red towel across the open hatch of her SUV to let it dry after washing dishes in the nearby stream.

Red. The color hit him like a needle sliding between his ribs, piercing something vital and electric. It spurred him like a cape waved before a bull, narrowing his world to that single splash of crimson against the metallic paint. His breath caught in his throat, and for a moment, he was eight years old again, clutching his grandmother's red blanket while hell erupted in the living room.

The girl had no idea what the color red meant to him. She didn't know what it awakened, what it called forth from the careful compartments where he kept his rage. To her, it was just a towel, a mundane object for drying hands and faces. She couldn't see how it pulsed like a heartbeat, how it whispered promises of completion and closure.

He dug his fingers deep into the forest floor to steady himself, his nails scraping through the decomposing leaves and soft earth until he reached the cool, damp soil beneath. It felt like the closet floor where he used to hide when the voices grew too loud, when furniture started flying, and glass began to shatter. Before the matches. Before his sanctuary turned to ash and something inside him crystallized into permanent winter.

The girl laughed at something on her phone, having finally found a bar of reception near a tall pine tree. She chatted with a friend or family member about her weekend plans. Her voice carried in the still air: "It's so peaceful out here. Nothing but trees and water and quiet. I needed this break from the city."

The killer licked his lips, tasting anticipation.

She felt safe in her designated campsite with its numbered marker and maintained fire ring. She trusted in the illusion of civilization that the state park provided, like restrooms within walking distance, a ranger station five miles down the access road, other campers scattered throughout the forest. She didn't know that safety was just a story people told themselves to sleep at night, that predators had always hunted in the spaces between human settlements.

The girl didn't fear the woods yet. She didn't know he watched her from the shadows, cataloguing her routines and vulnerabilities. People rarely sensed his presence. A skill learned in childhood, when invisibility meant survival.

He whispered numbers in his mind like a mantra. One. Two. Three. Four. Five. Six. Seven. Eight.

The counting steadied him, slowed his racing pulse, and helped him think instead of acting on pure instinct. Something tightened in his chest—anticipation mixed with a strange kind of hunger he'd never been able to name. But it wasn't time yet. He wasn't ready. The ritual demanded patience, planning, and the right circumstances. He'd know when the moment arrived, would feel it in his bones like approaching weather.

Instead of action, he pulled out his journal, a battered composition notebook with its cover long since torn away, the kind schoolchildren used for homework assignments. The pages were filled with dates and details written in careful block letters. Types of tents and campers, descriptions of vehicles, and license plate numbers when he could get close enough. Whether his subjects camped alone or in groups, their approximate ages, their routines, and blind spots.

Most importantly, he recorded the red items: towels, shirts, sleeping bags, camping chairs, coolers, anything that carried the color of memory and rage. Each crimson object was noted with particular care, sketched in the margins with colored pencils he'd stolen from a dollar store.

He flipped to a blank page and documented the girl with the lime green tent. Honda CR-V, Texas plates, early twenties, camping alone for the weekend, red towel currently hanging from the rear hatch. She'd brought enough supplies for three days based on the size of her cooler. Her campsite was situated in a natural depression that would conceal it from the main trail, accessible by a narrow path barely wide enough for her vehicle.

Perfect isolation. Perfect vulnerability.

The girl finished her phone call and began preparing dinner on her portable stove, still humming that tuneless melody. She seemed genuinely happy to be alone in the woods, unaware that solitude was the most dangerous luxury a person could indulge.

The next time she hung her red towel, he'd be ready. Waiting. Watching from the spaces between the trees where darkness gathered even in daylight, where the forest kept its oldest and hungriest secrets.

Chapter Two

Shea and Trevor dashed into Lucy's Diner the next morning to grab breakfast and escape the relentless rain that had been hammering Misty Hollow since dawn. Water dripped from their rain slickers onto the worn linoleum floor, adding to the puddles already tracked in by earlier customers. The bell above the door announced their arrival with a cheerful chime that seemed obscene given the circumstances.

Heads turned and conversations ceased when they entered, the usual morning chatter dying like a radio suddenly switched off. The silence stretched for three heartbeats before whispered discussions resumed, punctuated by furtive glances and the kind of speculation that spreads through small towns like wildfire. Questions about the double murder rippled from booth to booth—who were the victims, how had they died, was the killer still in the area?

"How did they find out so fast?" Shea scooted into their usual booth near the rain-streaked window, her voice tight with frustration. She'd hoped to keep details contained until they had more answers, but in a town of barely thirty thousand people, secrets had the lifespan of morning dew.

"A park ranger overheard the coroner on his CB radio yesterday afternoon," Lucy, the diner's owner and unofficial town gossip hub, said as she handed them well-worn plastic menus. Her Lucille Ball red hair was pulled back in the same messy bun she'd worn for twenty years, and her apron bore stains from the morning's pancake rush. "Didn't take long to spread the word after that. It's all over social media now—Facebook, Instagram, that Twitter thing. Shoot, my granddaughter posted something about it before I even knew what happened."

Shea frowned, scanning the familiar menu without really seeing it. She'd been ordering the same breakfast here for three years. "I'll have two biscuits and chocolate gravy."

"The hungry man special for me," Trevor said, handing back both menus. He waited until Lucy shuffled away, her shoes squeaking against the floor, before turning his attention back to Shea. "Are we ever going to talk about me telling you how I feel about you? It's been three months since I said it. You can't ignore this forever."

The conversation they'd been dancing around hung between them like smoke. Trevor had finally found the courage to tell her he loved her after they'd brought down the woman killing teenage girls she thought were acting immorally.

She'd been thinking about his words ever since, replaying them during sleepless nights and quiet moments in the patrol car. "Attachments are dangerous in our line of work. You know that," she said, watching raindrops race down the window. She wanted to tell him she felt the same way, wanted to let him know how the sight of his crooked smile could brighten her worst days, how she counted on his steady presence more than she'd ever admit.

But what if admitting her feelings somehow jinxed them? They'd both come close to death more times than she cared to count. Next time, they might not be lucky enough to walk away from the evil that seemed to gravitate toward Misty Hollow like iron filings to a magnet. "We've got two murders to solve, Trevor. Let's focus on that."

"Fine, but we're going to have this conversation eventually," he said, his blue eyes holding hers with an intensity that made her pulse quicken. "No matter what danger comes our way, it won't change how I feel about you." He dug his cell phone from his uniform pocket and began scrolling through social media feeds, his expression growing darker with each swipe. "Good grief. Photos of the crime scene and that red flag are posted everywhere. Someone must have snuck past the perimeter tape after we left."

A young server, whom Shea didn't recognize, approached their table, balancing their plates with the practiced ease of someone who'd been waiting tables for years. She couldn't be more than nineteen, with pink-streaked hair and multiple ear piercings that would have scandalized the older residents. "What does the red flag mean, Sheriff? Is it like a warning or something? A game?" The girl's eyes were wide with the kind of morbid curiosity that disasters inspired. "People on TikTok are saying the flag stands for something specific, like a code or a message."

"I can't discuss an ongoing investigation," Shea began,

then caught sight of the girl's name tag. "Sheila. We'll release information to the public as it becomes available through proper channels."

"But people are scared," Sheila pressed, lowering her voice conspiratorially. "Folks are saying the lake is cursed again, just like when those teenage girls died a few months back. My grandmother won't even let me drive past the park entrance anymore."

"Don't listen to gossip and rumors," Shea said firmly, though she felt her appetite disappearing with each word. "There's no such thing as a cursed lake. What happened was the work of a flesh-and-blood killer, and we're going to catch him."

"But my cousin Brittany—she works dispatch over in Baxter County—she says the killer is marking his territory by leaving those red flags. Like dogs marking trees, you know? She thinks there's gonna be more bodies."

Trevor rolled his eyes at the girl's amateur psychology but didn't comment until she'd moved on to refill coffee cups at other tables. He held up his phone for Shea to see, his expression grim. "It's worse than I thought."

The screen showed a live news broadcast from Channel 7, complete with a reporter standing in the rain at the lake's edge. The chyron at the bottom of the screen screamed "RED FLAG KILLER: CURSE OR COPYCAT?" in bold red letters that seemed to pulse with malevolent energy.

Shea waved Sheila away when she approached with the coffee pot and leaned closer to watch the newscast. The sound was muted, but she could read the reporter's lips well enough to catch the gist of her breathless commentary.

A woman in a rain-soaked blue suit spoke earnestly into the camera, gesturing toward the lake behind her. The audio cut in just as she was saying, "—comparison to the killings perpetrated by Marilyn Townsend, when she systematically drowned several teenage girls in these very waters before her arrest. Some locals claim the lake itself is cursed, and that these new murders are part of a grim legacy that has haunted Misty Hollow for generations."

The broadcast cut to file footage of the Townsend house, a small house used as the parsonage for a local church. "Authorities have not confirmed any connection between the recent deaths and the drownings," the reporter continued, "nor have they explained the significance of the red camping flag found at the scene. Some experts suggest it could be a ritualistic marker, similar to symbols used by serial killers to claim responsibility for their crimes."

"What experts?" Shea muttered, stabbing at her biscuits with unnecessary force. "They're just making stuff up for ratings."

The camera panned across the lake's surface, gray and choppy under the storm clouds, before returning to the reporter. "The residents of Misty Hollow are taking precautions—locking their doors, avoiding the lake area, and some are even considering leaving town temporarily until this nightmare ends. We'll have more coverage of this developing story tonight at five and eleven. This is Rebecca Martinez, Channel 7 News."

Shaking her head in disgust, she signaled Lucy for a to-go box and pushed her barely touched breakfast away. The thought of food made her stomach turn. Outside, rain continued to hammer the diner's window.

Back at the sheriff's office, Shea slammed the door behind herself and Trevor hard enough to rattle the frosted glass. She threw herself into her desk chair with enough force to send it spinning, then grabbed the stress ball her predecessor had left behind and squeezed it until her knuckles went white.

"Now we've got half the county thinking we're dealing with some supernatural curse instead of a flesh-and-blood killer. Others are treating this like entertainment, like it's some true crime podcast come to life."

Trevor nodded grimly as he settled into the chair across from her desk. "And the other half think that flag is some signature calling card. We're going to have copycats and thrill-seeking idiots out there planting red flags just for social media attention. I can see it now—fake crime scenes popping up all over the county, each one requiring resources we don't have to investigate."

Before Shea could respond, her phone rang with the shrill urgency that meant trouble. She grabbed the receiver on the second ring. "Sheriff Callahan."

"Sheriff, this is Mayor Ferguson." The mayor's voice carried the particular brand of panic that politicians developed when their carefully managed public image was threatened. "What exactly are you planning to do about this media circus? My phone hasn't stopped ringing since that news report aired. This kind of sensationalism and misinformation is going to destroy our tourism industry. People are already canceling their fall camping reservations, and you know that after the brutal heat we've had this summer, autumn tourism is what keeps half the businesses in this town afloat."

Shea could picture him in his overly air-conditioned office, probably pacing behind his massive mahogany desk while his secretary fielded frantic calls from local business owners. Ferguson had been mayor for twelve years, elected on a platform of economic development that relied heavily on the town's reputation as a peaceful getaway destination.

"I understand your concerns, sir," she said, fighting to keep her voice level and professional. "We're doing everything we can with the resources we have. It's been less than twenty-four hours since the bodies were discovered. Trust us to do our jobs and catch this killer before he strikes again."

"Make it quick, Sheriff," Ferguson said, his voice carrying an edge of threat. "Before we have a full-scale panic on our hands and every news van in the state parked outside our city limits. I've got the city council breathing down my neck, and if this situation spirals out of control, heads are going to roll. Starting with yours."

The line went dead, leaving Shea staring at the receiver in her hand. She'd known Ferguson long enough to recognize when he was serious about his threats, and her job security had just taken a serious hit.

She rubbed her temples, trying to massage away the tension headache that had been building since she'd first seen that red flag fluttering in yesterday's crime scene. "We need to find out where that flag came from. It's the only real clue we have, and without it, we're just spinning our wheels while this person plans his next move."

"We will," Trevor said, reaching across the desk to slide her untouched breakfast closer to her. His fingers brushed hers briefly, a moment of contact that sent warmth up her arm. "We always figure it out eventually. Now eat something. I have a feeling you're going to need your strength before this day is over."

~

The killer sat cross-legged on the threadbare carpet of his two-bedroom rental house on the outskirts of town, thirty-seven dollars' worth of thrift store furniture surrounding him like the remnants of other people's discarded lives. The television, a boxy old Zenith he'd rescued from a curb three months ago, cast flickering shadows across walls decorated with nothing but water stains and the ghosts of previous tenants' picture frames.

He watched the five o'clock news with the focused intensity of a scholar studying scripture. The lovely woman in blue, Rebecca Martinez, according to the chyron, tried unsuccessfully to keep the excitement from her voice as she delivered her breathless report about the "Red Flag Killer." Her eyes sparkled with the kind of professional ambition that fed on human tragedy.

"Local authorities have yet to release the victims' names pending notification of next of kin," she said, her perfectly styled hair unmoved by the wind whipping across the lake behind her. "The only unusual evidence left at the scene was a red camping flag planted near the victims' tent. Residents are already connecting this latest killing to the infamous Misty Lake curse, and authorities fear they may be dealing with a serial killer."

He leaned forward, elbows resting on his knees, the corner of his mouth twitching upward in what might charitably be called a smile. The expression sat strangely on his face, like a mask that didn't quite fit.

Red. Flag. Killer.

The words rolled through his mind like a hymn, soft and rhythmic and alive with possibility. He'd never had a name before, not a real name, anyway. Tommy had died in that closet when his blanket burned. The foster system had given him a string of temporary identities that never stuck. But this name, this title born from his actions, felt right in a way nothing ever had.

The station cut to footage of yesterday's crime scene: yellow tape fluttering like prayer flags in the wind, uniformed figures moving with professional urgency, the sheriff and her deputy entering the tent where his handiwork waited. And there, captured in high definition against the gray sky, stood his flag—tall and proud and crimson as fresh blood.

For a moment, he reached out and touched the television screen, his fingertips remembering the texture of that fabric. Synthetic material, slightly rough, nothing like the soft wool of his childhood blanket. But the color was perfect, the exact shade of the safety his father had stolen from him all those years ago.

He remembered that night with crystal clearness, though everything else from his childhood existed in a haze of fear and confusion. The soft cocoon of his grandmother's blanket wrapped around his small body, the way he would pull it over his head to block out the sound of his parents screaming at each other in the next room. The crash of breaking dishes, his mother's sobs, his father's slurred curses echoing through their tiny apartment.

"Stop hiding, boy!" his father had roared, ripping the blanket away with such violence that Tommy had tumbled backward against the closet wall. "Stop being such a weakling!"

The fire had burned bright on the porch, fed by newspaper and cardboard from the recycling bin. The red wool had caught immediately, curling and blackening as the flames consumed his only source of comfort. The acrid smell of burning synthetic fibers had filled the night air while his father stood over the fire like some primitive god demanding sacrifice.

The boy had cried without making a sound, a skill learned through hard experience. He had learned to disappear into himself, to become so small and quiet that maybe the monsters wouldn't notice him.

The broadcast shifted to street interviews, locals gathered outside Lucy's Diner sharing theories and spreading fear with the casual efficiency that small towns had perfected over generations. A young reporter with an earnest expression and perfectly styled hair thrust his microphone toward anyone willing to talk.

"They say it's the curse again," an elderly woman in a faded housedress told the camera, her eyes wide with the kind of superstitious dread that ran through Misty Hollow like groundwater. "The lake takes what it wants, when it wants. Always has, always will."

"I heard he marks them with flags afterward," a middle-aged man in work clothes added, glancing nervously toward the lake as if the killer might be watching from the tree line. "Like trophies, you know? Like hunters do with deer heads."

The killer chuckled, a sound like dry leaves rustling. He liked that comparison. Trophies. The idea had merit.

Another reporter replaced the first, her makeup perfect despite the persistent drizzle, her voice professionally hushed as if she were narrating a ghost story around a campfire. "Criminal psychologists suggest we may be looking at ritualistic killings, with the flags serving as symbolic markers. They could represent blood, danger, or territorial claims. Given the town's dark history with the Townsend murders, the moniker 'Red Flag Killer' is already spreading across social media platforms."

The name felt right, settling into his consciousness like a key finding its lock. The town knew him now. They would remember him. He was no longer invisible, no longer the frightened child hiding in closets while the world burned around him.

He turned the television down and moved to the window, peering through blinds he'd never bothered to clean. The rental house sat on a dead-end street populated mostly by other forgotten people—elderly widows, disabled veterans, single mothers working two jobs to make rent. No one paid attention to their neighbors here. No one asked questions about the quiet man who kept to himself and paid his rent on time.

"Let them talk," he murmured to his reflection in the grimy glass. "I want them to be afraid. And now it's time to give them something more substantial to fear."

He grabbed his backpack from beside the door, military surplus, olive drab, purchased with cash from a pawn shop in the next county. Inside: rope, duct tape, a fixed-blade hunting knife with a seven-inch steel blade, latex gloves, and three more flags folded with military precision. He had everything he needed for the night's work.

At the campsite with the offensive lime green tent, he crouched at the tree line like a gargoyle, motionless as weathered stone. His breathing had slowed to the point where his chest barely moved, and small night creatures had grown comfortable enough with his presence to forage within arm's reach.

A battery-powered lantern glowed from inside the tent, creating a shadow puppet theater against the nylon walls. The girl was still awake, moving around her small space with the unconscious confidence of someone who'd never had reason to fear the dark. She hummed while organizing her supplies, that same tuneless melody he'd heard earlier, probably stuck in her head from whatever song had been playing in her car.

Her red towel hung from a low branch twenty feet away, fluttering like a beacon in the night breeze. Even in the darkness, its color seemed to pulse, calling to something primal and hungry in his chest.

He checked his watch—a cheap digital model that glowed green in the darkness. 11:47 PM. Late enough that any sounds would be muffled by distance and dismissed as nocturnal wildlife by other campers. Early enough that she wouldn't be in a deep sleep yet.

Moving with the patience learned through years of hunting both animals and humans, he began his approach. Each step was carefully placed to avoid dry leaves and brittle twigs. His boots, military surplus like his pack, made no sound on the forest floor.

A branch snapped under his weight.

The girl's humming stopped. She appeared in the tent's

opening like a deer scenting danger, her head cocked at an angle that suggested she was listening rather than looking. "Hello? Is someone out there?"

He froze, becoming part of the landscape, just another shadow among the pines. His heartbeat slowed until it matched the rhythm of the night insects.

After thirty seconds that felt like hours, she shook her head and ducked back inside, zipping the tent flap with the finality of someone who'd convinced herself she'd imagined the sound. The lantern dimmed as she settled into her sleeping bag.

He waited. Patience was the hunter's greatest weapon, more valuable than speed, strength, or even surprise.

When the forest had been silent for twenty minutes and no light showed through the tent walls, he moved forward with the fluid grace of a predator who'd found his prey.

The knife sliced through the tent's rain fly like silk, the sound no louder than a whisper. He stepped through the opening he'd created and found himself standing over his victim.

The girl's eyes opened just as the blade found her heart.

She fought harder than he'd expected; soft city living hadn't eliminated her survival instincts. Her fingernails raked across his cheek, drawing blood, and she managed a single soft gasp before the life dimmed from her eyes like a candle being snuffed.

He let her fall back onto her sleeping bag, then stepped outside to complete the ritual. The knife blade gleamed wetly in the moonlight as he wiped it clean on her red towel, the fabric absorbing her life with eager efficiency.

The fire caught quickly in the established ring, fed by dry kindling and the cotton towel that had called to him like a siren song. As the flames consumed the red fabric, he planted his flag in the soft earth nearby, another marker, another trophy, another message for those who would find her.

Smiling, he melted back into the woods with his heart steady and his soul thrumming with dark satisfaction. Tomorrow, they would find her. Tomorrow, the Red Flag Killer would claim his second victory.

And the town would learn that some monsters were very real indeed.

Chapter Three

Fog rolled across Misty Lake in soft tendrils that curled between the towering pine trees like ghostly fingers reaching for the shore. The early morning mist transformed the familiar landscape into something otherworldly, muffling sounds and creating pockets of gray silence that seemed to swallow footsteps and whispered words. Earl Miller, a lone fisherman who'd been working these waters for thirty-seven years, trudged along the muddy shoreline with the methodical persistence of a man who understood that patience was the difference between going home empty-handed and filling his cooler with bass.

His weathered boots squelched in the thick mud with each step, leaving deep impressions that would dry and crack under the afternoon sun. Earl had been fishing since before dawn, when the water was glass-smooth and the only sounds were the gentle lap of the waves against the shore and the occasional splash of a jumping fish breaking the surface tension. Now, as the sun climbed higher and burned through the morning fog, he'd stop every few yards to cast his line into promising-looking spots, near fallen logs where bass liked to hide, in the shadows of overhanging branches, anywhere the water looked deep and dark enough to harbor decent-sized fish.

When nothing took his well-worn lures, he'd reel in with the acceptance of a man who'd learned that fishing was as much about the quiet contemplation as it was about the catch. The ritual of casting and waiting had become a form of meditation over the decades, a way to process the small disappointments and occasional joys that life in a small town provided.

As he rounded a bend in the shoreline, Earl stopped at the edge of a designated campsite where the bright green of a modern tent caught his attention like a neon sign in the gray morning light. The color seemed wrong somehow, too vibrant against the muted earth tones of the forest. His weathered nostrils twitched at the acrid scent of smoke drifting from the site.

A red flag fluttered in the early morning breeze, its crimson fabric a stark contrast to the garish lime green of the tent. The flag hung from a plastic pole driven deep into the soft earth. "Well, ain't that something," he muttered to himself, shifting his tackle box to his other hand.

He'd seen flags at campsites before during his years of fishing these waters. Some folks put them out as an invitation for other campers to stop by and share stories around the fire, a kind of outdoors hospitality that Earl supposed was nice enough in theory. As for himself, he'd always preferred to camp alone when he stayed overnight, with no visitors to disturb his peace or interrupt his communion with the water and the woods. Too much talking scared away the fish, and Earl had never been much for small talk anyway.

He took a closer look at the smoldering remains of what appeared to be a red towel in the established fire ring, its edges still glowing with tiny orange embers that pulsed like dying stars. The synthetic material had melted and curled into grotesque shapes that reminded him uncomfortably of burned flesh. "We've got a burn ban on, you know?" he called toward the tent, his voice carrying the irritation of someone who'd seen too many careless campers nearly start forest fires. "Idiotic people don't read the signs."

When no response came from the tent, Earl kicked dirt over the embers until they hissed and died, leaving behind only the smell of ash and melted plastic. The responsible thing to do, even if the camper was too lazy or ignorant to do it themselves. Fire was nothing to fool around with, especially during the dry months when a single spark could turn thousands of acres into an inferno.

He called out several more times in increasingly louder voices, trying to wake whoever was sleeping off what he assumed was a night of heavy drinking. "Hey! You in there. Your fire's still burning." His words seemed to disappear into the morning air without echo or response, swallowed by the fog that still clung to the low places near the water.

As he moved closer to investigate, a large rip in the side of the tent sent his stomach plummeting. The tear looked deliberate, too clean and straight to be accidental damage from wind or animals. Something cold and sharp settled in his chest, the same feeling he'd gotten years ago when he'd found his neighbor's dog dead on the side of the road. Not hit by a car, but killed by something with teeth and claws and malicious intent.

"Hello?" Earl's voice cracked slightly as he pushed aside the tent flap with one shaking hand, his fishing pole forgotten on the ground behind him. The interior of the tent was dim after the growing brightness of morning, and it took his eyes a moment to adjust to the shadows.

When they did, Earl Miller saw something that would haunt his dreams for the rest of his life.

"Oh, Jesus." Bile rose in his throat, burning and acidic, and he stumbled backward so quickly that he nearly fell over his own tackle box. His hands shook as he fumbled for the flip phone attached to his belt, an ancient device he'd refused to upgrade despite his daughter's constant nagging about getting something more modern.

The 911 call took three attempts because his fingers kept hitting the wrong buttons, and when the dispatcher finally answered, Earl could barely form coherent sentences through his shock and revulsion.

~

Shea's phone buzzed at 6:17 AM, dragging her from the restless half-sleep that had become her norm since the first murders. She'd been dreaming about red flags, her subconscious mind chewing over the case details like a dog worrying a bone. Even in sleep, she couldn't escape the feeling that she missed something important, some crucial connection that would make the killer's motivation clear.

Already half awake with the details of the previous murders whirling through her mind like a tornado of facts and theories, she answered on the first ring. "Sheriff Callahan."

Jason Martinez, the local park ranger whose voice

she'd come to know well over the past few days, crackled through the connection with an urgency that made her stomach clench. "Sheriff, we've got another body at Misty Lake. Solo female camper, early twenties by the look of her. A fisherman found her about ten minutes ago." He rattled off the campsite number, his professional calm barely masking the strain in his voice.

Swinging her legs out of bed, Shea was already reaching for the clothes she'd laid out the night before, a habit developed during her years as a detective when middle-of-the-night calls were a regular occurrence. "Secure the scene. Keep everyone back at least fifty yards, and don't let anyone else near that tent until I get there. I'll be there in fifteen minutes."

She placed a quick call to Trevor, knowing he'd be awake despite the early hour. Insomnia was an occupational hazard in their line of work, then she threw on her uniform and gun belt with practiced efficiency. "Come on, Heidi," she called to her German Shepherd, who was already by the door with her tail wagging, somehow sensing that work was calling.

The drive to the lake passed in a blur of gray morning light and fog-shrouded trees. Shea's mind raced through possibilities and procedures, trying to prepare herself for what she was about to see while hoping against hope that this wouldn't be a repeat of the previous crime scenes. But the knot in her stomach told her otherwise. Serial killers didn't stop after two victims, and the ritualistic elements of the earlier murders suggested someone who was just getting started.

Her patrol truck crunched on the gravel shoulder near

the designated campsite, and she cut the engine with more force than necessary. The clean aroma of wet pine and lake water should have been pleasant and calming, but it was mingled with something far more repugnant. The cloying, metallic stench of drying blood seemed to coat the back of her throat like thick syrup.

A man clutching a fishing pole like a lifeline leaned against the rough bark of a massive pine tree, his face the color of old paper. He looked up as Shea approached, his eyes holding the thousand-yard stare of someone who'd seen something that changed their understanding of the world.

"Sir? I'm Sheriff Callahan."

"Miller. Earl Miller." His voice was hoarse, as if he'd been screaming, though Shea knew from experience that sometimes shock could steal a person's voice just as effectively as shouting. He cleared his throat then spat into the dirt.

Looking at Earl's trembling hands and ashen complexion, Shea made a quick decision. "Why don't you wait in my truck while we handle this? My dog could use the company, and there's a thermos of coffee on the passenger seat if you need something to settle your nerves." Anything to keep the poor man from witnessing any more of the horror that waited inside that tent, and to prevent him from contaminating the crime scene if his shock made him sick again.

Earl nodded, his fishing pole clutched against his chest like a talisman. "Okay. Yeah, I like dogs. Used to have a bluetick hound named Duke." His words came in disconnected fragments, his mind still processing what he'd seen. "I saw the flag first... then noticed the tent was all torn up. Before that... I tried to put out their fire because of the burn ban..."

"You did exactly the right thing, Mr. Miller. Go on now, get yourself some coffee and try to warm up." Shea watched him shuffle toward her truck with the unsteady gait of someone whose legs weren't quite obeying orders from his brain.

Trevor's squad car pulled up next to her patrol truck in a spray of gravel, and he emerged with the long-legged stride of someone accustomed to arriving at crime scenes. His sharp gaze immediately darted to the red flag, now drooping in the still morning air. "Same MO?"

"Looks like it." Shea snapped on a pair of latex gloves and began her initial scan of the scene, her trained eyes cataloguing details that would later be crucial for the investigation. Burned red towel in the fire ring, check. Neon green tent with apparent damage, check. Camping flag planted like a territorial marker, check. "No question it's our guy. I think we've got a serial killer on our hands."

The realization settled over her like a lead blanket. Three victims in two days, all killed in the same manner, all marked with red flags that seemed to mock law enforcement's inability to stop the carnage. This wasn't random violence or crimes of passion. This was someone with a plan, someone who was escalating, someone who wouldn't stop until he was caught or killed.

"Shea, over here." Trevor's voice carried an edge of excitement mixed with dread as he called from the tree line about thirty yards from the tent.

She joined him at the edge of the forest, where the pine

needles gave way to softer soil that held impressions like wet clay. Crouching low, she studied the ground with the intensity of a tracker reading a sign. Flattened pine needles formed a rough outline where someone had crouched for an extended period. A partial boot print was pressed deep enough into the dirt to suggest considerable weight and time. Someone had waited there for hours, patient as a spider in its web.

"He watched her," Shea said, the words coming out flat and cold. "Probably from the time she set up camp until he was ready to strike. This isn't opportunistic killing, as we first thought. It's more like he's hunting."

Trevor's jaw tightened as he studied the evidence, his hands clenched into fists at his sides. "He's turned murder into a spectator sport. What kind of sick mind gets off on watching someone's last normal evening alive?"

A sudden gust of wind caught the red flag, causing it to snap taut with a sound like a rifle shot. The unexpected noise made Shea jerk, her hand moving toward her service weapon. She straightened, fighting off the chill that had nothing to do with the morning air.

"Call the state forensics team," she ordered. "I want every inch of these woods searched—soil samples, fiber evidence, anything he might have dropped or left behind. And get me a cast of that boot print before the weather destroys it."

The red flag snapped again in another gust of wind, the sound sharp and demanding attention. To Shea, it looked less like a camping accessory and more like a battle standard planted by a conquering army, or a grave marker placed by someone who wanted the world to know that this ground now belonged to death.

"He's taunting us," she continued, staring at the crimson fabric as it danced in the breeze. "Leaving breadcrumbs for us to follow, daring us to catch him. But he's also getting sloppy, spending more time at the scenes, taking bigger risks. That's going to be his downfall."

Back at the sheriff's station two hours later, Shea and Trevor sat in the conference room surrounded by the detritus of an active investigation, case files stacked in precarious towers, crime scene photographs pinned to a large whiteboard, detailed maps of Misty Lake marked with red pins at each murder location. The fluorescent lights hummed overhead, casting everything in the harsh glare that made even the living look like corpses.

Shea pinned the latest victim's driver's license photo to the growing collection on the whiteboard. The girl's face smiled back at them with the carefree expression of someone who'd never imagined that a weekend camping trip would be her last act on earth. "Alexis Moore. Nineteen years old from Dallas, Texas. Drove up Friday afternoon, texted her mother Saturday morning to let her know she'd arrived safely. Camped alone, first time visiting Misty Lake. No apparent connection to our previous victims, and no reason for anyone to want her dead."

Trevor flipped through printed pages of the girl's social media accounts, his brow furrowed in concentration as he searched for any detail that might provide a clue to her killer's selection process. "College sophomore at UT Dallas, studying elementary education. Clean record, no enemies that we can find, plenty of friends who describe her as sweet and responsible. Same profile as the other two.

Just good people looking for a peaceful weekend in nature."

"Except for the red items at each crime scene," Shea said, adding Alexis Moore's information to the growing timeline on the whiteboard. "That's the only common thread we can find."

"Right. Red camping equipment that drew our killer's attention like a beacon." Trevor set down the social media printouts and leaned back in his chair, rubbing his eyes with the heels of his hands. "Three victims, two different cities, no shared employment or social connections. They didn't know each other, never crossed paths that we can determine. The only link is that they all had red items at their campsites and the misfortune to choose Misty Lake for their getaway."

Shea folded her arms and stepped back to get a better view of the whiteboard, hoping that distance might reveal a pattern she'd missed. "No shared jobs, no clubs or organizations, no mutual friends or acquaintances. Different ages, different backgrounds, different reasons for being here. The only constant is that damned red flag he leaves behind like a signature."

"And their proximity to the lake," Trevor added. "Both campsites were within a quarter-mile of the shoreline, in spots that would be visible from the hiking trails that circle the water."

"Which suggests he's using those trails to scout for potential victims." Shea turned to face the large map of the lake area, studying the network of hiking paths and camping areas marked in green ink. "He's not randomly stumbling across these people. He's actively hunting them."

The weight of that realization settled like smoke from a house fire. They weren't dealing with a disorganized killer striking targets of opportunity. This was someone with patience, planning, and a specific type of victim in mind. Someone who could blend into the background of a popular recreation area without attracting attention, watching and waiting for the right combination of isolation and red-colored camping gear.

"We need to understand the significance of those flags," Shea continued, her voice taking on the focused intensity that her deputies had learned meant she was formulating a plan. "Let's visit Misty Outdoor Supply, see how common these particular flags are, and whether anyone remembers selling them to someone who stood out."

Misty Outdoor Supply sat halfway between the center of town and the lake, occupying a converted warehouse that had once housed a lumber company. The building's metal siding was painted forest green, though rust stains had begun to creep down from the roof line like tears. Hand-painted signs advertised everything from fishing tackle to hunting licenses, and the gravel parking lot was dotted with pickup trucks and SUVs bearing the mud and scratches that marked them as belonging to serious outdoors enthusiasts.

A bell over the door announced their arrival with a cheerful jingle that seemed incongruous given the morning's grim discoveries. Shea immediately wrinkled her nose at the musty smell that permeated the store, a mixture of old canvas, rubber boots, and something vaguely fishy that might have been bait or might have been the building's questionable plumbing.

The interior was a maze of camping gear, fishing equipment, and hunting supplies arranged in a disorganized manner. Sleeping bags hung from ceiling hooks next to canoe paddles, while display cases filled with pocketknives sat beside racks of camouflage clothing. A dusty ceiling fan turned lazily overhead, stirring the stale air without actually cooling it.

From behind a leaning tower of plastic coolers in various stages of sun-fading emerged a balding, rail-thin man who moved with the nervous energy of someone who'd consumed too much coffee and not enough food. His clothes hung loose on his frame, and his eyes darted around the store as if he were expecting shoplifters to emerge from behind every display.

"Hank Worth at your service," he said, wiping his hands on a rag that had seen better decades. "What can I do for Misty Hollow's finest this fine morning?"

"Sheriff Callahan and Deputy Bolton," Shea replied, showing her badge out of habit though most local business owners knew her by sight. "We're investigating the recent murders at the lake. A red camping flag was found at each crime scene. Do you sell those here?"

Hank's expression shifted from casual friendliness to nervous concern in the space of a heartbeat. "Oh, those terrible killings. Yes, ma'am, I do carry camping flags. Got a whole selection over in the back corner." He led them through the cluttered aisles, past displays of Coleman lanterns and camp stoves, to a dusty corner where a battered cardboard box sat on the floor next to a display case filled with various camping accessories.

"Safety flags, mostly," Hank explained, opening the

box to reveal only four flags left from what had been a much larger shipment. "But folks have taken to writing the names of all the places they've camped on them, turning them into a kind of trophy or conversation starter. Invites other campers to stop by and share stories. It's becoming quite popular with the younger crowd."

Shea examined the remaining flags, noting their bright red color and the space at the bottom where campers could add their text. "How many of these have you sold in the past couple of weeks?"

Hank shrugged, his nervous energy making him shift from foot to foot. "Since they come twenty-four to a case, and I'm down to four... I'd say about twenty flags in the last two weeks. This is peak camping season, you know. Lots of families are coming through, and college kids are on weekend trips. Some folks buy multiple flags—one for their tent, one for their vehicle, extras in case they lose one."

"Anyone stand out to you recently?" Trevor asked, pulling out his notebook. "Someone acting nervous, asking unusual questions, making you uncomfortable?"

Hank rubbed his chin, leaving a streak of dirt from his grimy hands. "Well... there was a fellow a couple of nights back. Didn't actually come into the store, but he hung around the parking lot for quite a while. Smoked cigarettes and watched the road like he was waiting for someone, or maybe watching who came and went."

Shea felt her pulse quicken. "Can you describe him?"

"Average height, maybe a bit on the thin side. Wore a dark jacket with the hood up even though it wasn't cold that night. Didn't get a good look at his face, but something about him gave me the creeps. Way he moved, maybe, or how he kept to the shadows between the parking lot lights. When I finally went out to ask if he needed help, he just flicked his cigarette into the ditch and walked off into the woods."

Trevor was already moving toward the door. "Where exactly did he throw that cigarette?"

"Right over there by the drainage ditch, near the sign about burn bans." Hank pointed toward the front of the store. "Probably long gone by now, though. Been a couple of days and we've had some rain."

Shea followed Trevor outside, hope battling skepticism in her chest. DNA evidence from a cigarette butt would be a major break, but only if they could find it and if the killer had been careless enough to leave saliva on the filter. "Check the area anyway," she told Trevor. "Even if it's a long shot, we need to follow every lead."

Trevor nodded and began to search the weedy drainage ditch, while Shea returned to the store to finish questioning Hank. "This man who was watching your store—did you see which direction he went when he left?"

"Toward the lake," Hank replied without hesitation. "Followed that old logging road that connects to the hiking trails. Most folks don't know about it unless they've been coming here for years."

Back outside, Trevor held up an evidence bag containing what appeared to be a cigarette butt, partially protected from the rain by an overhanging bush. "Marlboro Red," he said, unable to keep the excitement from his voice. "If we're lucky, our guy's DNA is all over this."

Shea continued to stare in the direction of the lake,

though the water wasn't visible from the store's location. She could feel it, though. The presence of evil seemed to hang over the beautiful location like a storm cloud that never quite broke. The killer was still out there, probably already selecting his next victim, waiting for another flash of red to trigger whatever twisted psychological mechanism drove him to kill.

"Our killer is stalking that lake like a predator working a territory," she said. "He's watching campers as they set up, cataloguing their equipment and routines, waiting for the right combination of red items and isolation. This isn't random violence, it's systematic hunting."

Trevor sealed the evidence bag and labeled it with the date and location. "Think he'll strike again soon?"

Shea turned back toward their patrol vehicles; her jaw set in the determined line that her deputies recognized as her game face. "He won't stop until we catch him or until there's no one left to kill. And given how many people camp at that lake every weekend, we've got a limited window before he claims another victim."

~

He'd watched the fisherman first, hidden in the pre-dawn darkness among the pine trees like a shadow given substance. His breathing had been slow and controlled as Earl Miller worked his way along the shoreline, stopping periodically to cast his line into the gray water. The killer had held his breath when the fisherman stopped in front of the tent, close enough that he could have reached out and touched the man's weather-beaten jacket.

He could feel the exact moment when fear rippled through Earl Miller's body like electricity, the sudden stiffening of posture, the sharp intake of breath, the trembling that started in his hands and spread through his entire frame. The killer had to suppress a chuckle when the fisherman stumbled backward from the tent opening and fumbled for his ancient cell phone with hands that shook like autumn leaves.

That was the moment the killer lived for. The instant when innocence died and terror was born. Better than the actual killing, in some ways, because it proved his power to transform the world with nothing more than his presence. He was no longer the frightened boy hiding in closets while his father raged drunk through their house. Now he was the one who brought fear, who changed lives with a simple slash of his blade.

The fisherman's voice had shaken with panic as he called 911, the words tumbling over each other in his haste to report his discovery. "There's a body... at the lake... campsite fourteen... oh God, there's so much blood..." Even from thirty yards away, the killer could hear every word, could taste the man's terror like wine on the morning air.

Then he'd melted deeper into the forest when the sheriff's patrol truck arrived, his movements as silent as smoke drifting between the trees. He'd watched Sheriff Callahan step from her vehicle and march toward the crime scene with the professional composure that marked her as a worthy adversary. The deputy had arrived a minute after her, staying close to his superior with the protective instincts that suggested either romantic involvement or simply good training. The killer suspected romance.

From his concealed position, he had studied their investigative techniques with the clinical interest of a student observing a master class. They approached the tent, documented the scene , and, most importantly, found the spot where he'd maintained his vigil throughout the previous evening. Deputy Bolton had turned toward the killer's hiding spot once, his sharp eyes scanning the tree line as if some primitive part of his brain sensed a predator's presence.

But he hadn't seen anything.

The killer was invisible when he chose to be, a skill learned during childhood when survival depended on becoming part of the furniture, part of the walls, part of anything except a target for his father's rage. Now that childhood talent served a different purpose, allowing him to move through the world like a ghost, observing but unobserved, hunting but never hunted.

When Sheriff Callahan looked directly at his position without seeing the one she sought, the killer had felt a surge of power. Here was the person tasked with stopping him, the representative of law and order and civilization's thin veneer of safety, and she couldn't even detect his presence twenty yards away. He was not just invisible, he was invincible.

He'd almost laughed out loud when the snap of his red flag in the wind startled both law enforcement officers, causing the sheriff to jerk like she'd been shocked and reach instinctively for her weapon. The sight of authority figures jumping at shadows filled him with the same warm satisfaction he'd felt as a child when he avoided his father's attention during one of the man's drunken rampages.

Instead of giving in to the urge to reveal himself, to step from concealment and show them how close death had been standing, he'd pulled the hood of his dark jacket lower over his face and controlled his breathing until it matched the rhythm of the wind through the pine boughs. Patience was the hunter's greatest virtue, and he'd learned patience in a hard school where mistakes meant beatings and beatings sometimes meant trips to the emergency room with stories about falling down stairs or walking into doors.

When the forensics team arrived and began their examination of the crime scene, he'd withdrawn deeper into the forest with the fluid grace of someone who'd spent years learning to move without sound. But he hadn't gone far. Just far enough to avoid detection while maintaining visual contact with the proceedings.

He'd watched them photograph his work, document his message, and search for clues that would lead them nowhere. The red flag snapped in the breeze like a battle standard, and he'd felt an almost paternal pride. His creation. His statement. His proof that the frightened child in the closet had grown into something far more dangerous than his father had ever been.

Soon, when the time was right, he would give them another gift. Another red flag to mark another victory in his private war against the world that had failed to protect him when protection mattered most.

The hunt would continue until every last trace of red was burned from his memory, or until Sheriff Callahan proved herself worthy of the game by finally seeing the invisible man who'd been standing in plain sight all along.

Chapter Four

The sun rose over Misty Lake's surface like a golden coin emerging from navy velvet, casting ribbons of amber light across water so still it might have been polished glass. The early morning air carried the crisp promise of autumn, tinged with the earthy scent of decomposing leaves. A loon called from somewhere across the water, its voice mournful and distant, the kind of sound that made even seasoned outdoorsmen pause and listen to something older than civilization.

Greg Tanner, a weekend fisherman in his mid-forties with calloused hands and the permanent squint of someone who spent his leisure time staring at water, trudged toward the public kayak launch with his teenage son Eric trailing behind him. The boy carried paddles over his strong shoulders with the reluctance of someone who'd been drafted into early morning fishing expeditions since he could walk. Both wore the layered clothing of experienced anglers, moisture-wicking base layers under flannel shirts, with rain jackets tied around their waists against the possibility of afternoon storms.

The wooden planks of the dock were slick with

morning dew that had condensed in the cool pre-dawn hours, each board dark with moisture that would evaporate within an hour of full sunlight. Their boots made hollow sounds against the weathered lumber, and Greg automatically reached out to steady himself against the railing as they approached the water's edge. The familiar scents of pine needles and algae filled the air, mixed with the faint odor of fish and the petroleum tang of two-stroke engines from the boats that would arrive later in the day.

"Keep your voice down when we get out there," Greg said in the stage whisper that fathers used when imparting outdoor wisdom to reluctant teenagers. "Sound carries across water like you wouldn't believe. The fish will scatter to the deep water if we make too much noise talking." He adjusted the tackle box in his free hand, mentally cataloguing the lures he'd selected for the morning's expedition. "Your mother will be mighty pleased if we return with tonight's supper instead of another story about the one that got away."

Eric groaned with the theatrical suffering that only sixteen-year-old boys could muster at six in the morning, his breath forming small clouds in the cool air. Still half asleep despite the coffee his father had forced on him before they left the house, he tossed the paddles into their respective kayaks with more force than necessary, the aluminum shafts clattering against the fiberglass hulls. The sound echoed across the water like gunshots, causing a great blue heron fishing in the shallows fifty yards away to lift its head in alarm.

Eric reached down to untangle a bungee cord that had somehow wrapped itself around one of the kayak's deck fittings, his teenage coordination still compromised by sleep and resentment at the early hour. As he worked to free the elastic cord, he froze, his hands still as his eyes focused on something floating in the shadows beneath the dock.

At first glance, it looked like a bundle of dark clothing or rags that had snagged on one of the support pilings, the kind of debris that accumulated around docks after storms, when the wind drove all manner of floating objects into the protected coves. But as Eric's eyes adjusted to the dim light beneath the wooden structure, the shape resolved itself into something that made his stomach clench with a primal recognition of wrongness.

Then the current shifted, and the bundle turned, revealing a pale, water-swollen arm that hung loose and lifeless in the gentle movement of the lake.

Greg dropped his tackle box with a metallic clang that seemed to echo across the entire lake, sending a startled great blue heron exploding from the reeds with a harsh cry of alarm. The bird's wings beat heavily as it labored to gain altitude, disturbed from its patient hunting by the sudden intrusion of human panic into the morning calm.

"Dad..." Eric's voice came out as barely more than a whisper, his teenage bravado evaporating like morning mist. He stumbled backward from the edge of the dock, his feet sliding on the wet planks. "Dad, it's a person. There's a dead person in the water."

"Don't look, son." Greg's voice cracked with the strain of trying to maintain paternal authority while his mind reeled from the discovery. But even as he said the words, he found himself unable to turn away from the horror floating beneath their feet.

The face rolled into view with the lazy motion of something no longer governed by will or consciousness, revealing features that had been transformed by days in the water. The eyes were clouded like old windows, staring sightlessly at nothing, while the mouth hung slack in the final expression of someone who had died in terror or pain. Dark hair trailed around the head like black lakeweed, moving with the gentle current in a grotesque parody of life.

The dead woman bobbed gently against the dock piling with each small wave, the motion hypnotic and horrible. A diagonal slash mark gaped across her shoulder, the wound pale and bloodless after days of submersion, but visible as something inflicted by human hands rather than the teeth of fish or the scrape of underwater debris.

Then Greg's gaze moved beyond the floating corpse to the shoreline just a few feet away, and his blood turned to ice water in his veins. A red camping flag had been staked into the muddy bank, its crimson fabric fluttering in the morning breeze. The bright color seemed obscene against the gray morning light and the horror of their discovery, like a celebration banner planted at a funeral.

Eric thrust his cell phone into his father's trembling hands. Greg's fingers shook as he tried to punch in the numbers for the sheriff's station, his muscle memory struggling against the shock that had turned his hands into clumsy appendages. The phone's screen seemed impossibly small, the numbers dancing before his eyes as adrenaline flooded his system.

"Sheriff..." he managed to say when someone finally

answered, his voice barely recognizable even to himself. "There's another one. Here at the lake. A woman. She's..." His voice faltered as the wind caught the red flag and snapped it taut with a sound as sharp as a gunshot.

The unexpected noise made him jerk, and the phone slipped from his nerveless fingers to splash into the lake water below, disappearing beneath the surface with the same finality as the woman who floated there like some terrible offering to whatever dark god haunted Misty Lake.

~

Shea's patrol truck ate up the miles between the sheriff's station and the lake with an urgency that had become all too familiar over the past week. The radio crackled with updates from dispatch and the growing coordination of what was becoming the largest crime scene investigation in the county's recent history. Another victim. Another woman who had chosen to camp alone at what should have been a peaceful recreation area, except this time her body had been found floating in the lake rather than arranged in her tent like some macabre art installation.

The change in the killer's method of disposal bothered her more than she wanted to admit. Serial killers typically developed patterns and stuck to them with obsessive consistency. It was part of what made them both predictable and catchable. When they deviated from their established routines, it usually meant one of three things: they were evolving and becoming more dangerous, they were under pressure and making mistakes, or someone else was involved.

None of those possibilities offered much comfort.

Trevor had beaten her to the scene by ten minutes and

stood grim-faced near the dock, his notebook already filled with preliminary observations and his camera documenting the scene from multiple angles. He looked up as she approached with Heidi at her side, the German Shepherd's ears already alert to the scent of violence and death that seemed to cling to the morning air like fog.

"Father and son fishermen found the body about forty minutes ago," Trevor reported, his voice carrying the professional neutrality that cops developed to distance themselves from the human cost of violence. "Greg and Eric Tanner, locals who fish here most weekends. Body looks like it's been in the water at least twenty-four hours, maybe longer. Hard to tell with the lake temperature."

A dragonfly hovered above the gentle ripples where the body had disturbed the water's surface, its iridescent wings catching the gold of the rising sun as it dipped toward the lake as if to offer some final benediction to the dead. The insect's presence seemed both beautiful and terrible, a reminder that nature continued its ancient cycles regardless of human tragedy.

"It's different this time." Trevor pointed toward the floating corpse with his pen while keeping his distance from the water's edge. "Deep, jagged slashes instead of the precise stab wounds we found on the other victims. The cutting pattern is completely different. Less controlled, more frenzied. Could be we're looking at a copycat."

"Maybe." Shea's instincts already told her the story was more complicated than simple imitation. Her trained gaze swept the scene, cataloguing details that would later prove crucial. "Where was she camping?"

"Over there, about thirty yards from the water." Trevor

led her away from the dock to where crime scene technicians were already processing a small pop-up tent that had been erected in a clearing among the pine trees. "Not an official campsite, just a spot someone picked because it was isolated and had good lake access."

The tent was a modern backpacking model in muted earth tones, the kind favored by solo hikers who valued light weight over space. It sat in a small clearing that would have been invisible from the main hiking trails, accessible only by a narrow path that wound between the larger trees. Someone had chosen this spot, seeking privacy and solitude, which ultimately made them an easy target.

"Drag marks lead from the tent to the water." Trevor indicated disturbed earth and flattened vegetation that told the story of violence more clearly than any witness testimony. "She was killed here, next to her camp stove, then dragged to the lake and dumped. I also found this near the tent." He held up an evidence bag containing a cigarette butt. "Same brand as the one we found outside the outdoor supply store—Marlboro Red."

Some similarities to the other murders, but also crucial differences that made Shea's investigative instincts itch with unease. She peered into the tent through the open flap, searching for the red item that had triggered the killer's attention in previous cases. The interior was neat and organized. A sleeping bag rolled up military-style, camping gear arranged with the precision of someone accustomed to living out of a backpack, personal items stored in waterproof bags that suggested an experienced outdoors enthusiast.

But there was nothing red. No clothing, no equipment,

no camping accessories in the color that had marked every previous crime scene. The absence felt significant, like a missing note in a familiar melody.

They returned to the dock as the county coroner's team lifted the body from the water with the careful reverence reserved for the victims of violent crime. As the black body bag tilted on the stretcher, water poured from multiple wounds that became visible along the victim's back and shoulders. Long, diagonal slashes that spoke of frenzy rather than the controlled precision they'd seen in previous murders.

"We have to close the lake," Shea said, the words carrying the weight of a decision that would impact the entire community. "Whatever's happening here is escalating, and I won't have any more bodies on my conscience because we let people keep camping in a hunting ground."

Trevor nodded grimly. "Mayor Ferguson's going to have a conniption when the tourism revenue disappears, but you're right. We can't protect people if they keep walking into the killer's territory."

~

He loved the mornings more than any other time of day. The fog that rose from the lake's surface like the breath of sleeping giants, the silver quality of light that existed only in those precious minutes before the sun burned through the mist and transformed the world into a harsh reality. He crouched low in the shadows at the forest's edge, his knees growing damp from the moisture-soaked earth beneath him, feeling more at peace than he had since childhood.

His fingers twitched restlessly against the moss-covered log that provided his concealment, tracing idle patterns in the soft decay. At the same time, his gaze never wavered from the spot where the body floated like some pale flower blooming in dark water. The sight filled him with a satisfaction that was almost sexual in its intensity—not because of the death itself, but because of what it represented. Power. Control. The ability to transform the world according to his will.

The red flag he'd planted in the muddy shoreline flapped gently in the morning breeze, its crimson fabric bright as fresh blood against the muted colors of dawn. His calling card. A secret signal that only he truly understood, though others would try to decode its meaning with their limited comprehension of the forces that drove him.

He heard them before he saw them, the crunch of boots on gravel, the low mumble of a man's voice mixing with the sleepy responses of someone much younger. Father and son, from the sound of it. Perfect witnesses for the latest chapter in his ongoing masterpiece.

A smile tugged at the corners of his mouth as he anticipated their discovery.

The wooden boards of the dock creaked under their weight as they stepped onto the weathered structure. He could practically taste their casual conversation about fishing techniques and family expectations. Then came the moment he'd been waiting for, the sharp intake of breath, the sudden silence, followed by the boy's stammered exclamation and the metallic crash of dropped equipment.

The killer could taste their fear from where he knelt hidden among the trees, could smell the adrenaline that flooded their systems as their brains processed what their eyes were showing them. The father fumbled with his phone, hands shaking as he tried to summon help, and the killer found himself silently urging the man on.

"Call her," he whispered to himself, his voice barely audible even in the morning stillness. "Bring her to me."

The sheriff was the only one who mattered now. The only person in this backwater town who possessed the intelligence and determination to truly see him, to appreciate the artistry of what he was creating. The others, the mayor, the deputies, the frightened townspeople, were just background noise in the symphony he was composing.

Minutes passed with the slow weight of ceremonial time. The deputy arrived first in his squad car, but he was just a supporting player in this drama. The killer kept his attention focused on the access road, his pulse quickening with anticipation as Sheriff Callahan's patrol truck finally appeared through the trees.

She stepped out of the vehicle with the fluid grace of someone accustomed to arriving at crime scenes, her dark hair catching whispers of the morning light, her posture sharp and alert as she processed the scene. Even from his concealed position fifty yards away, he could read her body language like a familiar book, the slight tension in her shoulders that spoke of controlled anxiety, the way her eyes swept the area in systematic patterns that missed nothing.

He knew the exact moment she spotted his red flag. She froze for just a heartbeat, her gaze locking onto the crimson fabric like a predator recognizing another predator's territorial marker, then squared her shoulders with the determination that made her such a worthy adversary.

Good girl. The sheriff always kept her composure, even when confronted with horrors that would send ordinary people screaming into the night.

The deputy pointed out different aspects of the crime scene, his deep voice carrying across the water as he shared his preliminary observations. The killer leaned forward, straining to catch every word, and felt his satisfaction begin to curdle into something darker and more dangerous.

Copycat? They thought this was the work of a copycat?

His hands clenched into fists as he processed the implications of their conversation. Someone had dared to imitate his work, to muddy the waters of his carefully crafted message with their crude approximation of artistry. The slashes on this body were wrong. Jagged and frenzied, his kills were precise and controlled, driven by passion rather than the cold calculation that marked actual predators.

This wasn't art. This was vandalism.

Someone had come along and ruined his work, corrupted his message, turned his elegant statement into a crude scrawl. Worse, they were making the sheriff doubt the purity of his vision, making her question whether she dealt with one killer or multiple threats.

The sheriff turned toward his hiding place as if some primitive part of her brain sensed his presence among the trees. Her gaze slid over his position, so close to discovering him that he could practically feel the heat of her attention. So perfect. So infuriatingly unaware of how close she was to the truth.

He would have to fix this. Make her see the difference between his work and this crude imitation. The next kill would be like the others, clean, precise, artistically perfect. Then she would understand that she was dealing with someone who operated on a level far above common murderers.

But first, he needed to find what was missing from this scene. Where was the red item that should have been here? Every one of his previous victims possessed something crimson that called to him like a beacon, that triggered the ancient rage that lived in his chest like a caged animal. Had the imitator taken it as some sick souvenir? Had they failed to understand that the red was essential, that it was the entire point of everything he was trying to accomplish?

The thought of someone else touching his trigger, possessing the crimson totems that belonged to him, filled him with a fury that made his vision blur around the edges. Whoever had dared to copy his work would pay for their presumption.

Soon.

~

Trevor frowned as he ended the call and slipped his phone back into his uniform pocket. "Potential witness just called in with a name," he reported, consulting his notes. "Boyd Winters. He owns some rental cabins on the other side of the lake and rents them out to campers who want more amenities than tent camping provides. Witness claims he saw Winters walking around this area before sunrise, maybe an hour before the body was discovered."

"Let's pay Mr. Winters a visit." Shea led the way toward her patrol truck. "We can retrieve your squad car later."

The dirt road that led to Boyd Winters' property barely deserved the name, being more of a logging trail that had been widened just enough to allow passage of pickup trucks and ATVs. Tree branches scraped against the sides of Shea's vehicle as they navigated the winding path, creating a sound like fingernails on a chalkboard. The canopy of pine and oak overhead blocked most of the morning sunlight, creating a tunnel of green shadows that seemed to press in from all sides.

"Tell me what we know about Winters," Shea said, tightening her grip on the steering wheel as she maneuvered around a particularly tight curve that brought them uncomfortably close to a drop-off that plunged toward the lake below.

Trevor pulled up information on his phone, scrolling through database records and background checks that painted a picture of someone existing on the margins of society. "Forty-six years old, Army veteran with three tours in Afghanistan. Moved to Misty Hollow six years ago and purchased the cabin property with what looks like disability payments and some settlement. Two assault charges over the past four years, both stemming from bar fights at Murphy's Tavern, but neither has stuck in court. Victims declined to press charges both times."

"Interesting. What's his business model?"

"Apparently, he rents cabins to people who want to camp at the lake but don't want to sleep in tents. Does everything online through one of those vacation rental websites. Advertises 'rustic accommodations for the outdoor enthusiast who values privacy and solitude.' No reviews mention ever meeting him face-to-face."

"Then what was he doing at the public boat launch this morning?" Shea mused as they emerged from the tree tunnel into a clearing that contained what could charitably be called a homestead. "If he's making money keeping people away from his property, why risk being seen at a crime scene?"

"That's what we're here to find out." Trevor suspected this would turn out to be another dead end. Someone in the wrong place at the wrong time, whose only crime was poor timing and suspicious neighbors.

The clearing contained a central cabin that looked like it had been constructed by someone with more enthusiasm than skill, surrounded by one smaller structure. The cabin was built from logs that had weathered to a silvery gray, with a metal roof that showed patches of rust . A narrow porch ran along the front, supporting a collection of mismatched furniture that looked like it had been rescued from various yard sales.

Trevor stepped out of the patrol truck onto a yard where weeds had won the war against grass years ago, his trained gaze scanning the property for potential threats or escape routes. The isolation of the location would make Winters dangerous if he chose to be, no neighbors to hear gunshots, no witnesses to whatever might happen in these woods.

The front door of the cabin slammed open with enough force to rattle the windows, the sound echoing across the clearing like a gunshot. Trevor's hand moved toward the service weapon on his hip as a tall, gaunt figure emerged onto the porch.

Boyd Winters looked like someone who'd been carved from weathered wood and left outside too long. He stood well over six feet tall but couldn't have weighed more than one-sixty, giving him the appearance of a scarecrow dressed in faded flannel and worn denim. His gray beard was unkempt, and his sunken eyes held the wariness of someone who'd learned not to trust authority figures. A chipped ceramic mug steamed in his hands, filling the air with the rich scent of coffee that seemed at odds with his hostile demeanor.

"You're trespassing," he announced without preamble, his voice carrying the flat authority of someone accustomed to being left alone.

Shea stepped forward and flashed her badge. "I'm Sheriff Callahan, and this is Deputy Bolton. We need to ask you a few questions about the recent killings at Misty Lake."

Winters studied them for a long moment, his pale eyes moving from Shea's face to Trevor's position near the truck. Finally, he took a slow sip from his coffee mug and shrugged with elaborate indifference. "I didn't kill anybody."

"Mind if we come inside?" Shea asked, her tone suggesting that refusal wasn't an option despite the polite phrasing.

Winters hesitated, and for a moment Trevor thought he might refuse and force them to obtain a warrant. Then the man's shoulders sagged slightly, and he jerked his head toward the open door. "I guess. But wipe your feet. I just mopped that floor."

The interior of the cabin hit them with a wall of

competing odors, motor oil, mildew, cigarette smoke, and strong coffee, all mixed together in a combination that spoke of a man living alone without much concern for social niceties. Newspapers sat stacked on every available surface, some dating back months, creating fire hazards. A gun rack hung over the stone fireplace, displaying a collection of hunting rifles and shotguns that looked well-maintained despite the general disarray of the living space. A mounted deer head stared down at them with glass eyes that seemed to follow their movement around the room.

Trevor's attention focused on a hunting knife lying on the kitchen table, its blade easily eight inches long with a serrated edge that could certainly have created the type of wounds they'd observed on the latest victim. "Interesting knife." He moved closer to examine it without touching the potential evidence.

Shea nodded but kept her primary attention on Winters, who had settled heavily into a recliner that looked like it predated the Clinton administration. The man rubbed his temples as if fighting off a headache, or perhaps trying to organize thoughts that unexpected visitors had scattered.

"You think I'm the one planting those red flags around dead bodies?" Winters asked, his voice carrying a mixture of incredulity and weary resignation. "I don't even like people camping at the lake in the first place. They leave trash everywhere, play their music too loud, and generally disturb the peace I moved out here to find. I only rent the cabins because it's decent money and keeps me from having to work for somebody else."

"Where were you last few nights between midnight and sunrise?" Trevor pulled out his notebook to record whatever alibi Winters might offer.

"Right here, same as every night for the past six years. I don't go out after dark unless there's an emergency, and I sure don't go wandering around the lake looking for people to murder."

"Can anyone vouch for that?"

Winters looked at Trevor as if he'd asked whether the sky was blue. "Are you hard of hearing, deputy? I said I was alone. That's the whole point of living out here. To be left alone."

"Mind if we take a look around your property?" Shea gestured toward the back door .

The man stood with the creaking joints of someone whose body had absorbed more punishment than it was designed to handle. "Guess not. You're already here, ain't you?" He led them outside through a back door that opened onto a path connecting the main cabin to the rental units. "Only other building of any size is the maintenance shed where I keep tools and supplies. Knock yourselves out."

The shed was a prefabricated metal structure that looked like it had been assembled from a kit, its walls lined with pegboard that held an impressive collection of hand tools. Rusty shovels and rakes competed for space with more modern power tools, while shelves along the back wall held everything from paint cans to camping equipment that former renters had probably left behind.

Trevor's flashlight beam landed on another knife hanging from a nail on the wall, this one in a leather sheath that showed considerable wear. He carefully pulled the blade free, noting its condition and design. "This one's seen a lot of use," he observed, angling the steel to catch the light filtering through the shed's single window.

Shea moved to examine a pile of firewood that had been stacked against the far wall, noting that the logs were streaked with damp mud and debris. "These were moved recently," she said, running her finger along one of the pieces and coming away with fresh dirt. "Within the last day or two, I'd say."

"That's what I was doing at the lake." Winters crossed his arms. "Gathering wood."

Trevor opened an old military surplus ammo box that sat on one of the workbenches, revealing a collection of items that made his pulse quicken. Red shop rags stained with what looked like motor oil, a coil of rope that could have been used for restraining victims, and several camping flags identical to the ones they'd been finding at crime scenes.

"This doesn't look good for you, Mr. Winters," Trevor said, photographing the contents of the box with his phone before carefully bagging each item as potential evidence.

Winters stepped closer. His expression shifted from resigned cooperation to genuine alarm as he saw what Trevor had discovered. "Now hold on just a cotton-picking minute. I collect stuff that campers leave behind when they clear out of here. Happens all the time. People forget things, or they decide they don't want to pack wet gear, or they abandon stuff they don't think is worth keeping. Those flags have the names of different campsites printed on them, not blank like the ones you've been finding at your murder scenes."

He was right. Shea examined one of the flags more closely and saw that it bore a list of state parks and campgrounds in small print along the bottom edge, the kind of souvenir that serious campers collected to commemorate their adventures. Still, the presence of multiple red flags in the possession of someone with no alibi and a history of violence was too much of a coincidence to ignore.

"Someone is murdering people out there, Mr. Winters," Shea said. "And whoever it is wants to be seen. They're sending a message with those flags, claiming responsibility for their kills. Right now, you look like a man with no alibi, a history of violent behavior, and a collection of the exact items we've been finding at murder scenes."

Winters worked his jaw as if he were chewing something bitter, his eyes moving between the evidence bags and the two law enforcement officers who were rapidly becoming his biggest problem. "Except for the printed names of campsites," he said finally. "Don't forget that detail, Sheriff. These flags are souvenirs, not the blank ones your killer's been using."

Trevor took a slow breath, his gloved fingers still wrapped around the handle of the knife he'd taken from the wall. Something made the hair on the back of his neck stand up, and it wasn't just the claustrophobic atmosphere of the shed or the potential evidence they'd uncovered.

The forest around them had fallen silent in a way that felt unnatural, as if even the birds and insects were holding their breath. He stepped from the shed and let his gaze sweep the tree line that surrounded Winters' property, every instinct developed over years of police work screaming that something was wrong.

Someone watched them. And it wasn't Boyd Winters,

who stood barely three feet away, arguing with Shea about the significance of printed camping flags.

Trevor's hand moved to rest on his service weapon as he continued to scan the shadows between the trees. Somewhere out there, hidden among the pines and oak trees, the real killer observed their investigation with the patience of a predator waiting for the perfect moment to strike.

The question was whether they would figure that out before it was too late.

Chapter Five

The little girl hung her red beach towel over the back of a folding lawn chair, the crimson terry cloth bright against the light of late afternoon. She smoothed the fabric with small hands before turning to where her family had gathered around a concrete picnic table for their evening meal. The familiar sounds of camping filled the air, the hiss of the propane camp stove, the rustle of paper plates being distributed, the gentle lapping of lake water against the nearby shore.

A sharp crack echoed from the woods. The unmistakable snap of a heavy boot breaking a dead branch. The sound drew her attention to a dense thicket of pine trees and wild undergrowth that bordered their campsite like a green wall. Between the trunks, shadows moved and shifted in ways that made her eight-year-old imagination conjure all manner of forest monsters.

"Daddy, are there bears out here?" Her voice carried the mixture of fear and fascination that children brought to discussions of dangerous wildlife.

Her father glanced up from flipping hamburger patties on the camp stove, grease spattering and hissing on the hot surface. He was a big man with gentle hands and laugh lines around his eyes, the kind of father who could make any situation feel safe with just his presence. "I'm sure there are, sweetie. Black bears, most of them harmless if you leave them alone. Why do you ask?"

"I heard something moving around over there." She pointed toward the tree line. "Something big."

Roy followed her gaze to the forest edge, his expression shifting from casual interest to mild concern. Bears were indeed common in this part of Arkansas, and while attacks on humans were rare, a surprised or cornered animal could be dangerous, especially with children around. "Do you still hear it, Emma?"

The girl tilted her head and listened for several seconds, her small face scrunched in concentration. Birds called from the canopy overhead, and somewhere in the distance a fish jumped in the lake with a soft splash. But from the woods came only the normal sounds of evening, the rustle of leaves, the distant hoot of an owl preparing for its nightly hunt. "No, not anymore."

"Probably just a squirrel foraging for nuts," he said. "I'll make sure to seal the camp food up tight before going to bed tonight. Lots of critters in these woods, and they can make quite a racket when they're digging around in the undergrowth."

He handed Emma a paper plate loaded with a hamburger and a generous helping of the potato chips his wife had opened, the kind of camp meal that tasted better outdoors than it ever did at home. His wife emerged from their pop-up camper carrying a tray of french fries that had been warming in the small oven they'd brought along for the weekend.

Her dark eyes swept the campsite with the automatic vigilance of someone accustomed to supervising twenty-five third-graders at once, and she caught the movement in the trees that her husband had missed.

"Roy?" Her voice carried a note of tension that made him look up from the camp stove. "Something is definitely out there. In those trees by the water."

"Daddy said it was a squirrel," Emma said around a bite of hamburger, ketchup and mustard mixing on her chin in a way that would have horrified her grandmother.

"That's not a squirrel." The woman set the tray of fries on the picnic table with more force than necessary. She grabbed her cell phone from a nearby camp chair, her fingers moving to the emergency contact list she'd programmed before they left home. "I told you we shouldn't go camping after everything that's been happening at this lake. People getting murdered, that serial killer running around loose. I'm calling the sheriff's department right now."

"You're overreacting,, Karen," Roy said, though his own eyes had moved to scan the tree line with more attention than he'd given it moments before. He shut off the propane valve on their camp stove and carried the remaining hamburgers to the table, his movements deliberate and calm in the way that men learned when they wanted to project confidence they didn't entirely feel. "It's probably just some other camper walking through the woods, maybe looking for a lost dog or trying to find the bathroom facilities."

Their son, twelve years old and possessed of the

invincible confidence that came with being almost a teenager, pushed through the screen door of their camper with his dark hair still damp from a quick shower. A blue bath towel was draped around his shoulders, and drops of water fell onto the wooden deck they'd assembled outside the camper's entrance.

He grabbed his sister's red towel from the back of her chair as he passed, ignoring her indignant protest. "You're getting the camp chairs all wet, Emma. Mom told us to keep the furniture dry." He headed toward the trees with both towels in hand, intending to hang them on low branches where they could finish drying in the evening breeze. "I'll put these somewhere they won't drip all over everything."

He didn't see his sister stick out her tongue at his retreating figure in the universal gesture of sibling defiance, but someone else did. From the darkness between the pine trees came a sound that was unmistakably human. A low chuckle of amusement that carried just enough malevolence to transform innocent family banter into something altogether more sinister.

The killer had been watching their domestic scene unfold with the patience of a predator studying its prey, cataloguing their movements and routines while his attention focused with laser intensity on that splash of red fabric. The sight of the towel triggered something deep in his damaged psyche, calling up memories of another red cloth from decades past. The soft wool that had meant safety and comfort before it became fuel for flames and the birth of monsters.

When the boy with the blue towel grabbed the red one

and started walking toward his hiding place, the killer felt a surge of anticipation so intense it was almost painful. Here was his chance. A child walking into darkness, carrying the very symbol that drove him to kill, moving away from the protection of his family with the innocent trust that predators had exploited since time began.

But then that chuckle had escaped him, a sound born from the dark amusement of watching innocence walk toward its destruction. The noise was quiet, barely more than a breath, but in the stillness of evening it carried like a gunshot.

The boy froze mid-step, his survival instincts screaming warnings that his conscious mind couldn't yet process. The forest around him had gone silent in the way that meant a predator was near, and some primitive part of his brain recognized the danger even as his rational thoughts struggled to catch up.

"Dad?" His voice cracked with the first real fear he'd felt since they'd arrived at the campsite, the confident swagger of near-adolescence evaporating like morning mist. "Dad, there's someone out here."

The terror in his son's voice sent Roy moving with the speed that only parents possessed when their children were threatened. He crossed the distance between the picnic table and the tree line in four quick strides, his hands already reaching for Michael's shoulders to pull the boy back toward the safety of their campsite.

"Who's there?" Roy called into the darkness, his voice carrying the authority of someone prepared to defend his family regardless of the cost. "Show yourself. I know you're out there."

The killer heard the challenge in the man's voice and recognized it as the sound a wolf made when protecting its pack. This was no longer a hunting opportunity. It was a confrontation that could only end in violence or retreat. Without the element of surprise, without the victim isolated and vulnerable, the risk had become too great.

He turned and bolted through the forest with the fluid grace of someone who had spent years learning to move through dense undergrowth without making unnecessary noise. Branches whipped at his face and arms as he ran, and he could hear Roy crashing through the woods behind him, cursing and calling for help.

But the killer knew these woods better than any weekend camper, knew every game trail and hidden path that would lead him back to safety. Within minutes he had vanished into the darkness like smoke dissipating in wind, leaving behind only the sound of Roy's labored breathing and the distant crying of a little girl who had just learned that monsters were real.

He would be back when the family wasn't on high alert, when their vigilance had been worn down by exhaustion and the false comfort of familiar surroundings. The red towel would still call to him, and next time he would be ready.

~

Shea drove toward the campsite with Trevor in the passenger seat, her patrol truck kicking up clouds of dust. The radio crackled with updates from dispatch and the growing coordination of what had become a county-wide manhunt, though she knew their chances of catching the killer in the vast wilderness surrounding Misty Lake were slim to none.

Thank God the potential victims had made the emergency call instead of someone stumbling across more bodies. She'd been dreading another crime scene, another family destroyed by senseless violence, another red flag planted like a grave marker in soil that was becoming saturated with blood.

A family of four huddled inside their camper when Shea and Trevor arrived, the parents' faces visible through the screen windows as they tried to comfort two children who had just experienced their first real brush with evil. The father, a heavyset man with graying hair and worried eyes, emerged from the camper as soon as the patrol truck's doors slammed shut.

Roy Patterson was visibly shaken, his hands trembling as he rushed toward the approaching officers. He began talking before Shea could even close her truck door, words tumbling over each other in his haste to share what had happened. "Someone was here, watching us from the woods. We saw him, or at least heard him clear as day. My son almost walked right into him." His voice cracked with the strain of maintaining composure while his mind processed how close his family had come to tragedy. "Was it that killer? The one who's been murdering people?"

Why anyone would choose to go camping when a serial killer hunted these woods was beyond Shea's comprehension, but she managed to keep her frustration from showing in her voice. People had a remarkable capacity for believing that bad things happened to other families, that their vacation plans somehow exempted them from the danger that stalked this particular paradise. "You did the right thing calling us, Mr. Patterson. What exactly did you see or hear?"

Roy ran a hand through his hair, leaving it standing up in nervous spikes. "My daughter Emma heard something moving around in the woods at first, but I brushed it off as being a squirrel or maybe a raccoon. Then my wife Karen saw actual movement between the trees. Something too big and too deliberate to be an animal. It wasn't until my son Michael went to hang up some towels..."

His gaze moved to the picnic table where a red beach towel lay crumpled next to a blue bath towel, both forgotten in the chaos of their hasty retreat to the camper. "Michael heard someone laugh. Not a nice laugh, you understand. Something that made his skin crawl. When I went to check on him, whoever it was took off running through the woods, making enough noise to wake the dead. Definitely human, definitely watching us."

"Why don't you finish packing up your gear while Deputy Bolton and I take a look around?" Shea's voice carried the gentle authority she'd learned to use with traumatized civilians. "We'll process the scene and see what we can find."

Roy nodded and began loading camping equipment into the back of his SUV with the methodical urgency of someone who wanted to put as much distance as possible between his family and this place. His wife emerged from the camper to help, her arms wrapped protectively around their two children as they gathered their belongings.

"Red towel," Trevor observed as they approached the area where the Patterson family had encountered their uninvited observer. "Just like all the other crime scenes.

Whatever triggers this guy, it's connected to that specific color."

"No question about it." Shea whistled for Heidi, and the German Shepherd leaped from the patrol truck to pad silently to her side, nose already working to process the complex scent picture that every crime scene presented.

They stepped into the gathering darkness of the forest, where the canopy of pine and oak branches filtered the remaining daylight into a green twilight that made every shadow potentially dangerous. Despite the fact that sunset was still an hour away, Shea switched on her powerful LED flashlight and began sweeping its beam across the forest floor in systematic patterns.

It didn't take long to discover where the killer had maintained his surveillance. The evidence was written in the disturbed earth and vegetation as clearly as words on a page for anyone trained to read the signs.

Flattened pine needles formed a rough outline where someone had knelt or crouched for an extended period. Deep boot prints were pressed into the soft soil, the heel marks indicating someone who had shifted his weight repeatedly while maintaining his position. The toe of each print pointed directly toward the Patterson family's campsite, confirming that their observer had been focused intently on their activities.

A patch of churned dirt showed where the watcher had changed position at least once, probably when the family's movements brought them closer to his hiding spot. Then, leading away through the undergrowth, a clear trail of broken branches and disturbed earth marked the killer's hasty retreat when his presence had been discovered.

"He was here for quite a while." Trevor knelt beside the most clearly defined boot print and used his phone to photograph it from multiple angles. "Watching their entire dinner routine, probably waiting for the right moment to strike." He moved to examine the smaller footprints that marked where young Michael Patterson had approached the tree line. "The boy got within arm's reach. If the killer had wanted to grab him, nothing could have stopped him."

The thought made Shea's blood run cold. She'd seen enough crime scenes to know how quickly violence could erupt, how a moment's inattention could transform a family camping trip into a nightmare that would haunt survivors for the rest of their lives. She glanced over her shoulder to where Karen Patterson held her children close, the mother's eyes never leaving the forest edge where death had been waiting in the shadows.

"We need to get this family to the station to give formal statements," Shea decided. "And then I'm closing down the entire campground. No more camping, no fishing, no recreational activities of any kind between sunset and sunrise. Maybe not even during daylight hours, if this continues."

Trevor looked up from his examination of the evidence, his expression reflecting the same frustration that had been building in both of them as the killer continued to evade capture. "Mayor Ferguson is going to lose his mind when he hears about this. The tourism industry is already hemorrhaging money from all the cancellations."

"I don't care if the mayor spontaneously combusts," Shea replied with more heat than she'd intended. "This family was lucky. They had a twelve-year-old boy with good instincts and a father willing to chase a potential threat through the woods. The next family might not be so fortunate."

Within an hour, a convoy of recreational vehicles and passenger cars filed out of the campground like refugees fleeing a war zone. Park rangers strung bright yellow tape across access roads and hiking trails, transforming what had once been a destination for outdoor enthusiasts into something that looked more like a quarantine zone.

The silence that settled over the area was profound and unsettling. Where laughter and conversation had filled the evening air just hours before, now only the natural sounds of forest wildlife remained. Even those seemed muted, as if the animals themselves sensed that something predatory had claimed this territory.

Shea stood at the edge of the lake, watching the last traces of sunlight dance across the water's surface like scattered diamonds. The beauty of the place seemed almost obscene when measured against the violence that had transformed it into a hunting ground. Somewhere out there, hidden among the trees or perhaps watching from across the water, the killer probably observed her efforts to deny him his prey.

The thought made her skin crawl, but it also strengthened her resolve. If this had become a personal battle between law enforcement and a predator, she was prepared to fight it on those terms.

~

The killer returned after midnight, moving through the forest with the silent grace of someone who had learned to hunt in darkness. He followed game trails and logging roads that most people never knew existed, his night vision aided by years of practice and an intimate knowledge of every tree and rock formation in these woods.

But as he approached the campsite where the red towel had called to him like a beacon, something felt wrong. The forest was too quiet, the air too still. None of the normal sounds of human habitation reached his ears. No voices, no music, no crackling of campfires or hum of RV generators.

He stopped at the edge of the clearing and frowned, his hand moving to the handle of the knife sheathed at his belt. The campsite stood empty and abandoned, stripped of everything that had made it a target for his brand of violence.

No firelight danced in the established fire ring. No camping chairs sat arranged in conversational clusters around picnic tables. No laughter or music drifted on the evening breeze. Most importantly, no red towel swayed in the night air, taunting him with memories of another piece of red fabric that had been stolen from him decades before.

Just emptiness. Just the hollow echo of an opportunity denied.

His heart hammered with a rage so pure and intense that it threatened to overwhelm his careful self-control. He stepped into the deserted campsite, his boots crunching on pine needles and scattered leaves that had already begun to reclaim the space where a family had been preparing to sleep just hours before.

The fire ring was nothing but cold gray ashes, as lifeless as the dreams of the victims he'd claimed in previous hunts. The cheerful checkered tablecloth was gone from the picnic table, along with the camping chairs and the small personal touches that had made this place feel like a temporary home.

No camper was connected to the electrical and water hookups that the campground provided for the comfort of its guests. Everything that had made this site a target for his obsessions had been swept away as if it had never existed.

He had waited and watched with the patience of a true predator. He had almost felt the weight of that red towel in his hands, could practically hear the child's whimper of terror that would have sounded so much like his own cries from long ago, when he had been the victim rather than the predator.

The ritual had been broken. For the first time since he'd begun his crusade against the color that haunted his dreams, he had failed to kill when red fabric beckoned to him. The sheriff had somehow managed to snatch his prey away just when the moment of culmination had been within his grasp.

Bright yellow police tape stretched across the hiking trail that led to this campsite, the plastic barrier fluttering in the night breeze like a challenge banner. The sight of it fueled his anger until his vision blurred around the edges and his hands shook with the need to destroy something, anything, that would relieve the pressure building in his chest.

He yanked the tape down with vicious satisfaction, wadding the plastic into a ball and hurling it into the darkness. His breathing quickened as he fought to regain the icy control that had made him such an effective killer, but the rage continued to burn in his belly like swallowed acid.

The ritual had been broken, but that didn't mean the war was over. There were other campsites, other lakes, other opportunities to continue his work. He wouldn't leave Misty Hollow. Not when things were just getting interesting between himself and the sheriff who had dared to interfere with his plans.

In an act of defiance that felt as necessary as breathing, he pulled a red camping flag from his backpack and stabbed it deep into the cold ashes of the abandoned fire ring. Let the sheriff find this message and understand that her small victory had only delayed the inevitable.

This was war now, and wars were won by whoever was willing to pay the highest price for victory.

~

The next morning, Shea returned to the empty campsite before heading to her office, wanting to verify that her closure orders were being respected and that no foolhardy campers had decided the rules didn't apply to them. What she found made her mouth go dry with a mixture of fear and professional satisfaction.

The red flag fluttered from the cold fire ring like a battle standard planted by an occupying army, its crimson fabric bright as fresh blood against the gray ashes. He had come back, just as she'd known he would. The yellow police tape lay scattered on the ground like the molted skin of some plastic snake, torn down in what could only be interpreted as an act of deliberate contempt.

She pushed open her truck door and commanded Heidi to stay close, her hand resting on her service weapon as she scanned the tree line for any sign that the killer might have remained in the area to observe her reaction to his message.

Moving with the careful precision of someone who had processed dozens of crime scenes, she documented the evidence with her phone camera while studying the story written in disturbed earth and scattered debris.

Fresh boot prints marked where the killer had marched into the clearing, the deep heel impressions suggesting someone walking with purpose rather than stealth. The same tread pattern they'd found at previous crime scenes, confirming that their primary suspect had indeed returned to claim this territory as his own.

But there was something different about these tracks, something in their spacing and depth that suggested emotion rather than the cold calculation she'd observed at previous murder sites. The killer had been angry when he'd planted this flag, frustrated by her interference with his plans.

She smiled grimly as she photographed the evidence, knowing that she had managed to disrupt his ritual and deny him at least one victim. It was a small victory in what was shaping up to be a long campaign, but sometimes small victories were all that stood between civilization and chaos.

She called the ranger station from her patrol truck, requesting immediate implementation of round-the-clock surveillance of the entire lake area. She'd closed public access to the campgrounds and hiking trails, but experience had taught her that some people considered themselves exempt from inconvenient regulations.

Late-night fishermen would try to sneak onto the lake under the cover of darkness, convinced that their hobby trumped public safety concerns. Teenage couples would view the closure as an exciting opportunity for privacy and adventure. Even serious hikers might decide that their outdoor recreation was worth the risk of encountering a serial killer.

All of them would become potential victims if the killer decided to expand his hunting grounds or change his methods. And judging by the angry message he'd left in the ashes of that fire ring, change was coming to Misty Hollow.

Chapter Six

The killer moved like a shadow through the towering mountain pines that carpeted the slopes of Misty Mountain in a dense blanket of green. Ancient trees rose toward the star-scattered sky, their trunks scarred by decades of weather and wildlife, their branches forming a canopy so thick that moonlight barely penetrated to the forest floor below. The air carried the sharp scent of pine needles and the mineral smell of mountain streams that wound their way down from the peaks above.

It had taken him three days of careful thought and planning before deciding that the vacation cabins scattered across these slopes would provide new opportunities for the color red to beckon him forward. Three days of pacing his rental house like a caged animal, studying topographical maps and vacation rental websites, searching for the perfect hunting ground to replace the lake that had been denied to him by police tape and round-the-clock surveillance.

Misty Mountain offered everything he needed. Isolated cabins filled with families seeking peaceful retreats, winding hiking trails that provided concealment and multiple escape routes, and terrain rugged enough to hide a dozen bodies without discovery. Best of all, the mountain cabins catered to a different type of vacationer than the lakeside campgrounds. Families with young children who valued comfort over wilderness adventure, people who brought along creature comforts that might include the red items that called him like sirens in the night.

Through the maze of pine trunks, he spotted a cluster of rental cabins perched along a gentle slope that overlooked the valley below. Each structure was designed to blend with the natural surroundings while providing modern amenities that city dwellers expected during their mountain getaways. Warm light glowed from multiple windows, casting golden rectangles across the forest floor and illuminating patches of fern and wildflower that grew in the spaces between trees.

The cabins sat far enough apart to provide privacy for their occupants while remaining close enough for mutual assistance in case of emergencies. Perfect conditions for a predator who understood how to exploit the illusion of safety that isolation provided.

He crouched behind a massive fallen log that had probably toppled during some long-ago storm, his gaze locked on cabin number six like a sniper studying his target through a scope.

Inside, a man and woman moved through their evening routine with the comfortable synchronization of a couple who had shared domestic spaces for years. The man stood at the kitchen sink washing dinner dishes, his sleeves rolled up and his attention focused on scrubbing a cast-iron skillet that had probably seen service in preparing the kind of hearty mountain meal that vacation rental websites promised their guests.

The woman folded blankets in the living room, her movements calm and nurturing as she arranged the colorful fabrics on furniture that had been chosen more for comfort than style. The domestic scene radiated the kind of peace and contentment that normal families took for granted but that had been stolen from the killer before he was old enough to understand what he was losing.

On the kitchen counter, partially hidden behind a coffee maker and a basket of mountain apples, lay a red oven mitt that snagged his vision like a fishhook catching flesh. The bright crimson fabric seemed to pulse with an internal light, calling to the damaged parts of his psyche that could never heal, never forget, never forgive the night his father had turned his childhood sanctuary into ash and smoke.

He had been called. The ritual could begin.

After watching the cabin for half an hour, cataloguing the family's routines and identifying potential complications, he approached the back door with the confidence of someone who had done this before. The lock was a simple residential deadbolt, the kind that provided psychological comfort rather than absolute security against someone with basic lock-picking skills and unlimited time to work.

Stupid people who lived their lives believing that death required an invitation, that evil respected locked doors and window latches. They moved through their safe little worlds, never understanding that predators had been watching from the shadows since the first human settlements, learning their patterns and weaknesses with the patience of apex hunters.

The back door opened with barely a whisper of sound, well-oiled hinges swinging inward to reveal a mudroom equipped with hiking boots and rain gear that spoke of a family that took their mountain vacation seriously. Beyond that lay a kitchen where the dishwashing husband had moved on to wiping down counters with the thoroughness of someone who had learned that vacation cleanup was still cleanup.

But the man had finished his chores and retreated to the living room, where the killer found him sprawled on a leather couch with one arm dangling toward the floor and his head tilted back against the cushions. A television cast a pale blue light across his relaxed features. At the same time, some late-night comedy show provided background noise for the kind of peaceful evening that millions of families enjoyed without ever considering how fragile such moments could be.

The killer approached with the slow patience of a cat stalking a sleeping bird, his footsteps muffled by carpet that had been chosen to absorb the sounds of vacation revelry. He drew the hunting knife from its sheath with surgical precision, the blade reflecting television light like captured lightning.

One clean thrust to the throat, angled upward toward the brain stem. The man jerked once as his nervous system registered the catastrophic damage, made a wet gurgling sound as blood filled his airway, then slumped lifeless into the couch cushions with the boneless collapse that marked the transition from person to corpse.

The killer paused and listened to the night sounds of

the cabin. The hum of the refrigerator, the whisper of air through heating vents, the distant murmur of a television in another room. Then he heard what he was waiting for: movement from somewhere down the hallway that led to the cabin's bedrooms. The soft pad of bare feet on hardwood flooring, approaching with the casual confidence of someone who had no reason to fear what might be waiting in the darkness.

He slipped around the corner into the hallway and pressed his back against the wall, becoming part of the shadows that pooled between the cabin's overhead lighting fixtures. His breathing slowed to match the rhythm of someone in deep sleep, and his grip on the knife handle adjusted to provide maximum control for the strike that would come in seconds.

The woman appeared at the end of the hallway, her hair tousled from an evening of relaxation and her feet bare against the polished wood floor. She wore the kind of comfortable clothing that spoke of vacation ease. She wore soft cotton that moved with her body and colors chosen for comfort rather than fashion.

As if some primitive part of her brain sensed the presence of evil lurking in her family's temporary sanctuary, she paused at the threshold between hallway and living room. Her head tilted in the universal gesture of someone trying to identify a sound or smell that didn't belong, and for a moment, the killer thought she might turn and flee back toward the bedrooms where her children slept in blissful ignorance.

But the moment passed, and she took another step forward, moving toward the living room where her husband's body waited in its mockery of peaceful sleep.

The killer lunged from the shadows with the explosive violence of a coiled spring suddenly released. His left hand clamped over her mouth before she could draw breath to scream, while his right hand drove the knife into her throat with surgical precision.

Her scream emerged as nothing more than a sharp intake of breath that was choked off by the blade that opened her carotid artery and severed the vocal cords that might have summoned help. But unlike her husband's swift and merciful death, hers became a frenzied ballet of violence that spoke to something more profound and more personal than simple murder.

He stabbed her three more times, each strike faster and more desperate than the last, his control slipping as memories of another woman flooded through his damaged psyche. His mother's face superimposed itself over his victim's features, and for a moment, he was eight years old again, watching helplessly as his father's fists reduced love to bruises and terror to silence. His mother had done nothing to save her son or herself from his father's wrath.

Chest heaving with exertion and emotion, he stepped back from the carnage and tried to regain the icy control that made him such an effective predator. Blood covered his hands and clothes, and the metallic smell of spilled life filled the cabin's recycled air like incense at some unholy altar.

The soft blue glow of a nightlight beckoned from somewhere deeper in the cabin, drawing him like a moth toward flame with the promise of completing his ritual. He followed the gentle illumination down the hallway until he reached a doorway that opened into a child's bedroom.

Two small forms huddled under blankets decorated with cartoon characters, their soft snores filling the air with the innocent sounds of childhood sleep. Two boys, he realized. Siblings close enough in age to share a room during family vacations. The older child appeared to be maybe ten years old, while the smaller figure couldn't have been more than six or seven.

He approached the bed where the younger child slept and gazed down at a face that could have been his own from three decades past. The same dark hair, the same button nose, the same expression of absolute trust in the safety of family and home that he had once possessed before his father had taught him that monsters were real and that they sometimes lived in your own house.

The hand holding the knife began to tremble as competing impulses warred in his damaged mind. The ritual demanded completion. These children wore red clothing, he could see the crimson fabric of the younger boy's pajama top beneath the cartoon blanket. They were part of the tableau that had called him to this place, integral components in the ceremony that would help him reclaim the power that had been stolen from him so many years ago.

But they were also children, as helpless and innocent as he had been when his childhood ended in flames and ash. They had done nothing to deserve the violence that had already claimed their parents. They represented the victim he had once been rather than the victimizer he had become.

The knife trembled in his grip as he stared down at the sleeping boy who might have been himself in another life, another family, another set of circumstances that didn't include a drunken father and a red blanket burning on a back porch.

He withdrew from the bedroom with harsh, ragged breaths that sounded like sobs in the cabin's sudden silence. Some lines could not be crossed, even by someone who had already crossed so many. Some boundaries were held even when everything else had been destroyed.

Without looking back at the children who would wake tomorrow to find their world transformed into a nightmare, he dashed through the cabin and into the surrounding forest where darkness could hide his retreat and pine trees could absorb the sounds of his flight.

~

"Sheriff, this is Boyd Winters." The voice on the phone carried the shaky quality of someone fighting to maintain control over emotions that threatened to overwhelm rational thought. "I've got... uh... I found some dead folks in one of my rental cabins. You need to get over here right away, Sheriff. Cabin number six up on Misty Mountain. And there are kids here. Two little ones who somehow made it through whatever happened to their parents."

The line went dead with an abrupt click that left Shea staring at her phone in disbelief. After three days of relative quiet, three days during which she had dared to hope that the killer had moved on to terrorize some other community, he had instead found a new hunting ground.

She motioned to Trevor as she headed for the door, filling him in on the details of Winters' call while they grabbed their gear and prepared for what promised to be another journey into the heart of human darkness. The drive up the winding mountain road passed in tense silence, both officers lost in their thoughts about what they might find waiting for them in cabin number six.

When they arrived at the scene, Boyd Winters paced the cabin's wraparound porch like a caged animal, a cigarette dangling from his lips. At the same time, his eyes darted between the forest and the door he had closed behind him after discovering the carnage inside. Two young boys sat huddled together on the porch steps, wrapped in blankets that had probably come from their parents' bed, their eyes holding the thousand-yard stare of trauma victims who had seen things no child should ever witness.

"I don't know how to handle kids," Winters said, grinding out his cigarette beneath his boot heel before immediately lighting another one with hands that shook like autumn leaves. "Never had any of my own, you know? I put them out here on the porch so they couldn't see what's inside that cabin. Figured that was better than leaving them in there with... that."

"You did exactly right." Trevor placed a steadying hand on the older man's shoulder before stepping toward the cabin's front door. "We'll take it from here."

Shea stopped just inside the doorway, her trained eyes taking in the frozen tableau of violence that greeted them. The cabin looked like a crime scene photograph come to life. The television still flickered with late-night programming, the sound muted, but the images continued their endless cycle of entertainment that no one would ever watch again.

An acrid smell drifted from the kitchen where

something had been left burning on the stove, filling the cabin's air with the smell of charred food that mixed with the copper scent of spilled blood to create an olfactory signature that would haunt both officers' memories for years to come.

Blood had painted abstract patterns across walls and furniture, speaking to violence that went far beyond simple murder into the realm of personal vendetta or psychological breakdown.

Trevor knelt beside the body sprawled on the leather couch, his examination quick but thorough as he processed the evidence that would help them understand the sequence of events. "Single wound to the throat," he reported, his voice carrying the clinical detachment that police officers learned to maintain when confronted with the aftermath of extreme violence. "Precise placement, probably severed the carotid artery and damaged the brain stem. He never saw it coming. Probably never even knew he was in danger."

"Can't say the same for the woman." Shea studied the carnage that marked where the killer's second victim had fought for her life. "Multiple stab wounds, defensive injuries on her hands and arms. This was personal somehow, more violent than his usual pattern. Why kill the husband quickly and make the wife suffer?"

The question hung in the air between them as they continued their preliminary examination of the crime scene. Shea made her way down the hallway toward the children's bedroom, dreading what she might find but needing to understand why two young boys had survived when their parents had not.

The bedroom told its own story of miraculous survival.

Two beds had been arranged to create a cozy sleeping space for siblings, with nightlights providing gentle illumination and cartoon decorations creating the kind of cheerful environment that parents worked to make for their children's happiness.

But there was no blood in this room, no signs of violence or struggle. Whatever had happened here, the killer had made a conscious decision to spare the children who had slept through their parents' murder just yards away.

Back outside, Shea leaned against her patrol truck while they waited for the crime scene technicians and medical examiner to arrive from the county seat. Social services would need to be contacted to arrange emergency custody for two children who had lost everything in a single night of senseless violence.

"He's changing his pattern." she watched as Heidi approached the two traumatized boys with the gentle instinct that made German Shepherds such effective therapy animals. "This isn't his usual methodology. Have you found a flag anywhere?"

Trevor shook his head as he made notes in his field book. "Haven't had time for a thorough search yet, but usually he plants them in plain sight where they can't be missed. This feels different somehow."

"Could be that he's unraveling." Shea watched as small arms wrapped around Heidi's neck and found comfort in the dog's steady warmth. "The stress of being hunted, the change in his hunting grounds, the fact that we've disrupted his rituals—all of that could be causing psychological deterioration."

"Ever notice how different mountain air smells after a murder?" Trevor's gaze moved across the forest that surrounded them like a green wall. "It's like the world looks the same and sounds the same, but something fundamental has changed that you can't quite identify."

Social services arrived within the hour, their van climbing the winding mountain road with the cautious speed of city drivers navigating unfamiliar terrain. As they prepared to take custody of the two survivors, the blanket wrapped around the smaller boy slipped from his shoulders to reveal a red and white striped shirt that had probably been chosen by loving parents who wanted their child to look nice during their mountain vacation.

Red. The color that triggered every one of the killer's previous attacks. Yet he had let these children live despite their possession of the very thing that called to his damaged psyche like a beacon in the darkness.

"I'm going to search the surrounding area." Shea pushed away from her truck with renewed purpose. "There's something here we've missed, some piece of evidence that will help us understand why he broke his pattern."

She walked the perimeter of the cabin. The footprints near the back door had already been photographed and marked by Trevor, and black fingerprint powder covered the door frame where the killer had gained entry to the family's temporary sanctuary.

She stepped back inside the cabin and retraced the killer's path from the mudroom through the kitchen to the living room where the husband had died, then down the hallway toward the children's bedroom where some internal mechanism had caused him to spare two lives when he could have easily taken them.

As she knelt to examine the area around the children's beds, something caught her eye—a flash of red fabric protruding from beneath the smaller bed like a tongue of flame against the hardwood floor.

Her blood froze as she recognized the shape and color of a camping flag identical to the ones that had marked every previous crime scene. She pulled the flag free and held it up to the cabin's artificial lighting, confirming that this was indeed their killer's signature calling card.

"Sheriff Callahan?" The voice from behind her carried the pompous authority that she had learned to associate with political interference in police investigations.

She straightened and turned to find Mayor Ferguson standing in the bedroom doorway, his presence at an active crime scene both inappropriate and potentially dangerous to the integrity of their investigation. "This is a crime scene, Mr. Ferguson. You have no business being here."

"This is my town, Sheriff. These are my constituents who've been murdered, and I have every right to be informed about what's happening in my jurisdiction."

"These are my people too," Shea replied, her voice carrying an edge of warning that most smart people recognized as a signal to back down. "It's my responsibility to keep them safe and to catch the person who's been terrorizing our community. Which means you need to stop interfering and let me do my job."

She marched past him with the red flag clutched in her evidence-gloved hand, her patience with political meddling exhausted by weeks of pressure and criticism from people who had never worked a homicide case in their lives.

"Found the flag." She tossed the evidence onto the hood of her patrol truck where it could be properly photographed and documented.

"We'll get him, Shea," Trevor said, his voice carrying a conviction that helped steady her nerves in a way that political promises and bureaucratic procedures never could.

She looked up to meet his eyes, and for a moment, the professional barriers she maintained between them seemed as fragile as morning mist. There was something in his expression—a mix of professional trust and emotional support that made her chest ache with feelings she had no business entertaining while standing over the bodies of murdered parents.

The moment stretched between them, heavy with unspoken possibilities, until the arrival of the county coroner interrupted their connection and returned them to the grim business of processing evidence and documenting violence.

By the time they returned to the sheriff's office, full darkness had settled over Misty Hollow like a blanket thrown over a birdcage. Most of the day shift staff had gone home to their families, leaving the building quiet except for the night dispatcher and the hum of fluorescent lights that never slept.

Shea tossed her hat onto her desk and pulled her hair free of the ponytail that had contained it through another day of confronting humanity's capacity for evil. The scent of the mountain cabin seemed to cling to her clothes and hair like smoke from a campfire. An olfactory reminder of violence that would follow her home and into her dreams.

"I can still smell that place." She rubbed her temples where a headache had been building since they'd first walked into the cabin's blood-soaked interior.

Trevor nodded with the understanding of someone who had shared the same traumatic experience. "Blood and pine sap and children's shampoo," he said. "Not a combination that's going to fade from memory anytime soon."

They moved into the conference room where the growing collection of evidence and crime scene photographs had transformed one entire wall into a shrine to the killer's escalating violence. A map of Misty Lake and the surrounding mountains was peppered with red pins that marked each location where death had visited their community, while photographs of victims stared down at them with the accusing eyes of the unavenged dead.

The two officers stood in silence before this monument to their failure to stop a predator who seemed to move through their jurisdiction like a ghost, striking without warning and vanishing without trace. The weight of responsibility settled on their shoulders like a physical burden, made heavier by the knowledge that somewhere in the darkness, another family might be preparing for a peaceful evening that would end in blood and terror.

"You holding up okay?" Trevor asked, his voice gentle in the way that suggested he was asking as a friend rather than a colleague. "No breathing problems?"

"This cooler weather is better for my asthma. Not as many flare-ups. This is a heavy burden to carry," Shea admitted, her voice barely above a whisper. "I can't pretend otherwise."

"You don't have to carry it alone." He stepped closer in a way that made her aware of his physical presence in the small room. "I'm here to share whatever weight you need help with."

For a moment, the professional wall she kept between them developed cracks that threatened to become permanent breaks. She found herself really looking at him, noting the tight line of his jaw that spoke to his stress and exhaustion, the steady eyes that had seen too much but hadn't lost their capacity for compassion, the warmth that radiated from him like heat from a banked fire.

Her chest ached with feelings that had no place in a police station conference room while a serial killer stalked their community. She swallowed hard and forced herself to turn back toward the evidence board, using professional necessity to rebuild the barriers that kept her personal and professional lives from becoming dangerously entangled.

"We need a psychological profile," she said, her voice steadier than she felt. "Someone who understands the kind of mind we're dealing with, who can help us predict his next move."

"You thinking about calling in the federal authorities?" Trevor asked, though his tone suggested he already knew the answer.

"I don't see how I can avoid it." Shea stared at the red pins that marked a growing trail of violence across their jurisdiction. "This is bigger than our small department can handle on its own. We need resources and expertise that we don't have access to locally."

The admission felt like failure, but it was also the recognition of reality that good leaders had to make when the stakes became too high for pride to matter more than results.

Chapter Seven

Rain streaked the window outside the conference room in the sheriff's office, each droplet creating wavering paths down the glass like tears on a grieving face. The weather wasn't uncommon for early fall in Arkansas, when the seasons couldn't decide whether to hold onto summer's warmth or surrender to autumn's chill. Gray clouds had settled over Misty Hollow like a shroud, casting everything in the muted light that made even familiar places seem foreign and unwelcoming.

Shea perched on the edge of the heavy oak conference table, arms crossed over her uniform shirt, and studied the case board with the same methodical intensity she'd brought to this ritual every morning for the past two weeks. The collection of crime scene photographs, victim profiles, and evidence markers had grown into a sprawling testament to their failure to stop a predator who moved through their jurisdiction like smoke through a forest fire.

Red pins dotted the large map of Misty Lake and the surrounding mountains, each one marking a location where death had visited their community. Photographs of the dead stared back at her from the corkboard—Rebecca Martinez and David Kim from the first campsite, Alexis Moore from the lakeside tent, the unnamed woman from the copycat killing, and now the mountain cabin family whose children would grow up haunted by memories of the night their world ended in blood and violence.

She studied the timeline they'd constructed, the pattern analysis that should have revealed some insight into the killer's psychology, the geographic profile that was supposed to help them predict his next move. But the board remained as cryptic as a foreign language, offering no revelations despite hours of staring at its contents.

The door opened behind her with the soft click of the latch mechanism, and she turned to see Trevor entering the room. He carried a thick stack of papers under one arm while balancing a steaming cup of coffee in his free hand. His uniform showed the wrinkles and creases of someone who'd been working through the night, and dark stubble covered his jaw and chin in a way that spoke of forgotten meals and missed sleep.

"Got the purchase records from all three outdoor gear shops within a thirty-mile radius." He set the stack of papers on the conference table with the satisfied thud of someone who'd finally made progress on an impossible task. "Took most of the night to cross-reference credit card transactions with customer databases, but I think we might have something."

Shea felt her pulse quicken with the first genuine hope she'd experienced since this nightmare began. "Please tell me there's a thread we can pull, something that connects our crime scenes to a specific individual."

"Maybe more than maybe." He flipped through several

pages before finding the one he wanted, then slid it across the table toward her. "Most of the purchases are exactly what you'd expect—families buying camping gear for weekend trips, tourists picking up supplies they forgot to pack, hunters stocking up for the season. All normal, everyday transactions."

He paused and pointed to a highlighted section near the bottom of the page. "But this name jumped out at me during the cross-reference check. Thomas LaCrosse. Thirty-three years old, and his purchase history is... interesting."

Shea leaned forward and read the typed notes that Trevor had compiled from multiple sources, her eyes widening as each detail painted a picture that was both terrifying and heartbreakingly familiar. The subject had been recently released from Glenvalley State Psychiatric Hospital after a seven-year commitment following what the records described as a "severe psychotic break with violent ideation."

The clinical language couldn't disguise the horror of what she read. Victim of severe childhood abuse at the hands of an alcoholic father. History of being locked in small spaces as punishment. Documented fixation on fire and burning objects. Current residence listed as cabin 9 on North Ridge Road, less than two miles from the lake where his killing spree had begun.

But it was the psychological profile that made her blood run cold. Recurrent nightmares of being trapped in a closet while violence erupted around him. Expressed violent impulses toward anyone he perceived as an intruder in his personal space. Most damning of all, the psychiatrist's notes documented an obsession with red cloth objects that stemmed from a childhood trauma involving the destruction of a security blanket.

She looked up to meet Trevor's eyes, her voice barely above a whisper. "He fits the profile. Too well to be coincidence."

Trevor moved closer, leaning over her shoulder to point out additional details in the file. "Look at the timeline. He was released from Glenvalley just three weeks before our first murders. His therapist recommended continued outpatient treatment, but he never showed up for a single appointment."

The proximity of Trevor's presence made Shea suddenly aware of details she'd been suppressing for months. The clean scent of rain and coffee that clung to his uniform, the subtle woodsy cologne he wore that reminded her of autumn mornings, the warmth that radiated from his body in the cool conference room. A pulse of shared adrenaline sparked between them, the electric connection that formed between partners who'd faced danger together and learned to trust each other with their lives.

She forced herself to focus on the papers in front of her, using professional necessity to maintain the boundaries she'd established between personal feelings and police work. But her awareness of his presence remained, a constant hum of attraction that she couldn't quite silence despite years of practice.

"This is him." Trevor's voice carried the conviction of someone who'd spent enough years in law enforcement to recognize patterns that others might miss. "This is our killer. Every instinct I've developed tells me we've found our man."

Shea reached for the phone on the conference table and dialed the number she'd memorized for the regional FBI field office in Little Rock. The call connected after two rings, and she recognized the voice of Agent Sarah Snowe, a behavioral analyst she'd worked with on a kidnapping case three years earlier.

"Agent Snowe, this is Sheriff Callahan down in Misty Hollow. We're dealing with an active serial killer situation, and we need federal assistance immediately." She glanced at Trevor, who nodded encouragingly. "Three confirmed murder scenes, five victims total, including two children who were spared. All crime scenes show elaborate staging with red fabric objects as apparent triggers."

She paused to flip through Trevor's research notes. "We've identified a primary suspect through retail purchase records and psychological profiling. Thomas LaCrosse, thirty-three years old, recently released from Glenvalley Psychiatric Hospital. He has a documented history of violent tendencies and childhood trauma specifically tied to red objects being destroyed."

Agent Snowe's voice carried the professional calm of someone accustomed to dealing with the worst aspects of human nature. "Send me everything you have, Sheriff. Crime scene photos, witness statements, and the suspect's psychiatric records, if you can obtain them legally. I'll have a team en route to your location within six hours."

"We need federal support for surveillance and behavioral analysis," Shea continued. "This individual is escalating rapidly, and our local resources aren't sufficient to monitor him around the clock while protecting potential victims." She felt the weight of responsibility settling on her shoulders like a physical burden. "Agent Snowe, if we don't stop him soon, more families are going to die."

After ending the call, she set the receiver back in its cradle and released a long breath that seemed to carry weeks of accumulated tension. Her hand lingered on the phone for a moment before she rubbed her forehead, trying to massage away the headache that had become her constant companion since this investigation began.

"We're on the right trail now," Trevor said, his voice carrying a confidence that helped steady her nerves. "For the first time since this started, we're ahead of him instead of reacting to his moves."

"I hope you're right. But I'm worried about what happens if we spook him before we can put together a proper arrest plan. A cornered predator is always the most dangerous kind."

Her gaze met his across the conference table, and for a moment, the professional wall she'd built around her heart developed cracks that threatened to become permanent breaks. The isolation of command, the pressure of being responsible for her community's safety, the accumulated stress of weeks spent hunting a killer—all of it pressed against her carefully maintained composure like water against a dam.

"I hate this part of the job." And the vulnerability in her voice that few people ever heard. "Waiting for a killer to make his next move, feeling helpless to protect anyone until he reveals himself by hurting someone else. It goes against every instinct I have as both a police officer and a human being."

Trevor stepped forward and rested his hand on her shoulder, the contact warm and reassuring through the fabric of her uniform shirt. "You're not facing this alone, Shea. You don't have to carry all this responsibility by yourself."

His touch lingered longer than professional courtesy required, and she found herself leaning slightly into the comfort he offered. The weight of everything they'd been holding back, weeks of shared danger, mutual respect that had deepened into something more personal, the growing awareness that their partnership had evolved beyond mere professional collaboration, pressed them closer together in the small conference room.

The moment stretched between them like a held breath, filled with possibilities that had no place in a police station while a serial killer stalked their community. Shea wavered on the edge of decisions that could change everything, torn between the loneliness of command and the warmth of human connection that Trevor represented.

Then the front door chimes echoed through the building, shattering their private moment like glass breaking against stone. Both officers stepped apart with the guilty speed of teenagers caught by disapproving parents, professional boundaries snapping back into place with almost audible force.

Deputy Butler appeared in the conference room doorway, his presence a reminder that they existed in a world where personal feelings had to be subordinated to public duty. "FBI's confirmed their arrival time." He consulted a notepad he'd pulled from his shirt pocket. "Agent Snowe and a behavioral analysis team will be here by morning, along with tactical support specialists."

Shea nodded and turned back toward the wall of red pins and crime scene photographs, using the familiar ritual of case review to rebuild the professional composure that had momentarily slipped. "Good. Once they arrive, we'll coordinate surveillance on Thomas LaCrosse while building a psychological profile that can help us predict his next target."

The hunt for their suspect had officially gone federal, bringing resources and expertise that their small department couldn't match. But it also meant acknowledging that the evil stalking their community had grown beyond their ability to contain it alone.

~

The killer gripped the military surplus binoculars until his knuckles went white with strain, the rubber eyepieces pressed so hard against his face that they would leave circular impressions on his skin. His eyes watered from the combination of wind and the pure hatred that coursed through his system like liquid fire, but he refused to lower the optical device that had become his window into the world of potential victims.

From his concealed position on a rocky outcrop overlooking the southern shore of Misty Lake, he could survey the entire cluster of rental cabins that dotted the hillside. Each structure represented a family seeking peaceful retreat from urban chaos, blissfully unaware that death watched them through military-grade optics with the patience of a sniper selecting targets.

A family sedan was parked outside cabin number seven, its out-of-state license plates marking the occupants as tourists who'd traveled hundreds of miles to find the kind of natural beauty that postcards promised but rarely delivered. Children's toys were scattered across the cabin's front deck. A bicycle with training wheels, a collection of beach balls, the stuff of family vacation that spoke to parents who'd planned this trip months.

But it was the red shirt hanging over the porch railing that captured his complete attention, the crimson fabric fluttering in the evening breeze like a flag of surrender. The sight of it triggered memories that had been buried but never forgotten. The soft wool of his grandmother's blanket, the security it had provided during those terrible nights when his father's rage had transformed their home into a battlefield.

Red. The color that called to him across decades of damage and pain. Red like the camping flags he'd planted at each crime scene, territorial markers that proclaimed his ownership of death itself. Red was his color, his signature, his pathway to the power that had been stolen from him when he was too young to defend himself.

His heart hammered against his ribs as he imagined the scene that would unfold tomorrow night. The family inside that cabin had no idea they'd been selected for his brand of ritual violence. They were probably sitting around their dinner table at this very moment, planning hiking trips and lake activities, making memories that would end in screams and blood.

He could picture Sheriff Callahan standing in her conference room, studying her collection of red pins and crime scene photographs with the intensity that had made her such a worthy adversary. She'd probably spent hours staring at that evidence board, searching for patterns that would lead her to his door.

The thought of her frustration filled him with dark satisfaction. Let her plot and plan with her federal allies. Let them bring their behavioral analysts and surveillance specialists. He'd been invisible for weeks, moving through their jurisdiction like a ghost, and he could remain invisible for as long as necessary.

But he knew they were getting closer. He'd seen his old name, Thomas LaCrosse, taped to their evidence board during his midnight reconnaissance of the sheriff's office two nights earlier. The identity he'd worn during his years of institutionalization, the label they'd used to categorize and medicate and analyze him until he'd learned to tell them what they wanted to hear.

They thought they knew who he was, but Thomas LaCrosse had died in that psychiatric hospital along with the frightened child who'd once believed in safety blankets and parental protection. What remained was something new, something evolved, something that had learned to hunt the very thing that had once tortured him.

He was no longer Thomas or Tommy or any of the names that others had used to define him. He was himself—the one who brought fear, who transformed peaceful evenings into nightmares, who proved that monsters were real and sometimes they won.

"Catch me if you can, Sheriff," he whispered to the wind that carried his words toward the distant lights of Misty Hollow.

He slid backward into the dense pine forest that had become his natural habitat, moving with the fluid silence of a predator who'd learned to exist between the spaces that civilization monitored. His passage through the undergrowth left no trace that he'd ever been there—no broken branches, no disturbed earth, no scent trail that tracking dogs could follow.

Tomorrow night, when darkness provided the cover he needed and the family in cabin seven had settled into the false security of vacation routine, there would be more red added to the sheriff's collection. Another pin for her map, another photograph for her evidence board, another failure to add to her growing list of people she couldn't protect.

The hunt would continue until every trace of red had been purged from his memory, or until Sheriff Callahan proved herself worthy of the deadly game by finally seeing the invisible man who'd been standing in plain sight all along.

But for tonight, he would retreat to his cabin and plan the ritual that would transform another family's paradise into his purgatory. The mountains held many secrets, and he intended to add a few more before his work was complete.

Chapter Eight

Shea's cruiser tires crunched up the narrow dirt road that wound through dense forest toward the north ridge, each pothole and rut jarring her spine as they climbed higher into the mountains that surrounded Misty. Ancient pines towered overhead, their branches so thick they blocked most of the pale morning sunlight, creating a tunnel of green shadows that seemed to press in from all sides.

The cabin appeared between the trees like something from a fever dream. A structure so weathered and neglected that it seemed to be melting back into the forest that surrounded it. The building leaned at an angle that suggested structural damage or simply the weight of years pressing down on rotting timbers, its cedar siding streaked with moss and black mildew that spoke of moisture and decay.

The place radiated wrongness in a way that made Shea's skin crawl. It wasn't just the neglect or the isolation that bothered her, though both were unsettling enough. Something deeper disturbed her about this cabin, some quality of menace that seemed to seep from the building itself like poison from a wound.

Weathered shingles curled away from the roof like dead skin, and several windows were cracked or missing entirely, their openings covered with plastic sheeting and duct tape that fluttered in the mountain breeze. A tangle of rusted wind chimes dangled from the sagging front porch, their discordant music creating an eerie soundtrack that mixed with the whisper of wind through pine boughs.

But it was the red bath towel draped over the porch railing that made her blood freeze. The crimson fabric hung limp in the still air, its bright color a splash of violence against the muted browns and greens of the deteriorating structure. After weeks of finding red objects at crime scenes, the sight of that towel felt like a taunt, a message left for her to find.

Shea glanced at Trevor, who sat rigid in the passenger seat, his hand already moving toward the service weapon on his belt. His usually calm demeanor had been replaced by the tense alertness of someone preparing for violence, and she could see her unease reflected in his expression.

"Ready for this?" she asked, though the question felt inadequate given what they might be walking into. "This is it—the moment we've been building toward."

Trevor's fingers drummed against his holster as he studied the cabin through the windshield, his trained eyes cataloguing potential threats and escape routes with the automatic assessment that came from years of police work. "Looks like something out of a nightmare." His voice carried an edge she'd rarely heard from him. "Like the kind of place where bad things happen and nobody ever talks about them afterward."

"Stay, Heidi," Shea commanded as she opened her door, leaving the German Shepherd in the relative safety of the patrol car. The dog whined, her instincts apparently as disturbed by this place as her human partner's, but she remained in her position as trained.

They approached the cabin with the careful steps of soldiers advancing through a minefield, their hands hovering near their weapons while their eyes swept the surrounding forest for signs of ambush or surveillance. The wooden steps creaked ominously under their weight, and Shea couldn't shake the feeling that they were being watched from the dark windows that stared down at them like hollow eyes.

The front door was solid wood that had once been painted green but now showed more bare timber than color, its surface scarred by weather and what looked like deliberate damage—gouges that knives or claws might have made, though she couldn't tell which. A single window beside the door had been covered from the inside with newspaper, blocking any view of the interior.

Shea's knock echoed through the cabin with a hollow sound that seemed to go on longer than physics should have allowed. The silence that followed stretched until she began to wonder if anyone was home, despite the fresh tire tracks they'd spotted in the muddy driveway and the sense of presence that seemed to emanate from the structure itself.

After what felt like an eternity but was probably only thirty seconds, the door opened just wide enough to reveal a sliver of pale face and one restless eye that darted between the two officers like a trapped animal looking for escape routes. The man behind the door had the gaunt appearance of someone who'd forgotten to eat regularly, his hair hanging in greasy strands that looked like they hadn't seen shampoo in weeks.

What she could see of his clothing appeared to be a military surplus jacket that had seen better decades, the fabric stained and worn until its original color was anyone's guess. The smell that drifted through the crack in the door was a mixture of wood smoke, unwashed human, and something else—something chemical and sharp that made her nostrils burn.

"Mr. LaCrosse?" Shea kept her voice level and professional, though every instinct screamed that she was talking to a predator who was evaluating her as potential prey. "I'm Sheriff Callahan, and this is Deputy Bolton. We'd like to ask you a few questions about some incidents that have occurred in the area. Mind if we come inside?"

Something hard and calculating flickered behind his eyes, an intelligence that seemed at odds with his disheveled appearance and the obvious signs of mental instability. For just a moment, she caught a glimpse of the mind that had planned and executed multiple murders with cold precision, and the sight of it made her hand drift closer to her weapon.

"You got a warrant?" His voice was rough, as if he hadn't spoken to another human being in days or weeks. "Because if you don't have a warrant, then you're just trespassing on my property, and I don't much care for trespassers."

The threat in his words was subtle but unmistakable, delivered with the casual tone of someone discussing the weather rather than implied violence. Shea felt Trevor shift slightly beside her, his body language indicating his readiness to draw his weapon if the situation escalated beyond words.

"Do we need one?" She matched his casual tone while her mind raced through the legal implications of what they were doing. They had circumstantial evidence and psychological profiles, but nothing that would hold up in court without additional proof. "We're just here to talk, to clear up some questions about your whereabouts during certain dates."

"What's this about?" His tone suggested he already knew why they were standing on his doorstep. "What dates are you so interested in?"

"Are you Thomas LaCrosse?" Shea studied his reaction to the name that appeared on psychiatric records and purchase receipts. "The Thomas LaCrosse who was recently released from Glenvalley State Hospital?"

His expression shifted in a way that was both subtle and deeply unsettling, as if multiple personalities were fighting for control behind his eyes. When he spoke again, his voice carried a different quality. Older somehow, more distant, as if the words were coming from somewhere deep underground.

"Not anymore." He shook his head with a motion that seemed more like a nervous tic than a conscious gesture. "Thomas burned up a long time ago, right along with his parents and everything else that mattered. What you're looking at now is what crawled out of the ashes."

Shea frowned, her training in crisis negotiation and psychological assessment telling her that she was dealing with someone who had constructed an elaborate defense mechanism around his trauma. "What should we call you then?"

A smile played at the corners of his mouth, the expression devoid of any warmth or humanity. "Whatever you want, Sheriff. Invincible, invisible, inevitable…the list goes on and on. Names don't matter much when you've learned to become something that exists between the spaces where normal people look."

Despite every professional instinct telling her this was a dangerous situation that required backup and tactical support, the man stepped back from the door and gestured for them to enter his domain. The invitation felt like a spider welcoming flies into its web, but they needed evidence, and evidence required taking calculated risks.

The interior of the cabin was a shrine to obsession and madness. Newspaper clippings about the Misty Lake murders covered every inch of a large corkboard that dominated one wall, connected by red string in patterns that probably made sense only to their host. Headlines screamed about serial killers and camping deaths, while crime scene photographs, some that looked suspiciously like official police evidence, were arranged in careful chronological order.

An entire wall had been dedicated to rows of red camping flags, dozens of them arranged in precise military formation like battle standards in some twisted war room. Each flag was identical to the ones they'd found at crime scenes, and the sight of so many gathered in one place made Shea's stomach clench with the realization of how long this man had been planning his campaign of terror.

Under a battery-powered camping lantern sat a folded

piece of scarlet fabric that looked like it might once have been part of a blanket or towel. The edges were burned and blackened, and the sight of it triggered something in their host's behavior. He moved protectively toward the fabric as if shielding it from their gaze.

"Don't touch my things." His voice carried a warning that made both officers tense. "The red keeps the voices calm. Without it, they get so loud that I can't think about anything else."

"What voices?" Shea suspected she already knew the answer. Trauma victims often reported auditory hallucinations related to their abuse, and this man showed every sign of someone whose childhood had been a battleground between innocence and cruelty.

His gaze flitted toward the window as if he could see something in the forest that remained invisible to normal people. "The ones that come when it gets too quiet." His words took on a singsong quality that suggested he was quoting something he'd heard many times before. "The ones that make me remember things I'd rather forget. They whisper about fire and pain and the sound a little boy makes when his whole world burns down around him."

"Let's sit down and talk about this." Shea guided him toward a chair that looked like it had been salvaged from a junkyard. Trevor remained standing nearby, his protective presence a comfort in this place where reality seemed to bend around the occupant's damaged psyche. "You've been to the lake recently, haven't you? Maybe camping or just visiting the area?"

He began rocking in the chair with a motion that reminded her of institutionalized patients she'd encountered during her years in law enforcement. "Whispers in the night." His words sounded like nonsense but carried an undertone that made the hair on the back of her neck stand up. "Red calling to me across the water, begging me to come and make everything right again."

The rocking increased in tempo, and she could see him retreating into whatever mental space he'd constructed to protect himself from memories that were too painful to process. But beneath the signs of psychological damage, she sensed a calculating intelligence that was watching and evaluating her reactions.

"Did you hurt anyone, Thomas?" she asked, using his original name deliberately to see how he would respond to the identity he claimed to have abandoned.

His head snapped toward her with predatory speed, and for a split second, she saw through the performance of madness to the cold intelligence underneath. "Thomas is dead!" His voice carried a fury that seemed to come from someplace much deeper than conscious thought. "He died screaming in a closet while his father burned everything that ever mattered to him!"

The mask of insanity slipped just enough for Shea to glimpse the real person hiding behind it, and what she saw chilled her to the bone. LaCrosse might act disturbed to the point of incompetence, but there was nothing wrong with his ability to plan and execute complex schemes. The man sitting in front of her was a cold-blooded killer who knew exactly what he was doing when he stalked families with red camping gear.

As if realizing he'd revealed more than he intended, he lowered his head and resumed the rocking motion that seemed to calm whatever demons drove him. They wouldn't get anything else useful out of him during this visit, but Shea knew with absolute certainty that she was sitting next to the predator who had terrorized her community for weeks.

"He's completely unstable," Trevor observed as they walked back toward their patrol car, his voice low enough that their suspect couldn't overhear from inside the cabin. "Whatever happened to him as a child, it broke something fundamental in his mind."

"No," Shea replied, her voice carrying the conviction of someone who had looked into the abyss and recognized what stared back. "He's toying with us, playing a role he thinks will keep him out of prison. He knows exactly what he's saying and what he's not saying. Every word was calculated for maximum effect."

Trevor's hand brushed against hers as they reached the car, a moment of contact that provided silent reassurance in the middle of their growing frustration. The touch was brief and professional, but it carried the weight of a partnership forged in dangerous circumstances and mutual trust built through months of facing the worst aspects of human nature together.

The mountain air seemed to hang heavy with the knowledge that their primary suspect remained free and in control, that despite their breakthrough in identifying him, the law required evidence that they didn't yet possess. Somewhere in the forest around them, death waited with the patience of a natural predator for the right moment to strike again.

Back at the sheriff's station, FBI Agents Snowe and

Larson were waiting in the conference room, their federal resources spread across the table in neat folders that represented the best that modern law enforcement could bring to bear against a serial killer. The agents had arrived that morning with crime scene analysis equipment, psychological profiles, and surveillance technology that dwarfed anything the local department could access.

Shea hung her damp jacket over a chair and immediately began briefing the federal agents on their encounter with Thomas LaCrosse. "He's our killer," she said with absolute certainty. "Every instinct I've developed over my years of police work tells me we just met the person responsible for terrorizing our community."

She described the shrine to the murders he'd constructed in his cabin, the collection of red flags that matched their crime scene evidence, and most importantly, the glimpse she'd caught of the calculating intelligence hiding behind his performance of mental illness.

Agent Snowe listened with the professional attention of someone accustomed to hunting the worst predators humanity could produce, but his expression remained skeptical even after hearing their report. "It certainly sounds suspicious," he agreed, "but we need more than suspicious behavior and circumstantial evidence. We need physical proof that directly connects him to the crime scenes, or we need a confession that will hold up in court."

He gestured toward the files spread across the conference table. "A good defense attorney will argue that he's just a disturbed individual collecting newspaper clippings and souvenirs related to crimes that fascinate his sick mind. Without DNA evidence, fingerprints, or witness testimony placing him at the scenes, we don't have enough to make charges stick."

Shea's frustration boiled over into anger, and she slammed her hand on the table hard enough to make the coffee cups jump. "Meanwhile, he's out there free to continue killing, growing stronger and bolder with each successful hunt. How many more families have to die while we build a case that satisfies legal requirements?"

Trevor stopped his restless pacing and turned to face the group. "He's bound to make a mistake eventually." His tone suggested he wasn't entirely convinced of his own words. "Killers like this get overconfident, start taking risks that expose them to capture."

"And when he slips up, we'll be ready." Shea crossed her arms as she stared at the evidence board that had become a monument to their failure to stop a predator who moved through their jurisdiction like smoke through a forest fire. "But I'm not willing to wait for more bodies to pile up while we hope he gets careless."

The weight of command had never felt heavier than it did in that moment, with federal agents questioning her instincts and a killer walking free in the mountains that surrounded their community like the walls of a hunting preserve.

~

Hidden among the towering pines that covered the ridge overlooking Misty Hollow, Thomas LaCrosse watched the faint lights of town twinkle in the valley below like fallen stars scattered across dark velvet. In his lap lay a fresh red camping flag, the smooth synthetic fabric soft against his work-roughened hands as he traced its edges with the obsessive attention that had become his only form of prayer.

He hummed tunelessly as he rocked back and forth, a sound that might have been soothing if it weren't mixed with the whispered words that spilled from his lips like poison from a broken bottle. The forest around him was alive with the sounds of nocturnal creatures beginning their nightly hunt, and he felt a kinship with every predator that stalked through these mountains in search of prey.

"She thinks she knows me now," he murmured to the darkness that had become his closest companion. "She thinks she can catch me by putting a name to what I've become. But Thomas LaCrosse died in that fire thirty years ago, and what crawled out of the ashes is something she's never encountered before."

The memory of Sheriff Callahan's eyes as she'd looked through his performance of madness still sent electricity through his nervous system. For just a moment, he'd let her see the real predator hiding behind the mask of mental illness, and the recognition in her expression had been more intoxicating than any drug the doctors had ever forced down his throat during his years of institutionalization.

He tucked the flag into his jacket pocket and crawled through the underbrush toward the cluster of rental cabins that dotted the southern shore of Misty Lake. His movements were fluid and silent, the result of decades spent learning to move through the world without leaving traces that others could follow.

A sedan with out-of-state plates sat in the driveway of cabin number twelve, and a red hooded sweatshirt hung from the porch railing where it had been left to dry after the afternoon's rain. The sight of that crimson fabric made his heart rate increase until he could feel his pulse hammering in his temples, and the familiar whispers began their nightly chorus in the spaces between his thoughts.

The final night flashed across his memory like frames from a film reel that a madman had spliced together. He'd been eight years old, small for his age and already wise in the ways that fear could teach a child who learned early that home was the most dangerous place in the world.

His grandmother had given him a new blanket for Christmas. A soft red wool that smelled like lavender and safety, the kind of gift that spoke to unconditional love in a house where affection was rationed like wartime supplies. He'd taken to hiding in the bedroom closet when his father's drinking transformed their small house into a battlefield, wrapping himself in that blanket like armor against the violence that erupted with increasing frequency as the man's demons grew stronger and more demanding.

That last night, he'd huddled in his sanctuary while his father's bellowing voice and his mother's terrified sobs created the soundtrack of domestic warfare that had become as familiar as breathing. His older brother Daniel, the favorite child who could do no wrong in their father's alcohol-clouded eyes, was probably sitting in the living room watching television while pretending not to hear the horror that played out just down the hallway.

The boy had often wondered if it was somehow his fault that his birth had left his mother unable to bear more children, if his very existence was the source of his father's rage and his family's dysfunction. The adults whispered about complications during delivery, about damaged parts that couldn't be repaired, about dreams of large families that had died in a hospital room along with his mother's ability to give his father the sons he'd wanted.

Heavy footsteps had approached the closet with the measured pace of someone who'd grown tired of the hunt and was ready to finish what he'd started. The boy had pulled his red blanket tighter around his small body and tried to become invisible, to disappear into the walls and shadows where pain couldn't find him.

But the closet door had been yanked open with enough force to tear it from its hinges, and his father had loomed there like a monster from the deepest nightmares, reeking of sweat and beer and the rage that came from a life that had disappointed at every turn. His eyes held the flat darkness of someone who'd learned to hate everything, especially the small, frightened boy who represented all his failures as a husband and father.

"I should have known you'd be cowering in there like the worthless little coward you are," his father had snarled, the words thick with the alcohol that had become his primary companion in recent years. "You're just as pathetic as your mother, hiding from the world instead of facing it like a man."

He'd yanked the blanket away with vicious satisfaction, tearing the soft wool from the boy's desperate grip and leaving him exposed to the cold air and colder hatred. "If I ever see another one of these security blankets in my house, I swear I'll make you pay in ways you can't even imagine, boy."

But something had changed in that moment, some fundamental shift in the balance of power that had defined their relationship since birth. Instead of the familiar fear and helplessness, a rage stronger than anything the boy had ever felt began to burn in his chest like swallowed fire. He'd watched his father carry the blanket outside to the burn barrel they used for trash, watched the flames consume the only source of comfort and safety he'd ever known.

But this time would be different. This time, he wouldn't be the victim cowering in corners while monsters ruled his world.

He'd waited until his father passed out in his recliner, the empty whiskey bottle rolling across the floor like a discarded weapon. Only then had he pulled a small corner of what was left of his blanket from the fire bin and crept to the storage shed where his father kept the gasoline for the lawn mower and other tools that required fuel to function.

His small hands had shaken as he'd carried the red gas can back into the house, the weight of it almost too much for his eight-year-old frame to manage. But determination had given him strength, and he'd methodically drizzled the accelerant from the front door down the hallway, then back to create a ring around his father's chair where the man snored in drunken oblivion.

The first match hadn't struck properly, his fingers too small and unsteady to create the friction needed for ignition. But the second match had flared to life like a tiny star, and he'd dropped it into the gasoline without hesitation or regret.

The flames had run like liquid lightning, fast and hungry and beautiful in their destructive power. They'd eaten the cheap carpet and climbed the walls with eager appetite, consuming everything they touched with the same indiscriminate violence that had defined his childhood.

Tommy had dashed back outside and hidden behind the large magnolia tree in the front yard, watching as the night sky turned orange with the glow of justice finally served. No one had screamed from inside the burning house. No one had appeared at windows begging for rescue. For several minutes, he'd allowed himself to believe that his nightmare had finally ended in the most permanent way possible.

But then his brother Daniel had crashed through a second-story window, landing hard enough to break his ankle but not hard enough to silence his cries for help. "Tommy!" he'd screamed, his voice raw with pain and terror. "Help me. I can't walk."

The boy had stood frozen behind his tree, torn between the satisfaction of watching his tormentor's house burn and the ingrained habit of protecting his older brother despite years of casual cruelty and deliberate indifference. In the end, family bonds had proven stronger than the desire for complete revenge, and he'd dragged Daniel far enough from the burning structure to ensure his survival.

Sirens had wailed through the night as fire trucks and police cars raced up their gravel driveway, but their efforts had been too little and too late. By the time the flames were extinguished, nothing remained of the house or its primary occupants except ash and charred timber and the smell of smoke that would linger in his memory forever.

People had called it a tragic accident, the inevitable result of an alcoholic falling asleep with a cigarette or knocking over a space heater during one of his binges. No one had cared enough about the no-good LaCrosse family to investigate too closely into the deaths of a worthless drunk and the frightened woman who'd been too damaged to leave him.

Tommy and Daniel had been placed in foster care, where they'd learned new forms of survival. The boy had carried his secret through a succession of temporary homes and temporary families, nurturing his rage like a flame that could never be extinguished.

It hadn't been until his early twenties, when he'd burned down another house in a moment of uncontrolled fury, that the authorities had finally connected him to the pattern of destruction that followed him like a shadow. The psychiatric hospital had been his home for seven years, a place where doctors had tried to medicate away the fire that burned at his core and therapists had attempted to convince him that his father's cruelty hadn't been his fault.

But they'd never understood the fundamental truth that the boy had learned that night when his red blanket turned to ash: his father had burned his sanctuary, so now he would burn everything else. The cycle of destruction wouldn't end until every trace of red had been purged from his memory, or until someone proved strong enough to stop him permanently.

Sheriff Callahan thought she could cage him with laws and evidence and federal agents, but she'd never faced anything like what he'd become. Tomorrow night, when darkness provided the cover he needed and the family in cabin twelve had settled into their false sense of security, there would be more red added to her growing collection of failures.

Chapter Nine

The next morning brought the kind of pale, watery sunlight that promised rain before noon, filtering through the windows of the sheriff's office and casting long shadows across the conference room table where Shea sat surrounded by stacks of paperwork that represented weeks of meticulous investigation. She flipped through ranger patrol reports with the methodical attention of someone who'd learned that the devil lived in the details, searching for patterns that might have been invisible during the initial chaos of active crime scenes.

With the campground officially closed and federal agents coordinating surveillance of Thomas LaCrosse, these reports had become their best record of anyone brave or stupid enough to sneak into the restricted areas around Misty Lake. Every ranger patrol, every maintenance check, every authorized visit had been logged with bureaucratic precision, creating a paper trail that should have revealed any anomalies in the normal rhythm of park operations.

The coffee in her mug had gone cold hours ago, but she continued sipping it anyway, using the bitter liquid as fuel for concentration while her eyes scanned columns of dates and times and locations. Somewhere in these mundane records lay the key to understanding how their killer had moved through the area without detection, how he'd selected his victims and planned his attacks with such precision.

Trevor entered the conference room carrying his stack of files. He'd been cross-referencing vehicle logs with GPS tracking data, a tedious process that required comparing electronic records with handwritten reports to identify discrepancies that might indicate deception or negligence.

"Something is off here." He dropped into the chair across from her and spread several files across the table like a card dealer preparing for a high-stakes game. "Ranger Binkley's patrol logs don't line up with the GPS tracking from his assigned vehicle, and the inconsistencies are getting worse over the past month."

Shea looked up from her paperwork, noting the excitement in Trevor's voice that suggested he'd found something significant. "How bad are the discrepancies?"

"Bad enough to make me wonder if we've been chasing the wrong suspect," Trevor replied, opening the first file and pointing to highlighted sections that told a story of systematic deception. "Two of our murders occurred on nights when Binkley claims in his written reports to have been patrolling the opposite side of the lake from where the bodies were found."

He flipped to another page covered with GPS coordinates and time stamps. "But here's where it gets interesting. There are no GPS pings from his assigned truck during the hours in question, which means either his vehicle's tracking system malfunctioned on multiple occasions, or he wasn't where he claimed to be in his official reports."

The implications hit Shea like a physical blow. Rangers had access to every inch of the park, knew the terrain better than anyone, and could move through restricted areas without arousing suspicion. Most importantly, they would know which campsites offered the best combination of isolation and vulnerability that their killer seemed to prefer.

"What about his supervisor?" Part of her already dreaded the answer. "Someone should have noticed irregular patrol patterns or questioned why his GPS data doesn't match his written reports."

Trevor consulted another file, his expression growing darker with each detail he uncovered. "According to the district supervisor, Binkley has been showing signs of stress over the past few weeks. Taking unscheduled breaks, calling in sick more frequently, general behavior changes that were attributed to personal problems."

He paused and looked directly at her, his voice carrying the weight of a revelation that could change everything about their investigation. "But here's the real bombshell. One of the patrol logs from the week when Alexis Moore was killed is missing entirely from the official files. Not misfiled or damaged—completely absent, as if it never existed."

Shea felt her pulse quicken as the pieces of a new pattern began forming in her mind. "What about the timing of these anomalies? When did Binkley's behavior start changing?"

"That's where this gets personal." Trevor leaned back

in his chair with the satisfied expression of someone who'd solved a complex puzzle. "I decided to run background checks on all the victims again, looking for any connections we might have missed during the initial investigation."

He pulled out a photograph of Alexis Moore—the young solo camper whose body had been found floating in the lake, the victim whose murder had marked an escalation in the killer's violence. The image showed a pretty young woman with dark hair and a confident smile, someone who'd had her whole life ahead of her before a predator had stolen it away.

"Binkley and Moore knew each other," Trevor continued, his voice taking on the clinical tone that police officers used when discussing evidence that might be emotionally charged. "A fellow ranger confirmed that they met last summer during one of her camping trips to the area. What started as a casual friendship developed into something more intimate."

Shea's tone sharpened as the implications became clear. A romantic relationship between a local authority figure and a young woman from out of state created precisely the kind of emotional complexity that could trigger violence when things went wrong. "How intimate are we talking about? Friendly dates or full-blown affair?"

Trevor hesitated for a moment, consulting his notes as if double-checking facts he'd already verified multiple times. "According to the ranger who provided the information, the relationship was physical. Moore would come up to the lake specifically to spend time with Binkley, usually camping alone in areas where he could visit her without being observed by other park staff."

The picture that was forming made Shea's stomach clench with the familiar mixture of anger and sadness that came with understanding how personal relationships could spiral into tragedy. "But something went wrong between them. What ended it?"

"She broke off the relationship about three months ago," Trevor said, his voice carrying the weight of information that had been painful to extract from reluctant witnesses. "According to the same source, Moore told Binkley that she was interested in someone closer to her own age, that their relationship had run its course, and she wanted to end things while they could still be friends."

Trevor paused and met her eyes across the table. "The source also said that Binkley didn't take the rejection very well. He became possessive, started showing up at her apartment in Little Rock unannounced, made it clear that he wasn't ready to let her go."

The pattern was becoming clear now, painted in the kind of toxic masculinity that turned rejection into rage and love into control. Shea had seen it before in domestic violence cases and stalking incidents, the mentality that treated women as property to be possessed rather than people with the right to make their own choices.

"Decision made," she said, grabbing her jacket from the back of her chair and checking her service weapon with the automatic gesture of someone preparing for potential violence. "Let's pay Ranger Binkley a visit and see how well his story holds up under direct questioning."

As they drove through the winding mountain roads that connected the sheriff's office to the ranger station, Trevor was behind the wheel this time, while Shea studied the case files and prepared her interrogation strategy. She found herself staring out at the forest that surrounded them like green walls. These woods held secrets and memories, places where violence had erupted and where predators still moved between the trees with impunity.

"Binkley knows these woods better than anyone." A dense canopy of pine and oak flashed past their windows. "Every trail, every hidden clearing, every spot where someone could dispose of a body without discovery. If he's involved in these murders, he's smart enough and experienced enough to cover his tracks in ways that would take us months to unravel."

Trevor navigated a particularly sharp curve that brought them closer to the lake, the water visible through gaps in the forest like fragments of a broken mirror. "Or maybe he thinks he's untouchable because he's part of the system." His voice carried an edge of anger at the possibility that someone sworn to protect the public had betrayed that trust in the most fundamental way possible.

He paused, then glanced at her with an expression that mixed professional concern with personal frustration. "Can I ask you something that's been bothering me about this whole investigation?"

"Shoot."

"Do you ever get the feeling that this killer, whoever he is, has been laughing at us? Like he's been watching our investigation unfold and enjoying our mistakes and false leads?"

The question hit closer to home than Shea wanted to admit. "Every single day," she replied, her voice carrying the weight of weeks spent chasing shadows while a predator continued to claim victims with impunity. "It's the worst part of this job—the knowledge that while we're following procedure and building cases, real people are dying because we haven't been smart enough or fast enough to stop someone who sees murder as a game."

The self-doubt that had been growing in her mind since the investigation began threatened to overwhelm her professional confidence. As with the serial arson case they'd solved a few months earlier, she'd started to question her abilities as sheriff, to wonder whether the previous sheriff's faith in her leadership had been misplaced.

Yes, her predecessor had vouched for her capabilities, had told her she possessed the intelligence and determination necessary to protect their community from the worst kinds of human predators. But if that was true, why was it taking so long to catch someone who seemed to move through their jurisdiction like smoke through a forest fire?

Trevor seemed to sense her internal struggle because he reached across the seat and briefly squeezed her shoulder, a gesture of support that carried more emotional weight than either of them wanted to acknowledge in the professional context of their partnership.

The ranger station appeared through the trees like something from a postcard. A squat log building situated near the lake's southern trailhead, designed to blend with the natural surroundings while serving as headquarters for the people tasked with protecting thousands of acres of wilderness from both natural disasters and human stupidity.

Rainwater dripped from the building's metal roof in a steady rivulet that had carved channels in the gravel parking area, and a single lamp glowed in the window like a beacon for lost travelers. The scene should have been peaceful and welcoming, but Shea felt her nerves tightening as they approached what might be a breakthrough in their investigation.

She pushed open the heavy wooden door, and the smell of wet pine mixed with freshly brewed coffee greeted them like an olfactory welcome mat. The interior was exactly what she'd expected from a working ranger station—functional furniture arranged around a central desk, walls covered with topographical maps and safety notices, the kind of organized efficiency that spoke to people who took their responsibilities seriously.

Roy Binkley sat hunched over paperwork at the main desk, his ranger uniform showing damp patches that suggested he'd been working outside despite the threatening weather. He was a man in his early forties with the weathered appearance of someone who'd spent years working outdoors, but there was something defeated about his posture that hadn't been there during their previous brief encounters.

A thermos sat beside his coffee mug, along with what appeared to be an empty whiskey bottle that he'd made no effort to conceal. The combination painted a picture of someone using alcohol to cope with stress or grief, and Shea filed the observation away for later use.

Binkley glanced up at their entrance, his eyes red-rimmed from either drinking or crying or lack of sleep and locked onto them with the startled expression of someone who'd been caught doing something they shouldn't. "Sheriff... Deputy." His voice carried a slight slur that confirmed her suspicions about his recent alcohol consumption. "Didn't know I was expecting company today."

Shea stepped up to his desk with the confident stride of someone who'd learned that hesitation could be interpreted as weakness during interrogations. The man across from her didn't look like a cold-blooded killer. Still, experience had taught her that predators came in all shapes and sizes, that evil could wear the uniform of authority as easily as it could hide behind the mask of mental illness.

Instead, Binkley resembled a man in mourning, someone who'd lost something precious and was drowning his sorrows in whatever alcohol he could find. But grief could be just as dangerous as rage when it came to motivating violence, especially in men who'd learned to see women as possessions rather than people.

"We'd like to ask you a few questions about your patrol schedules over the past few weeks," she said, her tone professional but carrying an undercurrent of authority that suggested cooperation wasn't optional. "Specifically, about some discrepancies we've found between your written reports and the GPS data from your assigned vehicle."

The ranger's gaze flickered nervously toward a stack of patrol logs on his desk, the involuntary movement confirming that he was aware of whatever inconsistencies they'd discovered. "Just routine checks and maintenance," he said, his voice carrying the careful neutrality of someone who'd prepared answers for questions he'd been expecting. "Nothing unusual or out of the ordinary for this time of year."

Trevor planted his hands flat on the desk and leaned forward with the aggressive posture of someone who'd decided that subtle questioning wasn't going to work with this suspect. "Maybe you can explain why your truck didn't register any GPS pings on the night Alexis Moore was killed," he said, his voice carrying an edge that made Binkley flinch back in his chair.

"Or why an entire patrol log from that week is missing from the official files," Shea added, watching the ranger's reaction with the trained eye of someone who'd learned to read guilt in facial expressions and body language. "Those are pretty significant oversights for someone who's supposed to be maintaining detailed records of his activities."

Binkley swallowed hard, his Adam's apple bobbing as he struggled to formulate a response that wouldn't incriminate him further. "GPS goes out all the time when you're working deep in the woods," he said, his hand twitching nervously as he gripped a pen like a lifeline. "The mountains interfere with satellite signals, and the equipment isn't as reliable as people think. The missing log must be some kind of clerical error—maybe it got misfiled or damaged."

His explanations sounded rehearsed, as if he'd been practicing them for days while dreading the moment when someone would come asking the right questions. But Shea could see the fear behind his eyes, the knowledge that his carefully constructed lies were falling apart under scrutiny.

"You knew Alexis Moore personally, didn't you?" she asked, switching tactics with the suddenness that often caught suspects off guard. "This wasn't just another camper whose name you might remember from a registration form."

Binkley's face darkened with an emotion that might have been shame or anger or some toxic combination of both. "Everyone knows everyone around here," he said, falling back on the kind of non-answer that small-town residents used when they wanted to avoid giving specific information. "It's a close community."

"She wasn't from around here," Shea pressed, leaning closer to invade his personal space in the way that made guilty people uncomfortable. "Alexis Moore lived in Little Rock, more than a hundred miles away. Don't play games with me, Roy. Deputy Bolton has already interviewed your fellow rangers, and they told us that you and Moore were much more than casual acquaintances."

The combination of shame and anger behind his eyes shifted toward the anger end of the spectrum. For a moment, she caught a glimpse of the rage that might have motivated violence when his relationship with Moore ended. "Yeah, so what if we knew each other?" he said, his voice carrying a defensive edge that suggested she'd hit a nerve. "We saw each other off and on for a few months, but it ended back in the spring. She said she wanted someone closer to her own age, that I was too boring and set in my ways."

The pain in his voice was genuine, but Shea had learned that pain could be just as dangerous as malice when it came to motivating violence against women who'd dared to exercise their right to end unwanted relationships.

Trevor crossed his arms and took on the role of bad cop with practiced ease. "You just let it go at that?" he asked, his tone suggesting he found that possibility unlikely. "A young woman tells you she doesn't want to see you anymore, and you simply accept it? You didn't follow her out to the lake that night? Didn't get angry enough to make her pay for rejecting you?"

The accusation had the desired effect. Binkley lunged to his feet with the sudden violence of someone whose self-control had finally snapped, his chair clattering backward as he rose to face them with clenched fists. "No!" His voice echoed off the log walls with desperate intensity. "I didn't kill her! I stayed away from her just like she asked me to. I do my job, I watch the lake, and I try not to think about what we used to have together."

"Then why lie on your patrol logs?" Shea stepped around the desk to close the distance between them while Trevor positioned himself to block any potential escape routes. "Why vanish from your assigned patrol areas when people are dying out there? Why disappear from the very places where you're supposed to be protecting the public?"

The questions hit him like physical blows, and she could see his carefully constructed defenses beginning to crumble under the pressure of confrontation. "I needed time off," he said, his voice dropping to barely above a whisper. "Personal time to deal with my problems without having to explain myself to supervisors who wouldn't understand."

He paused and looked directly at her, his eyes holding a pain that seemed to go deeper than simple romantic rejection. "Do you think I wanted to find her body? Do you think I wanted to see what some monster had done to someone I cared about?"

The admission hung in the air between them like

smoke from a gunshot, and Shea felt pieces of the puzzle clicking into place with sickening clarity. "You found Alexis Moore's body before it was officially reported." Shea's voice carried the certainty of someone who'd just solved a crucial part of the mystery. "You discovered her remains during an unauthorized patrol, and instead of calling it in, you fled the scene."

"So, you disappear the night she dies and still collect a paycheck for work you weren't doing." Disgust spread across Trevor's face added, "That's obstruction of justice at minimum, Roy, and it makes you look guilty of a hell of a lot more than just dereliction of duty."

Binkley slammed his pen down on the desk with enough force to crack the plastic casing, his composure finally shattering under the weight of weeks of guilt, alcohol, and sleepless nights. "I make mistakes, same as anyone else," he said, his voice cracking with emotion. "But I'm not the monster you're looking for. I'm just a broken man who lost the only good thing in his life and couldn't handle seeing what someone else had done to her."

Fear, shame, and something else flickered across his weathered features—guilt that went deeper than simple romantic loss but didn't quite reach the level of murderous rage. Shea studied his face with the trained eye of someone who'd interrogated hundreds of suspects over the years, and her instincts told her they were looking at a man who'd committed crimes of negligence and obstruction rather than violence.

But obstruction was still a crime, and his behavior had actively hindered their investigation into multiple murders. "We're booking you for obstruction of justice."

She nodded to Trevor to begin the arrest procedure. "Your lies and omissions may have cost lives, Roy. People might still be alive if you'd done your job instead of wallowing in self-pity."

Trevor moved forward with handcuffs, and Binkley didn't resist as the metal restraints clicked into place around his wrists. But instead of the relief or defiance that often accompanied arrest, the ranger simply stared out the window toward the lake where his former lover had died, his expression carrying the hollow emptiness of someone who'd given up fighting.

"You're wasting time," he said, his voice barely audible above the sound of rain beginning to fall against the station's windows. "The real killer is still out there, still watching and planning and choosing his next victims. While you're arresting me for being a coward and a drunk, he's getting ready to claim another family."

The words carried the weight of prophecy, and Shea felt a chill that had nothing to do with the mountain air seeping through the building's gaps and cracks.

~

Hidden among the dense pine trees that provided perfect concealment fifty yards from the ranger station, the killer pressed military surplus binoculars against his eyes and smiled with genuine pleasure as he watched Sheriff Callahan and Deputy Bolton escort the park ranger from the log building toward their patrol car.

The sight of Binkley in handcuffs filled him with satisfaction, proof that his careful manipulation of events had achieved exactly the result he'd intended when he'd begun leaving misleading evidence and false trails for the authorities to follow.

He pressed his back against the rough bark of an ancient oak tree, feeling the textured surface bite into his spine through his jacket, and closed his eyes for a moment as the thrill of absolute control washed over him like warm water. The binoculars hung heavy around his neck.

They'd taken the bait with the predictable enthusiasm of hunting dogs following a scent trail, never suspecting that the evidence they'd uncovered had been carefully planted to lead them away from the real predator who moved through their jurisdiction like smoke through a forest fire.

"Who's worthless now, old man?" he whispered to the ghost of his father, the words carrying the venom of decades-old rage that had never been properly satisfied. The drunk who'd burned his red blanket and called him weak would never see how strong his son had become, how perfectly he'd learned to hunt the very people who represented safety and authority in the world.

He slipped his hand into his jacket pocket and fingered the small scrap of wool that he carried everywhere. A piece of red fabric that had survived the fire that claimed his childhood home, rescued from the ashes and preserved as both a reminder and a talisman. The texture was rough and partially burned, but the color remained true, and touching it helped focus his thoughts when the whispers in his mind became too loud to ignore.

The red called to him across time and space, connecting him to every victim he'd claimed and every victim still to come. Each camping flag he'd planted had been a prayer to the memory of his grandmother's blanket, a ritual sacrifice offered to the part of himself that had died screaming in a closet while monsters ruled his world.

He moved through the woods with the fluid silence of someone who'd learned to exist between the spaces that civilization monitored, following game trails and deer paths that would leave no trace of his passage for tracking dogs or forensic teams to discover later. The forest was his natural habitat now, the place where he felt most comfortable and most powerful.

His destination was the cluster of rental cabins that dotted the southern shore of Misty Lake, isolated enough to provide privacy for whatever rituals he chose to perform but accessible enough that families still rented them for weekend getaways and summer vacations. The perfect hunting ground for someone who understood how to exploit the illusion of safety that civilization provided its most vulnerable members.

His gaze swept methodically across each structure until he found what he was searching for. A red hooded sweatshirt draped over a wooden rocking chair on one of the front porches, the crimson fabric bright as fresh blood against the weathered gray of the deck planking.

As he watched through his binoculars, a girl who appeared to be around ten years old emerged from the cabin and walked toward the rocking chair where the hoodie waited like bait in a trap he hadn't even needed to set. She was small and dark-haired, with the unconscious confidence of a child who'd never had reason to fear the world beyond her parents' protection.

But as she reached for the garment, something made her pause and turn toward the forest where he crouched in concealment. She froze like a rabbit that had suddenly caught the scent of a fox, her head tilted in the universal gesture of someone trying to identify a sound or movement that didn't belong in the usual pattern of their environment.

The killer's heart hammered as he realized the girl stared directly at his hiding spot, her young eyes somehow able to penetrate the shadows and undergrowth that had kept him invisible to adult observers for weeks. For a moment that seemed to stretch into eternity, predator and potential prey regarded each other across the distance that separated civilization from wilderness.

The forest seemed to hold its breath, as if even the trees and animals recognized that they were witnessing a moment when fate balanced on the edge of a knife. One movement, one sound, one decision could transform this encounter from mere observation into the kind of violence that would haunt a community forever.

But children possessed instincts that adults had learned to ignore, survival mechanisms that hadn't yet been dulled by years of assuming that monsters existed only in fairy tales and horror movies. After several seconds of mutual staring, the girl shrugged with the casual dismissal that kids used when they couldn't quite explain something that bothered them, grabbed her hoodie, and disappeared back inside the cabin.

The sound of the door slamming echoed across the water like a gunshot, and the killer slowly released the breath he'd been holding since their eyes had met across the deadly space between hunter and hunted.

He retreated deeper into the forest with the patience of someone who understood that the best predators never rushed their kills, that true power came from choosing the perfect moment rather than simply reacting to opportunity. The girl had seen him, but children were often dismissed when they reported strange encounters with shadowy figures in the woods.

Let Sheriff Callahan chase her false leads and arrest innocent men for crimes of negligence and stupidity. Let her federal allies waste their time building psychological profiles of suspects who existed only in their imaginations. Tomorrow night, when darkness provided the cover he needed and the family in that cabin had settled into their false sense of security, there would be more red added to the growing collection of evidence that proved his superiority over everyone who'd ever called him weak or worthless or broken.

The hunt would continue until every trace of red had been purged from his memory, or until someone proved worthy of the deadly game by finally seeing the invisible man who'd been standing in plain sight all along.

Chapter Ten

Shea sat at her desk in the empty sheriff's office as midnight approached, her third cup of coffee growing cold in her hands while she read through the latest reports that had accumulated during another day of chasing shadows and false leads. The building around her had settled into the quiet rhythm of night shift operations—distant radio chatter from dispatch, the hum of fluorescent lights that never slept, and the occasional creak of old timber adjusting to temperature changes.

She'd half expected to see FBI Agents Snowe and Larson still working in the conference room, but Doris, the veteran receptionist who seemed to know everything that happened in their small department, had informed her that the federal agents were following up on a lead that had taken them to Little Rock for the evening. Something about additional psychiatric records that might shed light on Thomas LaCrosse's mental state and potential triggers.

The paperwork spread across her desk represented weeks of meticulous investigation that had yielded frustratingly little concrete evidence. Witness statements that contradicted each other, forensic reports that raised more questions than they answered, and psychological profiles that seemed to describe half the population of disturbed individuals in Arkansas rather than pinpointing a specific suspect.

Her eyes burned from hours of reading the same facts over and over, searching for connections that might have been invisible during the initial chaos of active crime scenes. Somewhere in these mundane details lay the key to understanding how their killer selected his victims, planned his attacks, and moved through their jurisdiction without leaving traces that competent law enforcement could follow.

The phone rang with the sharp urgency that always made her pulse quicken, cutting through the office silence like a blade through silk. She reached for it with the automatic gesture of someone who'd learned that late-night calls in law enforcement rarely brought good news.

"Sheriff Callahan," she said, her voice carrying the professional alertness that came from years of handling emergencies at all hours of the day and night.

A pause stretched across the connection, filled with the kind of electronic silence that suggested someone weighing their words carefully before committing to a course of action that couldn't be undone. Then a male voice emerged from the static—rough and tight with nerves, carrying the tremor of someone who'd been wrestling with a difficult decision for days or weeks.

"You're looking at the wrong brother," the caller said, his words delivered with the clipped precision of someone who'd rehearsed this conversation multiple times before finding the courage to make the call.

Shea straightened in her chair, her hand tightening around the phone receiver as every instinct developed over fifteen years of police work screamed that this was the breakthrough they'd been waiting for. "Who is this?" she demanded, her voice sharp enough to cut through whatever hesitation might cause the caller to hang up.

The pause that followed was shorter this time, as if the caller had crossed some internal threshold and was now committed to revealing information that had been weighing on his conscience. "The man you should be looking for has burn scars on his left arm and neck." His voice gained strength as he continued. "He works maintenance at the state park under the name Daniel Hunt, but he used to be Daniel LaCrosse."

Shea's mind raced as the implications hit her like a physical blow. Another LaCrosse brother, one they'd never identified during their investigation into Thomas's background. Someone with access to every inch of the park system, who would know the terrain better than any casual visitor, who could move through restricted areas without arousing suspicion.

"Are you telling me that Daniel LaCrosse is here in our jurisdiction, possibly watching his brother's activities?" Her hand trembled as she set down her coffee mug and reached for a notepad to record every detail of this conversation.

But the line went dead before she could extract any additional information, leaving nothing but the electronic buzz of a severed connection and the sound of her own heart hammering against her ribs. The caller had revealed enough to transform their investigation but not sufficient to make the next steps obvious or easy.

The next morning brought the kind of crisp autumn air that promised winter was approaching the mountains of Arkansas, and Shea arrived at the office before dawn to find Trevor already at his desk, surrounded by the electronic glow of multiple computer screens and the detritus of an all-night research session.

She told him about the anonymous phone call, watching his expression shift from skepticism to excitement as the significance of the information became clear. Within minutes, he was typing with the focused intensity of someone who'd finally found a thread worth pulling in a case that had been unraveling their sanity for weeks.

"Found him." Trevor's voice carried the satisfaction of a hunter who'd finally spotted his quarry. "Daniel LaCrosse, age thirty-five, treated for severe burn trauma to his left arm and neck when he was twelve years old. Medical records show he was placed in emergency foster custody at the same time, then later transferred to Jefferson County where he aged out of the system."

He paused to scroll through additional screens of information. "No criminal record, which is probably why he never showed up on our initial background checks. But here's the interesting part—he legally changed his name to Daniel Hunt six years ago, right around the time he started working seasonal jobs for the state park system."

Shea perched on the edge of his desk, her mind processing the timeline and trying to understand the family dynamics that had led one brother to a psychiatric hospital and the other to a life of quiet anonymity in government service. "So, here's what we know," she said, organizing her thoughts out loud. "Thomas LaCrosse is the mentally unstable brother who was recently released from Glenvalley State Hospital. Daniel, now using the name Hunt, has followed him to our area and taken a low-profile job that gives him access to everywhere his brother might choose to hunt."

Trevor leaned back in his chair and crossed his arms, his expression thoughtful as he considered the implications. "The question is why Daniel would put himself in this position. Is he trying to keep an eye on Thomas? Trying to keep him safe from the consequences of his actions? Or does he know his brother is a killer and he's been covering for him somehow?"

"Don't forget we have an anonymous caller who specifically directed us toward Daniel." Shea's investigative instincts were telling her that nothing about this situation was as simple as it appeared. "That could be Daniel's conscience finally getting the better of him, or it could be someone else entirely who's been watching this family drama unfold and decided to manipulate our investigation."

She pushed off from the desk and headed toward her office to retrieve her jacket and service weapon. "Let's find Daniel Hunt and get some answers straight from the source."

Her first call was to the state park administration office, where a sleepy supervisor confirmed that Daniel Hunt was scheduled to work a maintenance shift that morning but hadn't shown up for his assigned duties. The supervisor provided a home address from personnel files, along with the grudging observation that Hunt had always been a reliable employee who'd never missed work without calling in advance.

They raced through the mountain roads toward the address, both officers silent as they prepared themselves for what might be another dangerous confrontation with someone whose connection to multiple murders remained unclear. The address led them to a small cabin in a cluster of rental properties that catered to seasonal workers and others who needed temporary housing without the complications of credit checks or long-term leases.

The cabin looked empty from the outside, but through a window, they could see the sparse furnishings of someone who lived like he might need to leave at a moment's notice—a military surplus cot, some worn clothes draped over a chair, and a half-packed duffel bag that suggested either recent arrival or imminent departure.

Shea tried the front door and found it unlocked, which immediately raised her suspicions. People who lived in remote cabins and worked jobs that required solitude tended to be careful about security, especially if they had secrets they wanted to protect.

Inside, the cabin's interior confirmed their impression of temporary occupancy. The furnishings were minimal and impersonal, but scattered across a small table were photocopies of what appeared to be official documents— psychiatric release papers bearing Thomas LaCrosse's name and signature, along with a detailed map of the lake region marked with red X's at various locations.

"These match our crime scenes," Trevor observed, comparing the marked locations to his notes about where bodies had been discovered. "All of them except the most recent murder at the mountain cabin."

Shea studied the map with growing unease, noting that the marks weren't random but followed a pattern that suggested systematic surveillance or planning. "He's been tracking his brother's movements," she said, though her tone suggested she wasn't entirely convinced of her conclusion.

"Or helping him select targets," Trevor replied, voicing the darker possibility that both of them had been considering since they'd discovered the evidence.

A shadow fell across the doorway, and they turned to find a middle-aged man peering into the cabin with the curious expression of someone who'd noticed unusual activity in his usually quiet neighborhood. "Y'all looking for Danny?" he asked, his voice carrying the casual friendliness of someone who knew all his neighbors and kept track of their comings and goings.

"We are." Shea stepped toward the man while keeping her hand near her service weapon. "Have you seen him recently?"

"Sure did. He headed out toward that maintenance shed behind the cabin about half an hour ago. Looked like he was in a hurry, carrying a big bag and walking fast like he had somewhere important to be."

Shea thanked the neighbor and motioned for Trevor to follow her toward the rear of the property, where a weathered storage shed sat among the pine trees. Their approach was quiet and cautious, weapons holstered but hands ready to draw at the first sign of danger.

She noted fresh boot prints in the muddy ground

around the shed's entrance, size eleven or twelve, with a tread pattern that matched impressions they'd found at several crime scenes. The discovery made her pulse quicken with the realization that they might finally be closing in on someone directly connected to the murders that had terrorized their community.

"Daniel Hunt," she called out. "This is Sheriff Callahan. I need you to step outside so we can talk."

A floorboard creaked inside the shed, followed by the sound of someone moving carefully among stored equipment or supplies. The response confirmed that someone was indeed inside, but the deliberate nature of the movement suggested calculation rather than panic.

"We're not here to hurt you," Shea continued, modulating her voice to project calm authority rather than aggression. "But you need to come out now so we can sort this situation out properly."

The metallic click of a latch being released preceded the slow opening of the shed door, revealing a figure standing in the shadows of the windowless interior. Daniel LaCrosse stepped into the daylight. Shea immediately understood why their anonymous caller had mentioned burn scars as identifying characteristics.

The left side of Daniel's neck and arm bore the twisted, discolored skin that spoke to severe trauma survived during childhood. Scars that told a story of pain and survival that connected him irrevocably to the house fire that had claimed his parents and transformed two young boys into something else entirely.

He wore the uniform of a state park maintenance worker, the kind of official clothing that allowed him to move through public spaces without attracting attention or questions. But there was something defeated about his posture that suggested he'd been expecting this confrontation for days or weeks, preparing himself for the moment when his careful anonymity would finally collapse.

"I'm not the one you're looking for." His voice carried the weary resignation of someone who'd been running from something for longer than he cared to remember.

"But you are Daniel LaCrosse." She studied his face for signs of deception or dangerous instability. "And we need to know where your brother Thomas is right now."

Daniel exhaled with the sound of someone releasing a burden he'd been carrying for far too long, then gestured for them to step inside the shed where they could continue their conversation away from the curious ears of neighbors who might be watching from their windows.

Skin prickling with the awareness of walking into a potentially dangerous situation, Shea stepped into the dim interior of the storage facility. Hand tools hung from pegboard walls with the organized precision of someone who took pride in maintaining his equipment, but her attention immediately focused on items that seemed out of place in a maintenance shed.

In one corner sat a large duffel bag packed with survival supplies—canned food, bottled water, detailed topographical maps of the region, and several burner phones that suggested someone planning to disappear into wilderness areas where everyday communication would be impossible.

"Looks like you're planning a trip somewhere."

Daniel slumped onto an overturned bucket. "I thought I could manage him," he said, his voice barely above a whisper. "Take him away from here before anyone else got hurt. Make sure he didn't have another complete breakdown like the one that landed him in the psychiatric hospital."

He paused and looked up at them with eyes that held the haunted quality of someone who'd seen too much violence and carried too much guilt. "I didn't know he'd started killing people again. Not at first, anyway. I just knew he wasn't handling his release well, and I wanted to keep him from doing something that would put him back in a locked ward."

"He's been murdering families for weeks." Trevor's voice carried undisguised disgust at the implications of what they were hearing. "Are you seriously telling us you had no idea what your brother was doing?"

The accusation seemed to age Daniel ten years in the space of a single breath, and Shea watched him struggle with emotions that went deeper than simple family loyalty into territory that touched on survivor's guilt and the kind of codependency that developed between trauma victims.

"I knew he wasn't mentally stable," Daniel admitted, his voice carrying the weight of someone confessing sins that had been eating him alive. "The fire damaged us both, but Tommy was always different afterward. Our father was cruel to him, blamed him for the complications during his birth that prevented our mother from having more children. When Tommy got released from Glenvalley, I followed him here because he'd always been drawn to wilderness areas where he could be alone with his thoughts."

He glanced up with an expression that mixed shame

and terror in equal measures. "But then people started dying, and I heard about the red camping flags being left at crime scenes. I recognized the significance immediately—Tommy had always been obsessed with red objects ever since our father burned his security blanket. I wanted to confront him about it, but the truth is he scares me now. What if he decided I was a threat? What if I became his next victim?"

Shea leaned closer, her voice taking on the edge that she used when dealing with people whose negligence had contributed to preventable tragedies. "And now he's escalating beyond anything you could have imagined. He's not just killing random campers anymore. He murdered parents while leaving their children alive to send some message. That's not your brother trying to stay quiet and avoid attention. That's someone who's completely lost touch with reality and is operating according to his twisted logic."

Daniel flinched as if she'd struck him physically, his hands trembling as the full weight of his brother's crimes settled on his shoulders like a crushing burden. "He's not the same person he was when we were children," he whispered. "He talks to himself constantly now, carrying on conversations with voices that only he can hear. He obsesses over red objects, fire, and hiding from imaginary threats. I think part of him is still trapped in that closet, still listening to our father scream at him about being weak and worthless."

Shea closed her eyes and took a deep breath before speaking again, using the moment to center herself and push down the anger that threatened to compromise her professional judgment. "You should have come to us the moment you realized your brother was killing innocent people and you knew where he was staying. Your silence may have cost lives, Daniel. Families might still be alive if you'd done the right thing instead of trying to protect someone who was beyond saving."

"I thought I could reach him somehow," Daniel said, his voice cracking with emotion. "I thought maybe if I could get him away from the triggers that were causing his episodes, he might stabilize enough for me to convince him to turn himself in or at least stop hurting people."

"He's beyond saving now," Shea replied with the finality of someone who'd seen too much evil to believe in easy redemptions. "The only thing that matters is stopping him before he kills again."

She motioned for Trevor to begin the arrest procedure, her decision made despite the sympathy she felt for someone who'd tried to carry an impossible burden. "Daniel LaCrosse, you're under arrest for obstruction of justice and accessory after the fact. You have the right to remain silent..."

"You won't find him hiding in these woods like some ordinary fugitive," Daniel said as Trevor placed the handcuffs around his wrists. "Tommy knows every cave system in these mountains, every abandoned structure, every place where someone could disappear for months without being discovered. You're not chasing a man anymore—you're hunting a ghost who learned to survive in places where normal people would die of exposure."

"Then help us. Give us something we can use to predict his next move or find his hiding places."

Trevor secured the handcuffs and checked them for proper placement. "This is for your protection as much as anything else. We're taking you into protective custody until we can figure out whether you're a liar, a coward, or the key to finding your brother before he kills again."

As they led him toward their patrol vehicle, Daniel's gaze drifted toward the tree line that surrounded the cabin like green walls holding back an ocean of wilderness. His expression held the haunted quality of someone who knew that monsters were real and that some of them wore familiar faces.

"He doesn't call himself Tommy anymore," Daniel said, his voice barely audible above the sound of wind through pine boughs. "That name burned up in the fire along with everything else from our childhood."

Shea opened the rear door of their patrol car and helped Daniel settle into the back seat, her movements careful but firm. "What does he call himself now?" .

"Red." The single word carried more weight than any lengthy explanation could have conveyed. "He calls himself Red, like the color that haunts his dreams and drives him to kill."

The revelation hung in the mountain air like smoke from a distant fire, and Shea felt pieces of the psychological profile clicking into place with sickening clarity. They weren't just hunting a disturbed individual— they were tracking someone who'd constructed an entire identity around the trauma that had shaped his childhood and continued to define his adult actions.

~

Thomas crouched on a rocky bluff that overlooked the

narrow ranger road winding through the valley below, his position carefully chosen to provide maximum visibility while maintaining concealment among the dense pine trees that covered the mountainside. The elevation allowed him to observe vehicle movement while remaining invisible to anyone passing beneath.

Through the gap in the forest canopy, he spotted the distinctive gleam of the sheriff's patrol car as it navigated the winding road toward the main highway. His military surplus binoculars brought the scene into sharp focus, revealing details that sent waves of rage coursing through his damaged nervous system like electricity through copper wire.

They were taking Daniel away in handcuffs, his brother's head hanging down in the defeated posture of someone who'd finally been caught carrying a burden too heavy for his shoulders to bear. The sight triggered memories and emotions that went deeper than conscious thought, reaching into the primitive parts of his brain where survival instincts and family bonds created chemical reactions that could drive rational people to irrational actions.

"They have him," he whispered to the forest that had become his congregation, his voice carrying the flat affect of someone processing information that didn't quite fit into his understanding of how the world was supposed to work. "They're taking him away from me. The golden son. The survivor who always managed to land on his feet while I got locked away in places where the walls had ears and the needles made the voices louder."

His hands trembled with barely controlled fury, one

clenched tight around a fresh red camping flag that he'd been preparing to plant at his next crime scene, while the other gripped the jagged bark of the pine tree he leaned against hard enough to drive splinters into his palm. The physical pain was welcome, a distraction from the emotional chaos that threatened to overwhelm his carefully maintained control.

Daniel had been the favorite child, the one who'd received foster homes instead of institutional care, schools instead of hospitals, regular meals instead of medication administered through injection or forced down reluctant throats. While Tommy had been locked in wards with magnetic door locks and observation windows, Daniel had been free to build a normal life despite carrying the same scars from the same fire that had consumed their childhood home.

The inequality had eaten at Tommy's soul during the seven years he'd spent in psychiatric facilities, listening to counselors talk about family dynamics and therapists explain how trauma could manifest differently in siblings who'd experienced identical events. They'd never understood that the difference hadn't been in their reactions to trauma but in how the system had chosen to treat them afterward.

"He thought he could watch me," Tommy continued his monologue to an audience of trees and mountain wildlife that had learned to recognize the sounds of human predators stalking through their territory. "Follow me around like some kind of guardian angel, keeping track of my activities and making sure I didn't do anything bad."

He began rocking back and forth with the motion that

had become his primary self-soothing mechanism during years of institutionalization, his body finding rhythm in the repetitive movement while his mind processed information and emotions that normal people would have been able to handle without physical manifestations.

"But he never understood that I let him follow me." His voice took on the singsong quality that emerged when he was talking to the voices that lived in the spaces between his thoughts. "I could have disappeared into these mountains months ago, could have become invisible in ways that would have made it impossible for anyone to track my movements or predict my actions. I allowed him to think he was watching me because it amused me to have an audience for my transformation."

The trees whispered their agreement with secrets that only he could understand, and he felt the familiar comfort of being surrounded by living things that didn't judge or medicate or try to convince him that his perception of reality was somehow flawed or incomplete.

His thoughts drifted to Sheriff Callahan, whose sharp eyes and determined expression had impressed him during their brief encounter at his cabin. She possessed the kind of intelligence and strength that his father would have despised in a woman. These qualities marked her as someone who would never allow herself to be victimized by men who used violence to compensate for their inadequacies.

"She's clever," he admitted to his forest congregation, his voice carrying a mixture of respect and anticipation that spoke to the predator's appreciation for worthy prey. "She smells like authority and control, like pine bark and thunder clouds gathering before a storm. The kind of woman who would have fought back against our father instead of cowering in corners and making excuses for bruises that couldn't be explained away."

But intelligence and determination weren't enough to protect someone from a predator who'd learned to hunt by studying the mistakes that had led to his capture and institutionalization years earlier. Sheriff Callahan didn't understand how the color red worked as a trigger, didn't comprehend the psychological mechanisms that transformed him from a merely disturbed individual into an apex predator with supernatural patience and tactical awareness.

He could picture his brother sitting in a jail cell, probably crying as he confessed secrets that had been eating at his conscience for weeks or months. Daniel had always been weak when it came to authority figures, too eager to please and too guilty about his own survival to maintain the kind of silence that protected family members from consequences they couldn't control.

The rage that had been building in his chest since he'd watched the arrest through his binoculars finally reached the combustion point that transformed emotion into action. He reached into his jacket pocket and pulled out a book of matches that he'd been saving for a special occasion, the kind of ceremonial moment that required fire to purify the world of things that had become corrupted by compromise and betrayal.

He struck one match and held it up to watch the tiny flame dance in the mountain breeze, so small and seemingly harmless but carrying within it the potential to consume forests and buildings and lives with equal appetite. "He was mine to burn," he whispered to the fire, "not theirs to catch and cage and process through their system of laws and procedures and therapeutic interventions."

The flame burned down toward his fingers, and he pressed it against his left wrist before it could reach the phosphorus that would cause it to die naturally. The pain was sharp and immediate, adding another small burn scar to the collection that mapped his psychological deterioration across the landscape of his flesh.

He straightened with the renewed focus that came from physical pain translating into mental clarity, his body moving with the fluid grace of someone who'd learned to exist in harmony with violence rather than fighting against it. The sheriff thought she was ahead now, that arresting his brother had given her some kind of advantage in their ongoing game of predator and prey.

But she didn't understand the fundamental truth that Daniel had been nothing more than an echo of the fire that had created them both, a shadow cast by the real flames that continued to burn in the spaces where his father's cruelty had consumed Tommy's childhood. Daniel had been a distraction, a false lead designed to waste law enforcement resources while the real predator continued to move through their jurisdiction like smoke through a forest fire.

This time would be different. This time, he wouldn't strike at random strangers who happened to possess red camping gear that triggered his damaged psyche. This time, he would target someone close to the sheriff herself, someone whose death would send a message that couldn't be misunderstood or deflected through arrests of peripheral figures.

The story of the LaCrosse brothers wouldn't end with handcuffs and arraignments and plea bargains negotiated by public defenders who'd never experienced the kind of trauma that created monsters from damaged children. It would end in flames and red, the way it had always been destined to end since the night an eight-year-old boy had learned that sometimes the only way to stop being a victim was to become something that victims feared more than their original tormentors.

And this time, he would go after someone close enough to Sheriff Callahan to make her understand that intelligence and authority and federal resources meant nothing when facing an enemy who'd learned to embrace the very darkness that normal people spent their lives trying to avoid.

Chapter Eleven

Shea's boots squelched through the thick mud left by recent mountain rains, each step creating sucking sounds that seemed to echo through the forest. The dark clouds overhead hung low and heavy, pressing down on the canopy of pine and oak with the promise of more precipitation before the day ended.

She knew she shouldn't have ventured into these woods alone, especially with a serial killer who'd already demonstrated an intimate knowledge of the terrain. But she'd been restless all night, pacing her small house like a caged animal. At the same time, her mind churned over the details of their investigation and the growing certainty that Tommy LaCrosse planned something far more personal than his previous attacks.

Trevor had been working eighteen-hour days for weeks without complaint, and she'd finally ordered him to take the morning off despite his protests that he was fine and wanted to continue pursuing leads. The dark circles under his eyes and the tremor in his hands when he reached for his coffee cup had told a different story, and good leaders knew when to force their people to rest before exhaustion led to mistakes that could prove fatal.

But solitude had never been her friend during active investigations, and by dawn she'd found herself studying topographical maps with the obsessive intensity of someone convinced that the answer lay hidden in geographic details they'd somehow overlooked. That's when she'd spotted the notation about an old trail that had been closed years ago due to erosion problems that made it too dangerous for casual hikers to navigate without serious risk of injury.

A trail that only locals with decades of experience in these mountains would know about, or a killer who'd spent months studying every possible route through terrain that could provide concealment and escape options when law enforcement finally closed in.

Her only companion was Heidi. The dog padded silently beside her, nose working constantly to process the complex scent picture that every forest presented to animals with the ability to read chemical signatures invisible to human perception.

Eyes alert and constantly scanning, Shea studied the abandoned trail. Her gaze swept back and forth across the path ahead, looking for signs of recent passage or anything that seemed out of place in the natural environment.

Heidi suddenly gave a soft woof, the kind of quiet alert that indicated she'd detected something worth investigating without creating enough noise to attract unwanted attention from anyone who might be listening from concealment nearby.

That's when Shea saw it. A brief glint of something metallic at ankle height, so subtle that it would have been invisible to someone moving at normal hiking speed through the dappled light filtering down through the forest canopy. She narrowed her eyes and moved closer, her hand instinctively drifting toward the service weapon holstered at her hip.

Stretched between two young saplings was a length of fishing line, nearly transparent and positioned precisely where someone walking the trail would step without looking down. The setup was so simple and effective that it spoke to someone with either extensive experience in wilderness survival or a natural talent for creating improvised weapons from common materials.

"Good girl, Heidi." She scratched behind the dog's ears while her mind processed the implications of finding a deliberate trap on a trail that hadn't seen official use in years.

Upon closer examination, she discovered the actual trap mechanism tucked beneath a carefully arranged pile of decaying leaves that would have appeared completely natural to anyone not looking for signs of human interference. A plank of rotted wood studded with rusty nails that had been sharpened to vicious points, all tilted upward to ensure maximum damage to anyone whose foot broke through the concealing vegetation.

But the most sophisticated element was a metal camping cup that had been rigged with additional string to create a primitive but effective alarm system. Anyone triggering the fishing line would cause the cup to jingle with enough noise to alert someone listening from a concealed position nearby, while the victim would be too focused on the sudden pain of puncture wounds to mount an immediate pursuit.

The killer had created more than just a trap. He'd built a silent alarm system designed to maim anyone who came looking for him while simultaneously announcing their presence so he could observe their reaction or plan his next move. The level of planning and tactical thinking involved spoke to someone with either military training or an intuitive understanding of predator-prey dynamics that went far beyond what most criminals possessed. But then again, Tommy had had a lot of time to study and research during his stint in the hospital.

Shea carefully stepped over the fishing line, her movements deliberate and controlled while her mind raced through the implications of this discovery. "Watch yourself, girl," she warned Heidi, though the dog had already detected the danger and moved with the careful precision that working animals developed when operating in hostile environments.

No one left a trap like this unless they wanted to prevent someone from finding them, or unless they wanted to control precisely how and when that discovery took place. Either the mechanism was very old, left by some long-departed hermit or survivalist, or Tommy LaCrosse had recently constructed it as part of whatever plan he was developing for his next phase of violence.

Given the freshness of the fishing line and the deliberate sophistication of the alarm system, she bet on the latter possibility. Which meant he was hiding somewhere further up the trail, possibly watching her at this very moment through binoculars while she examined his handiwork.

She pulled the radio from her belt to call for backup, her standard procedure when entering potentially dangerous situations without adequate support. But the device emitted only static, the mountain terrain and dense forest canopy combining to block the radio signals that worked perfectly well in town or open areas.

The hair on the back of her neck stood up. Heidi whined deep in her throat.

"You're watching me right now, aren't you, Tommy?" Her voice carried clearly through the forest silence. "You set this trap knowing I'd find this trail, knowing I'd be curious enough to investigate it despite the obvious risks."

A twig snapped behind her with the sharp crack of dead wood breaking under weight, and she spun toward the sound with her weapon clearing its holster in one fluid motion.

"Whoa!" Trevor burst through the underbrush. "Don't shoot. It's just me"

"Freeze right there."

Trevor skidded to a halt with his eyes wide, confusion and concern warring across his features as he realized how close he'd come to being shot by someone he trusted with his life on a daily basis. "Shea, why are you pointing a gun at me?"

She kept the weapon raised for another few seconds while studying his face and body language for signs that something was wrong, then slowly lowered it as her rational mind overrode the paranoid thoughts that active manhunts could generate in even experienced law enforcement officers.

"There's a trap." She pointed toward the nearly

invisible fishing line stretched across the trail. "I wanted to make sure you stopped. It's primitive but effective. Designed to maim whoever triggers it and alert the person who set it."

Trevor moved closer to examine the mechanism. "That could have done some serious damage to anyone walking this trail without knowing it was there," he observed. "Whoever built this has done similar work before. This level of planning and execution doesn't come from reading survival manuals."

"Speaking of planning and execution," Shea said, holstering her weapon but keeping her eyes on the forest around them, "why aren't you at home enjoying a leisurely cup of coffee and a few hours of sleep like I ordered? You're supposed to be taking a break from this investigation."

Trevor's expression carried the mixture of guilt and determination that she'd learned to recognize. "I could ask you the same question. But here you are, hiking through dangerous terrain alone with a serial killer who's already demonstrated a personal interest in making you his next target."

"I've got Heidi with me. She's the one who alerted me to the trap in the first place. I trust her senses to warn me if anyone is approaching our position."

Trevor looked like he wanted to argue the point, but the first fat raindrops began falling through the canopy overhead.

Shea's gaze landed on a patch of disturbed moss near the base of a large oak tree, the kind of scuffed earth that indicated recent human activity in an area that should have been undisturbed for months or years. Boot prints led away from the trail into dense brush that would provide excellent concealment for someone wanting to observe without being seen.

She followed the tracks for several yards, Trevor close behind her, until they reached a low ridge where a shallow depression in the ground suggested someone had lain prone for an extended period. The position would have provided a perfect vantage point for watching anyone who discovered the trap, while remaining invisible to casual observation from the trail below.

A cigarette still smoldered in the dirt beside the observation post, its ember glowing like a tiny red eye in the gathering gloom. The sight of it made her stomach clench with the realization of how close they'd come to walking into an ambush, and how lucky they were that Tommy had decided to withdraw rather than engage.

"He was here watching me. He knew I'd find this trail. He probably wanted me to find it."

Trevor studied the still-burning cigarette. "I don't think there's much you do that he isn't aware of at this point," he said, his voice carrying implications that made her skin crawl. "The level of surveillance and preparation we're seeing suggests someone who's been studying your habits and patterns for weeks or months."

He gestured toward the darkening sky where rain was beginning to fall with increasing intensity. "Come on. Let's get back to the station before we're completely soaked. This terrain becomes treacherous in wet weather, and I'd rather not have to explain to the mayor how his sheriff fell off a cliff while chasing ghosts through the forest."

Shea nodded. The abandoned trail was already becoming slippery, and one wrong step could result in either of them plummeting down steep slopes that would turn a manhunt into a rescue operation.

She followed Trevor's broad shoulders as he led them back toward where she'd parked her patrol truck, but her mind continued churning over the implications of what they'd discovered. Tommy had somehow known she would find the abandoned trail, had prepared for her arrival with traps and observation posts.

The question that bothered her most was whether he'd wanted her to find evidence of his presence, whether this entire encounter had been designed to send a message or lure her into some larger trap that she couldn't yet see. Because one thing was certain—she would find him eventually. She had no doubt about that. The only question was what horrors he prepared for their final confrontation.

Back at the sheriff's station, Shea took her customary place at the head of the conference table where FBI Agents Snowe and Larson had spread their latest psychological profiles and tactical assessments across the polished surface. The federal agents looked up expectantly as she entered, clearly hoping that her unauthorized solo reconnaissance had yielded information that would break their investigation wide open.

She told them about the sophisticated trap and the evidence that Tommy had been watching her approach from a carefully prepared observation post, while Trevor pinned photographs of the mechanism to their ever-growing case board that now resembled a shrine to law enforcement frustration.

The agents exchanged glances that spoke to their own growing concerns about an adversary who seemed to anticipate their every move while remaining invisible to conventional tracking methods. This wasn't the behavior pattern they'd expected from someone with Tommy's psychiatric history, and the tactical sophistication he was demonstrating suggested capabilities that went far beyond what hospital records indicated.

A knock on the conference room door interrupted their discussion, and Deputy Butler entered with Daniel LaCrosse in handcuffs. The man's appearance had deteriorated since his arrest. His clothes were rumpled, his hair unkempt, and his eyes held the red-rimmed look of someone who hadn't slept since being taken into custody.

"This guy said he wanted to talk to you specifically." Butler guided Daniel to a chair at the far end of the table. "Claims he has information that might help us locate his brother before anyone else gets hurt."

Shea studied Daniel's face, noting the mixture of guilt and desperation that suggested he was finally ready to reveal information he'd been holding back. "Talk." Her tone indicated that she was in no mood for games or partial truths.

Daniel's jaw twitched as he struggled with whatever internal conflict had been eating at him since his arrest. "I need you to understand something," he began, his voice barely above a whisper. "I knew about Tommy's involvement in these murders after the first couple was found at the lake. The red flags, the precise nature of the wounds, the ritual aspects. It all fit patterns I'd observed during his previous breakdown."

"Why didn't you come forward immediately?" Shea crossed her arms as she fought the urge to reach across the table and throttle a man whose silence had potentially cost innocent lives. "If you'd contacted us after the first murders, we might have been able to stop him before he killed again."

Daniel met her gaze without flinching, his eyes holding no defensiveness or self-justification, only the raw guilt of someone who'd made a terrible decision and would have to live with the consequences for the rest of his life. "Ever since the house fire that killed our parents—which I'm now certain he deliberately set—Tommy has been obsessed with fire as both a weapon and a form of purification. I'm actually surprised he's been using a knife to kill his victims rather than burning them alive."

He paused and took a shaky breath, his hands trembling as memories he'd tried to suppress for decades forced their way to the surface. "He started small when we were children—burning cigarettes and paper scraps and small animals that he'd capture in the woods. But as he got older, the targets became larger and more dangerous. When he graduated to burning occupied buildings, that's when the state finally stepped in and had him institutionalized."

Agent Larson leaned forward with the focused attention of someone who'd spent years studying criminal psychology. "What you're describing is a classic escalation pattern," he observed. "But the current murders don't fit that profile. Why would someone with pyromania switch to stabbing victims instead of using fire as his primary weapon?"

"Because he's learned to be more careful," Daniel

replied. "Fire attracts attention—smoke, sirens, investigators with specialized training in arson cases. Knife attacks can be concealed for days or weeks if the bodies are hidden properly. But I need to warn you about something more immediate."

His voice took on an urgency that made everyone in the room lean closer. "Once Tommy reaches this point in his psychological deterioration, he stops targeting random victims and starts focusing on authority figures. Specifically, the person in charge of investigating his crimes."

Shea felt her heart skip a beat as the implication hit her like a physical blow. "Me."

"Yes," Daniel confirmed, his voice carrying the weight of certainty born from a lifetime of watching his brother's behavioral patterns. "He'll be watching your every move from now on, studying your habits and routines, looking for the perfect opportunity to make you his final victim. In his mind, killing the person who's been hunting him will complete some kind of ritual that's been building since our childhood."

"And yet you still didn't come forward when you realized what he was planning," Shea said through gritted teeth, noting the angry expressions on the faces of the federal agents and Trevor. She wasn't the only person in the room who wanted to assault this man for his criminal negligence.

"No," Daniel admitted, his voice barely audible. "I didn't come forward because I thought he might come for me first. I've been living in terror for weeks, jumping at every shadow and sound, waiting for the moment when he'd decide that I knew too much to be allowed to live."

He took another ragged breath and seemed to gather what remained of his courage. "But there's something else you need to know. When I was able to observe him without being detected, I heard him muttering about a place he called 'his quiet.' I'm not entirely sure where it is, but based on his words, I believe it's somewhere underground. A cave or abandoned mine shaft or storm shelter that reminds him of the closet where he used to hide as a child."

Agent Larson immediately pulled out his phone and began coordinating with local resources. "We need to locate every abandoned mine, natural cave system, and storm shelter within a twenty-mile radius of the lake," he announced. "Based on his previous behavior patterns, he won't stray far from his established hunting grounds, especially if he's preparing to target Sheriff Callahan."

Shea shook off the cloak of dread that had been settling around her shoulders like a funeral shroud. "I'll get my deputies started on compiling locations immediately," she said, forcing her voice to project the kind of confidence that leaders needed to maintain even when facing their own mortality. "We'll coordinate with park service records and old mining surveys to create a comprehensive search grid."

Daniel stood as Deputy Butler prepared to escort him back to his holding cell, but he paused at the door and turned back toward Shea with an expression that mixed brotherly concern with absolute terror. "There's one more thing you need to understand, Sheriff," he said, his voice carrying the finality of someone delivering a death sentence. "Tommy doesn't fear death anymore. He embraced it years ago when he learned that being dead inside was the only way to survive what our father did to him and our mother. If you corner him in whatever hole he's chosen for his final stand, he won't hesitate to burn everything down around him, including anyone who gets in his way."

The warning hung in the air long after Daniel had been led away, and Shea found herself staring at the case board where photographs of victims gazed back at her with the accusing eyes of the unavenged dead.

~

Hidden in the shadow of an enormous pine tree that provided perfect concealment while allowing him to observe the sheriff's station through military surplus binoculars, Tommy LaCrosse felt a mixture of disappointment and admiration as he watched the last patrol car disappear down the mountain road.

She'd been so close to walking into his trap, so perfectly positioned for him to demonstrate his superiority over law enforcement officers who thought they could hunt him like some common criminal. If not for her dog's superior senses, he would have heard her scream as the sharpened nails punched through her boots and into the soft flesh of her feet, would have watched her stumble and fall while he decided whether to finish her quickly or allow her to suffer.

But she'd seen the fishing line, had recognized the sophistication of his alarm system, had known that it was intended specifically for her. The realization filled him with an almost paternal pride. She was indeed smart and strong, not like the other authority figures who'd tried to control and medicate and institutionalize him over the years.

She understood that he would come for her. She'd be waiting and prepared, which would make their final confrontation far more satisfying than simply ambushing some unsuspecting victim who never saw death approaching through the forest shadows.

But that deputy kept interfering, showing up at crucial moments and disrupting carefully laid plans with his protective instincts and tactical awareness. Trevor Bolton had become more than just an obstacle. He actively prevented Tommy from completing the ritual that had been building since childhood, and that kind of interference couldn't be tolerated indefinitely.

He sat among the pine needles and formulated various plans for dealing with the deputy problem, considering approaches that ranged from simple elimination to more elaborate psychological warfare designed to break the man's spirit before killing him. But the increasing rain soon sent him dashing toward his underground sanctuary.

Maybe not Deputy Bolton directly, he decided as he navigated the familiar path through dense undergrowth toward the concealed entrance to his subterranean refuge. Not yet, anyway. The man was too alert, too well-trained, and too closely connected to the sheriff to be easily isolated and eliminated without creating complications that might interfere with larger plans.

But there were other deputies, other law enforcement officers who worked for Sheriff Callahan and represented her authority in the community. Tommy could eliminate one of them instead, leaving their body in a location where it would send an unmistakable message to everyone involved in the investigation.

He would demonstrate that the sheriff's people were vulnerable, that her authority couldn't protect the men and women who served under her command. He'd take her deputies down one by one until she understood that her only choice was to face him alone, without backup or federal support or the comfortable illusion that civilization's rules applied to their final confrontation.

The message would be written in blood and fire, the way all important communications had been delivered since the night an eight-year-old boy learned that sometimes the only way to stop being a victim was to become something that victims feared more than their original tormentors.

Chapter Twelve

Doris burst through the door of Shea's office. The veteran receptionist's face was flushed from running, and her hands trembled as she gripped the doorframe to steady herself while delivering news that would transform their investigation from professional duty into personal warfare.

"It's Lisa Hensley." Her voice cracked with emotion that decades of working in law enforcement hadn't prepared her to handle. "The new deputy who was supposed to start tomorrow."

Shea glanced up from the personnel file she'd been reviewing on her desk, her mind automatically shifting to administrative mode as she processed what should have been routine information about a rookie officer's first day assignment. "Isn't she scheduled to begin orientation tomorrow morning? I was going over her training requirements."

"I don't think that's going to happen." Her eyes filled with tears. "A hiker called dispatch about twenty minutes ago. Found Deputy Hensley's body up by the north cove. She's dead, Shea. And there's a red flag planted right next to her campsite."

The mundane sounds of office life that had provided background noise suddenly became amplified in the terrible silence that followed. The hum of fluorescent lights overhead seemed to grow louder and more oppressive. The steady clicking of Trevor's fingers on his laptop keyboard stopped.

"Shea?" Trevor's voice carried a mixture of concern and barely controlled rage, the tone of someone who'd just realized that a predator had crossed a line that transformed professional investigation into personal vendetta.

Her gaze locked with his across the office space that had become their war room over the past weeks, and she saw her understanding reflected in his eyes. This wasn't another random victim who'd made the mistake of camping with red gear in Tommy LaCrosse's hunting territory. This was a deliberate escalation, a message written in blood and designed for her to find.

"It's one of us this time." They were no longer hunting a serial killer—they were engaged in a personal war with a predator who'd decided to make law enforcement his primary target.

The north cove where Lisa Hensley had chosen to spend her last night alive was tucked deep into the most remote section of the state park, accessible only by a narrow dirt road that wound through dense forest for miles before reaching the isolated clearing. The location offered no cell phone service and barely appeared on official maps, the kind of place that serious campers sought out when they wanted to experience true wilderness without the crowds and conveniences that defined most recreational areas.

When Shea and Trevor arrived at the scene, their

patrol cars kicking up clouds of dust that hung in the still air like smoke from a distant fire, the clearing possessed the profound silence that seemed to follow violent death like a shadow. Deputy Butler stood near his cruiser with the rigid posture of someone fighting to maintain professional composure in the face of personal tragedy, while a young man in his twenties sat on a boulder with his head buried in his hands, shoulders shaking with the aftershocks of discovering something that would haunt his dreams for years to come.

A blue and gray dome tent had been pitched close to the water's edge, its entrance flap gaping open like a mouth frozen in a silent scream. Inside, visible through the opening, was a red sleeping bag with hiking boots placed neatly beside it in the kind of precise arrangement that spoke to someone who took care of their equipment and planned to use it again.

Near the established fire ring, a scarlet camping flag stood perfectly staked in the soft earth, its crimson fabric fluttering in the mountain breeze like a banner marking conquered territory. The sight of it made Shea's stomach clench with rage and recognition—another calling card from a predator who turned murder into performance art.

But it was the body that transformed professional crime scene processing into something far more personal and devastating. Lisa Hensley lay in the grass nearby, her form covered by a bright red rain poncho that had been stretched over her with deliberate care. The waterproof fabric was shiny with morning dew, and four carefully selected rocks anchored the corners as if the killer had wanted to ensure his display would remain intact until law enforcement arrived to appreciate his handiwork.

Trevor knelt beside the covered form and lifted one corner of the poncho with the reverent care that officers reserved for fallen colleagues. Lisa's skin had taken on the pale, waxy appearance that marked the transition from person to evidence, but even in death, her face showed the determined expression that had impressed Shea during the interview process weeks earlier.

"Her wrists are bound with bright orange nylon cord." Trevor's voice carried the clinical detachment that police officers learned to maintain when processing scenes that threatened to overwhelm their emotional defenses. "Pulled tight enough to dig into her flesh and leave permanent marks. There's bruising along her jawline that suggests she fought back before he overpowered her."

Shea swallowed the bile that rose in her throat and crouched beside her deputy, forcing herself to study the evidence that would help them understand the killer's methods and potentially predict his next move. "No blood visible on the body or immediate surrounding area," she noted. "He killed her somewhere else and moved her here for the staging. Wanted her displayed exactly like this when we found her."

A crime scene technician waved to her from the tree line, and she left Trevor to continue documenting the body while she examined what appeared to be the actual attack site. The physical evidence told a clear story for anyone trained to read the signs that violence left behind.

Deep boot prints with a narrow heel matched the impressions they'd found at previous crime scenes, confirming that they were dealing with the same perpetrator despite the change in victim selection. A torn scrap of red fabric, identical to the material used for the poncho covering Lisa's body, hung from a thorny bush at shoulder height where it had been ripped away during struggle or flight.

And there, partially concealed beneath fallen leaves that had been hastily scattered to hide the evidence, was the blood they'd been looking for. Dark stains in the earth that spoke to violence inflicted in this secluded spot, where screams would echo off the surrounding mountains without reaching ears that might have summoned help.

"He grabbed her when she stepped into the trees for privacy." Shea reconstructed the sequence of events that had ended a promising career before it could begin. "Probably waited in concealment until she was far enough from her campsite that he could attack without worrying about evidence being visible from the main clearing."

This was different from his previous attacks, which had all been crimes of opportunity targeting strangers who happened to possess the red camping gear that triggered his psychological mechanisms. Tommy LaCrosse had deliberately stalked Lisa Hensley.

Her death wasn't random violence. It was a personal message directed at Shea, designed to demonstrate that he could reach anyone in her department regardless of their training or awareness of the danger he represented.

By the time they returned to the sheriff's station, news of the deputy's murder had spread through the small law enforcement community with the speed that tragic information always seemed to travel. The killer hadn't just claimed another life. He'd breached the department's inner circle and proved that badges and training and weapons meant nothing when facing a predator who'd learned to hunt the hunters.

Outside the office building, a crowd had gathered with the mixture of morbid curiosity and genuine concern that small-town tragedies always seemed to generate. Locals who'd known Lisa's family mingled with reporters who'd descended on Misty Hollow like vultures drawn to carrion, while a surprising number of tourists still lingered despite weeks of warnings about the danger that stalked anyone who ventured into the mountains.

News vans were parked bumper to bumper along the street that had never seen this kind of media attention, their satellite dishes and transmission equipment transforming the quiet mountain town into something resembling a war zone command center. Camera operators hoisted their equipment onto tripods while reporters checked their microphones and rehearsed the questions they'd been instructed to ask by producers who cared more about ratings than the human cost of the violence they were covering.

Shea stepped up to the cluster of microphones that had been arranged like flowers at a funeral, Trevor positioning himself at her side in a show of solidarity that spoke to a partnership forged through shared danger and mutual respect. The assembled media immediately focused their attention on her.

"This morning, we lost one of our own," she began. "Deputy Lisa Hensley was murdered while camping alone at the north cove. She was off duty and scheduled to begin work with our department tomorrow morning."

She paused to gather her thoughts and push down the rage that threatened to compromise her professional demeanor. "Deputy Hensley was not aware of the specific details of our ongoing investigation into a suspect who targets campers displaying red items, and she unfortunately chose to sleep in a red sleeping bag that attracted the killer's attention. Her death represents an escalation in this individual's pattern of violence and demonstrates his willingness to target law enforcement personnel."

The formal language felt inadequate for describing the loss of someone who'd been looking forward to serving her community and protecting the people who couldn't protect themselves. But press conferences required a certain clinical distance that helped maintain public confidence while providing information that might prevent additional victims.

"Effective immediately, I am again advising all residents and visitors to avoid Misty Lake and the surrounding campground areas. If you are currently camping anywhere in this county, remove all visible red items from your campsite immediately. The killer is using them as attractants to identify potential victims."

She glanced toward the mountains that surrounded their small town like the walls of a fortress. "I also suggest that property owners remove red items from their private residences and businesses. This individual has demonstrated a willingness to expand his hunting territory when his current area becomes too heavily patrolled or publicized."

The questions that followed came like machine gun fire, reporters shouting over each other in their eagerness to extract information that might advance their careers or satisfy the bloodthirsty curiosity of audiences who consumed violence like entertainment.

"Is this murder a direct message to law enforcement?"

"Has the FBI confirmed the identity of their primary suspect?"

"How long until you close the entire park system to public access?"

"Are you personally being targeted by this killer?"

Shea didn't answer any of the shouted questions. Instead, she backed away from the microphones. The reporters continued calling after her as she headed toward the office entrance, their voices creating a cacophony of demands for information that she couldn't provide without compromising their ability to catch a predator who seemed to anticipate their every move.

In her office, she leaned against her desk and gripped its edge hard enough to make her knuckles ache, the physical pain serving as an anchor against the emotional storm that threatened to overwhelm her professional judgment. Tommy LaCrosse had stayed two steps ahead of them throughout this investigation, anticipating their tactics and countering their strategies with the kind of tactical awareness that suggested either extensive military training or an intuitive understanding of how law enforcement operated.

The federal agents with their psychological profiles, surveillance technology, and behavioral analysis expertise had produced nothing but theories and speculation while real people continued to die at the hands of someone who seemed to exist in the spaces between their investigative procedures. Lisa Hensley's death proved that all their resources, training, and coordination meant nothing when facing an enemy who'd learned to hunt from the shadows.

Trevor appeared in her doorway with the careful approach of someone who'd learned to recognize when his partner was balancing on the edge of emotional breakdown. "I know I've said this before, but we will catch him. This time he made a mistake by targeting one of our own."

"When?" She whirled to face him. "How many more people have to die while we chase shadows and process evidence and build cases that never seem to lead anywhere? We have no idea what we're doing out there. I have no idea what I'm doing as sheriff!"

The admission felt like a physical wound, exposing insecurities that she'd been fighting since accepting the position and taking responsibility for protecting a community that had trusted her with their safety. Every victim represented a personal failure, and every red flag planted at a crime scene served as a monument to her inadequacy as a leader and investigator.

Trevor stepped closer and gripped her shoulders. "You're doing an excellent job as sheriff, Shea. The problem isn't your leadership or investigative skills. It's that we're dealing with someone whose psychological profile doesn't fit any of the conventional patterns that law enforcement is trained to handle. It's your weakness not to see that."

She jerked away from his touch. "A weakness that's getting innocent people killed."

"You aren't the one killing them," Trevor replied, moving toward her again with the patient persistence of someone who refused to allow a partner to self-destruct during a crisis.

She planted her palms against his chest and shoved him backward with enough force to make him stumble, the violence serving as a release valve for emotions that had been building to dangerous levels. "My failure to stop him is the same as holding the knife in my own hands. Every victim died because I wasn't smart enough or fast enough or ruthless enough to catch a predator who's been playing games with us since this investigation began."

Trevor steadied himself and studied her face with the expression of someone who'd learned to recognize when colleagues were approaching the breaking point that ended careers and destroyed lives. "Go home and get some rest. I can handle things here for the remainder of the day."

He made a move toward her again, but she shook her head with violent emphasis. "He specifically chose Lisa because she worked for me. Her death wasn't random—it was personal. He wanted to hurt me by killing someone under my protection. He made a tactical error by targeting law enforcement. Because now I'm coming for him without restraints, without the limitations that legal procedures impose on police investigations."

She moved toward the door. "Leave me alone, Trevor. Please." She opened the door and gestured for him to leave.

The door closed behind him with the finality of a coffin lid, leaving her alone with her rage and her grief and her growing certainty that Tommy LaCrosse's next victim would either be her or someone else who mattered enough to destroy what remained of her faith in justice.

~

Tommy LaCrosse sat cross-legged on the stained carpet of a cheap motel room that was rented by the week to people who preferred to remain invisible to authorities, his attention focused on the small television that sat on a wobbly dresser like an altar to the outside world he'd learned to observe from the shadows.

The local news anchor's voice carried the forced calm that professional communicators adopted when reporting on events that challenged their sense of safety, the kind of deliberate composure that barely concealed the fear underneath. "Sheriff Shea Callahan held a press conference this afternoon following the murder of an off-duty deputy at Misty Lake's north cove. Sheriff Callahan is warning all residents and tourists to avoid the lake area and remove any red items from their campsites immediately."

The image on the screen shifted to footage of the sheriff standing before a cluster of microphones, her uniform still bearing mud from the crime scene and her jaw set with the kind of determination that spoke to someone who'd been pushed beyond their breaking point. But it was her eyes that captured Tommy's complete attention. They were colder than he'd ever seen them, holding the flat emptiness that marked someone's transition from protector to predator.

He leaned closer to the television screen, not to hear her words or study her mouth, but to see the steel that had replaced whatever softness might have once existed beneath her professional facade. The transformation fascinated him in ways that simple violence never could.

He could see how exhausted she was, could read the

signs of sleepless nights and accumulated stress that had been wearing her down since the first murders. But this was different from the fatigue that came from overwork or professional pressure. This was the bone-deep weariness that came from carrying responsibility for failures that couldn't be undone or forgiven.

She finally understood that their game was no longer about random victims or camping equipment or even law enforcement procedures. It had become personal the moment he'd chosen to kill someone who worked for her, someone whose death would serve as a message that couldn't be misunderstood or deflected through official channels.

He closed his eyes and allowed his imagination to recreate the scene when she'd first looked at Deputy Hensley's carefully arranged body. That was the moment when intellectual understanding had become visceral knowledge, when she'd realized that he wasn't just another criminal to be processed through the justice system but a force of nature that had chosen to focus its attention on destroying everything she cared about.

On the floor beside him lay a piece of the red poncho he'd used to cover the deputy's body, torn from the larger piece during the struggle that had preceded her death. He picked up the fabric scrap and twirled it between his fingers until it tightened against his skin like a tourniquet.

The news footage cut to scenes of local residents pulling down anything red from their properties and tossing the items into garbage cans. Red windsocks disappeared from porches, garden flags were hastily replaced with neutral colors, and even children's toys were confiscated if they bore the wrong pigmentation.

But their precautions were meaningless because he'd already moved beyond the need for external triggers. If they removed all the red items from their environment, he would simply create his own opportunities in locations where Sheriff Callahan would have no choice but to respond personally rather than send subordinates to handle routine investigations.

A detailed park map lay spread across the motel room's threadbare carpet; its surface marked with notations and symbols that represented weeks of reconnaissance and tactical planning. A fresh red X marked a location nowhere near the lake, a hunting ground that law enforcement wouldn't be expecting because it fell outside the geographic profile they'd constructed based on his previous activities.

He picked up a black marker and wrote a single word on the back of a torn paper menu from the Chinese restaurant down the street. Just one word rendered in blocky, uneven letters that carried more weight than any lengthy manifesto could have conveyed.

SOON.

He folded the paper carefully and slipped it into an envelope that had already been addressed to the sheriff's office in the same deliberate handwriting. Tomorrow morning, she would find it waiting on her desk like a promise that couldn't be broken or delayed indefinitely.

The word represented more than a threat. It was a timeline that would force her to make choices about how far she was willing to go to protect people who couldn't protect themselves. Soon, she would have to decide whether to face him alone or watch more of her people die while she hid behind procedures and protocols that meant nothing to someone who'd learned to exist outside the boundaries of civilized society.

~

The conference room felt smaller than usual, compressed by the presence of federal agents who'd taken over half the table with their laptops, surveillance equipment, and behavioral analysis charts that reduced human violence to statistical probabilities. Agent Larson stood before a large topographical map of Misty Lake and the surrounding parklands that had been tacked to the wall like a battle plan in a military command center.

"If we assume his established pattern continues to hold," Larson said, pointing with his pen to locations marked with red pins that represented previous crime scenes, "he stages his displays within fifty yards of the victim's primary campsite. The red item serves as both a trigger and a territorial marker. The problem we're facing now is that media coverage has prompted half the camping population to remove red items from their sites."

He paused and looked around the room with the expression of someone delivering bad news to people who were already operating under maximum stress. "That won't stop him from killing. It will simply force him to adapt his selection criteria and possibly expand his hunting territory to areas we haven't been monitoring as closely."

Shea leaned back in her chair with her arms crossed, her attention drifting as the agent continued his analysis of behavioral patterns and geographic profiles that had failed to produce actionable intelligence throughout their investigation. All she heard was "blah, blah, blah".

The federal agents hadn't contributed anything substantive to their investigation beyond psychological profiles that could have described half the mentally unstable individuals in Arkansas. Their surveillance technology and behavioral analysis expertise had produced nothing but reports and recommendations. At the same time, real people continued to die at the hands of someone who existed in the spaces between their investigative procedures. They already knew who the killer was. All they had to do was find him.

A soft knock on the conference room door interrupted Larson's presentation, and Doris entered with the apologetic expression of someone who hated to disturb important meetings but had information that couldn't wait for a more convenient time.

"Sheriff, this just arrived in the mail." She held out an envelope that looked ordinary except for the absence of a return address and the deliberate block lettering that spelled out the sheriff department's address. "No postmark from our local post office, which means it was probably stuck in our mailbox during the night."

Shea took the envelope and noticed that the flap wasn't completely sealed, as if the sender had wanted to make opening it as easy as possible. The paper felt cheap and rough, the kind that came from fast-food restaurants or convenience stores rather than office supply companies.

"Want me to take a look before you open it?" Trevor asked. "Could be some kind of chemical or biological hazard designed to incapacitate whoever handles it."

"No, I can handle this myself." Her hands trembled as she tore open the envelope and extracted a single piece of paper that had been torn from something larger.

One word dominated the paper's surface, written in thick black marker with the kind of aggressive strokes that spoke to barely controlled rage. The letters were blocky and uneven, suggesting someone who'd either been intoxicated during the writing process or was deliberately trying to disguise their natural handwriting style.

SOON.

She tossed the paper onto the conference table, where it landed with the soft whisper of something that weighed almost nothing but carried the emotional impact of a physical blow. The room fell silent as everyone processed the implications of receiving direct communication from someone who'd been killing people in their jurisdiction for weeks without leaving any trace evidence that could lead to his capture.

Trevor's jaw tightened with barely controlled fury as he stared at the single word. "We'll process it for fingerprints and DNA evidence," he said, though his tone suggested he held little hope that someone who'd been this careful throughout his killing spree would suddenly become careless about leaving biological traces.

"We already know who sent it. Processing it for evidence is just another procedural step that will waste time while he continues planning whatever he's going to do next."

"But he's communicating directly with you now." Trevor's voice took on an urgency that made everyone in the room lean forward. "This isn't random violence anymore. It's personal contact between predator and prey. That suggests he's escalating toward some kind of final confrontation rather than continuing to kill random victims indefinitely."

She carefully folded the paper and slipped it into a clear evidence sleeve. "Fine, we'll run the standard tests. But this information doesn't leave this room unless I specifically authorize its release. The last thing we need is media speculation about direct communication between the killer and law enforcement."

She could picture Tommy LaCrosse sitting somewhere in the darkness, perhaps in a cheap motel room or abandoned building, writing that single word with the kind of deliberate care that transformed simple communication into psychological warfare. He would have smiled while imagining her reaction, would have taken pleasure in knowing that his message would create the exact combination of fear and rage that he'd been working to cultivate since the investigation began.

Under the table, Trevor's hand brushed against hers with the gentle pressure of someone offering reassurance without making their support obvious to the federal agents who were observing every interaction with professional interest. The brief contact carried more emotional weight than any lengthy conversation could have conveyed, a reminder that she wasn't facing this threat entirely alone despite the isolation that command responsibility inevitably created.

But the killer was closer than any of them wanted to acknowledge, close enough to hand-deliver messages and observe their reactions, close enough to strike at anyone in their department who might be vulnerable to someone who'd learned to hunt law enforcement personnel with the same tactical awareness he'd previously applied to civilian targets.

And now it wasn't just the investigation that hung in the balance, or even the safety of potential victims who might cross his path during future hunting expeditions. It was her life, and the lives of everyone who worked for her, and the growing certainty that their final confrontation would come sooner rather than later.

Chapter Thirteen

Shea spent several hours alone in her office after Trevor and the federal agents had departed for the evening, the building settling into the quiet rhythm of night shift operations. At the same time, she immersed herself in the accumulated evidence of their investigation. The fluorescent lights hummed overhead, and the distant sound of dispatch radio chatter provided a soundtrack to her solitary review of witness statements, crime scene photographs, and interview transcripts that had failed to yield the breakthrough they desperately needed.

She focused particular attention on the notes from Daniel LaCrosse's interrogation, reading through his carefully parsed admissions and psychological insights, convinced that the answer lay hidden in details she'd somehow overlooked during the initial questioning. The written transcript captured the words but not the emotional undertones, the hesitations, and fear that had marked every revelation about his brother's deteriorating mental state.

But it was the audio recording that provided the real treasure, and she listened to it multiple times while studying Daniel's body language and vocal patterns for signs of deception or information he'd been reluctant to share. Most of the conversation followed the same patterns she remembered from the live interview, but there was something, a slight mumble just as he was being escorted from the room, that she'd missed during the intensity of face-to-face questioning.

She rewound the digital file and played that section again, adjusting the volume and using noise-filtering software to isolate Daniel's voice from the background sounds of chairs scraping and footsteps on linoleum. This time, the words came through with crystal clarity, and she felt her pulse quicken as she recognized their potential significance.

"He stayed at that rundown motel outside of town for a while," Daniel had muttered to himself, probably thinking his words were too quiet to be picked up by the recording equipment. "Before he went into the woods to find whatever hole he's hiding in now."

The revelation hit her like a physical blow, and she leaned back in her chair to stare at the case board where photographs of victims and crime scenes created a mosaic of violence that had consumed her life for weeks. It made perfect sense that Tommy would have needed temporary housing after his release from Glenvalley State Hospital, somewhere cheap and anonymous where recently discharged psychiatric patients could transition back into society without attracting unwanted attention from authorities or social workers.

There were only two motels in Misty Hollow that fit the description of "rundown," both of them establishments that catered to people who preferred to remain invisible to mainstream society. The Pines Motor Lodge and the Mountain View Inn were the kind of places that rented rooms by the day, week, or month to construction workers, seasonal employees, and recently released felons who needed temporary shelter while figuring out their next move.

Neither establishment was the type of place where Shea would choose to spend a night, but they served a necessary function in small-town America by providing affordable housing for people who couldn't meet the credit requirements or background checks that conventional hotels imposed on their guests. More importantly, for her investigation, they were exactly the kind of businesses that wouldn't ask too many questions about a customer who paid in cash and kept to himself.

The first motel she visited was the Pines Motor Lodge, a collection of single-story buildings arranged around a gravel parking lot that looked like it hadn't been resurfaced since the Carter administration. The neon sign that advertised "Weekly Rates Available" flickered intermittently, and several of the room doors showed evidence of forced entry that had been repaired with mismatched paint and hardware store hinges.

The manager emerged from the front office before she could knock, a heavyset man in his sixties whose suspicious expression suggested he'd had numerous encounters with law enforcement over the years. His clothes were stained with what might have been motor oil or coffee, and his hands bore the permanent grime of someone who did his maintenance work without much concern for personal hygiene.

"Evening, Sheriff," he said, his tone carefully neutral in the way that people adopted when they wanted to appear cooperative without actually volunteering information. "What brings you out to our little establishment tonight?"

Shea showed him the photograph of Thomas LaCrosse that they'd obtained from hospital records, noting how the manager's expression shifted from wary cooperation to genuine recognition. "I'm looking for information about this man. He would have stayed here sometime in the past two months, probably paid in cash and kept a low profile."

"Sure, I remember that weird fellow," the manager replied without hesitation. "Gave me the creeps from the moment he walked through that door. Barely spoke above a whisper, but there was something in his eyes that made me want to keep my distance. Hold on a minute. I might have something that'll interest you."

He disappeared back into the office, leaving Shea standing in the parking lot while she studied the motel's layout and tried to imagine Tommy LaCrosse spending weeks in this depressing environment while planning the murders that would terrorize their community. The isolation and anonymity would have appealed to someone who needed time and space to develop his hunting strategies without interference from well-meaning social workers or parole officers.

She followed the manager into his office, a cramped space that looked like it hadn't been updated since the motel's construction decades earlier. A single desk lamp threw a weak cone of yellow light across a battered metal filing cabinet that probably contained records of every questionable transaction that had taken place on the property over the years.

The room carried the accumulated odors of old paper, persistent mildew, and the faint but unmistakable trace of cigarettes that had been smoked in violation of whatever fire codes might theoretically apply to this establishment. But what caught her attention were the dozens of photographs, mostly old Polaroid snapshots, that were pinned to the back wall like trophies from some bizarre collection.

"What's with all the photographs?"

"We get a lot of shady characters staying here, Sheriff." He pulled out manila folders and loose papers. "People who don't want to use credit cards or show government identification when they check in. I started taking pictures of everyone years ago. Insurance policy in case someone skips out on their bill or leaves behind evidence of illegal activities."

He pointed to a particular photograph near the center of the collection, and Shea's blood froze as she recognized the distinctive features of Thomas LaCrosse captured in grainy color film. The image showed a rail-thin man with shaggy dark hair and the vacant eyes of a predator, standing near a vending machine in what appeared to be the motel's common area.

"There's the guy you're looking for," the manager continued, seemingly oblivious to the significance of having documented a serial killer's temporary residence. "Took that picture when he was getting cigarettes from the machine, probably didn't even realize I was watching him from the office window."

The photograph provided their first clear image of Tommy's current appearance, confirming that he'd changed significantly from the hospital records they'd been using to construct their search parameters. He looked older than his chronological age, worn down by years of institutional living and whatever internal demons had been driving him toward increasingly violent expressions of his psychological damage.

"Found it." The manager held up a wrinkled photograph that he thrust toward her. "Discovered this under the bed when I went in to clean his room after he disappeared without paying for his last week. Figured he must have dropped it and forgotten about it in his hurry to get out of town."

Shea stared at the image with growing understanding of the psychological forces that had shaped their adversary into the predator who now stalked their jurisdiction. The photograph showed a little boy, perhaps six or seven years old, sitting stiffly on a weathered front porch with the rigid posture of someone who'd learned that relaxation could be dangerous.

Wrapped around the child's small frame was a red wool blanket, pulled tight as if it were the only source of warmth and comfort in a world that had proven itself to be cold and hostile. But it was the boy's eyes that told the real story—wide and frightened, focused on whoever was taking the photograph with the wariness of someone who'd learned that adults couldn't be trusted to provide safety or protection.

"Ever seen this child before?"

"Nope, never laid eyes on him. "

The photograph represented more than sentimental value. It was a window into the formative trauma that had created a serial killer from a frightened child who'd once believed that a red blanket could protect him from the monsters that ruled his world.

"I doubt he'll be returning to collect his belongings." Shea slipped the photograph into an evidence bag while her mind processed the implications of this discovery. "But if he does show up here again, please call the sheriff's department immediately. Do not attempt to interact with him or detain him yourself. He's extremely dangerous and has already killed multiple people in this area."

She glanced around the office, looking for anything red that might attract Tommy's attention if he decided to return to familiar territory during his escalating psychological breakdown. Her gaze landed on a red bandanna that had been casually draped over a chair, probably left behind by some previous customer and forgotten until now. "Get rid of that bandanna." He's specifically attracted to the color red, and having something like that visible from the parking lot could draw him back here when you least expect it."

The manager looked skeptical about the significance of a simple piece of cloth, but he nodded and moved to stuff the bandanna into a desk drawer where its color couldn't be seen from outside the office. "Anything else I should know about this fellow? Any other precautions I should take to keep him away from my establishment?"

"Just stay alert and call us if you see anything suspicious." She suspected that Tommy had moved far beyond the need for temporary housing in seedy motels. By now, he'd probably established a more permanent base of operations in whatever cave or abandoned structure Daniel had referred to as "his quiet."

Trevor stood up from his position on her front porch as she pulled into her driveway, his silhouette visible against the warm light spilling through her living room windows. The sight of him waiting for her provided a comfort that she hadn't realized she needed after spending hours immersed in the psychological horror of their investigation.

"I expected you back a while ago," he said, his voice carrying the mixture of concern and relief. "When you didn't answer your radio, I started thinking maybe our friend had decided to make his move ahead of schedule."

"Had to make a stop at one of the local motels." She pulled the evidence bag containing the childhood photograph from her jacket pocket. "Daniel let slip something during his interview that I missed the first time through the recording."

Trevor's expression shifted to alert attention as he recognized the significance of new evidence in a case that had been frustratingly devoid of actionable leads. "What kind of something?"

"The kind that might help us understand what we're dealing with," she said, but before she could elaborate, Trevor's posture changed in a way that suggested he had his revelation to share.

"I need to tell you something first." His voice took on the serious tone that meant he'd been wrestling with a difficult decision during the hours they'd been apart. "Maybe this isn't the right time with everything that's happening, but after what happened to Lisa and with LaCrosse getting closer to making you his primary target..."

He paused and took a deep breath. "I'm in love with you, Shea. This goes way beyond friendship or professional partnership or anything that could be explained away by the stress of working together during a crisis. I've been feeling this way for months, but I never found the right moment to tell you."

The admission hung in the evening air between them like smoke from a distant fire, and for a moment, she could only stare at him while her mind processed emotions that she'd been suppressing since the early days of their partnership. Her pulse quickened and her chest tightened with feelings that had no place in the middle of a manhunt for a serial killer who'd made their professional relationship into a personal target.

Instead of responding with words that might complicate an already dangerous situation, she stepped forward. She kissed him with the deliberate intensity of someone who'd been denying her feelings for far too long. The contact was soft at first, almost hesitant, then deeper as weeks of accumulated tension and unspoken attraction found expression in the kind of physical intimacy that changed everything between partners.

When she finally pulled back, Trevor's eyes held a mixture of surprise and satisfaction that made her realize how long he'd been waiting for some sign that his feelings might be reciprocated. Sure, they'd danced around their feelings before, but now they were out in the open. The practical part of her mind immediately began calculating the risks that personal involvement would create during an active investigation.

"If Tommy finds out about this, he'll come for you next." He's already demonstrated that he'll target people who matter to me, and this would make you an even more attractive victim."

Trevor smiled. "Let him try. He won't catch me by surprise the way he did Lisa. I know what I'm dealing with now, and I'll be ready for whatever he has planned." His expression grew more serious as he studied her face for signs of how she'd received his declaration. "Does this mean you feel the same way about me?"

"I won't say that." Instead of pursuing the conversation further, she showed him the photographs she'd obtained from the motel manager, both the current image of Tommy as an adult and the devastating childhood picture that revealed the origins of his psychological damage.

"At least we have a face to go with the name now."

"It's hard to imagine this scared little boy growing up to become a cold-blooded killer." Trevor compared the two photographs. "The transformation from victim to predator must have taken years of accumulated trauma and institutionalization."

He handed the pictures back to her and pulled out his phone to show her something he'd discovered during his research into the LaCrosse family history. "I found a newspaper article about the fire where the brothers lost their parents." He scrolled to a digitized news story from decades earlier. "The details are pretty sparse, but it confirms some of what Daniel told us and fills in gaps that hospital records didn't cover."

The article was brief. "House fire claims two lives, leaves two minors orphaned," read the headline, followed by a few paragraphs that described the basic facts without delving into the psychological complexities that would emerge years later.

"According to this story, both parents were found burned inside the house," Trevor continued. "Two male minors survived and were taken into protective custody. Fire investigators determined that an accelerant had been used. Still, they initially focused on external causes, maybe an insurance fraud scheme or revenge by someone with a grudge against the family."

He paused. "But here's the crucial detail that explains everything we've been seeing. Tommy was found wrapped in a partially burned red blanket, and at first, the authorities didn't consider him a suspect because of his age and apparent trauma. It wasn't until he started setting fires during his placement in foster care that investigators went back and determined he'd been responsible for the original fire that killed his parents."

Trevor's jaw tightened. "What kind of abuse must he have suffered to drive an eight-year-old boy to commit double murder by arson? And how does someone recover from that level of psychological damage?"

"They don't recover." Shea shook her head. "We're not just looking for a killer, Trevor. We're hunting a man whose entire identity was forged in the flames that consumed his childhood and everything he'd once believed about safety and family and protection."

The red blanket had started everything, the symbol of security that had been stolen from him by an abusive father, then literally burned before his eyes as a demonstration of power and control that had taught a frightened child that love could be destroyed as easily as fabric could be consumed by fire.

She unlocked her front door and gestured for him to follow her inside, suddenly needing the comfort of familiar surroundings and the illusion of security that her own home provided. "Want a beer?"

"Absolutely."

~

Tommy sat in his stolen pickup truck with the windshield wipers working steadily against the rain that had begun falling as evening settled over Misty Hollow like a shroud. The rhythmic sound of the rubber blades against glass provided a hypnotic backdrop to his surveillance of the sheriff's modest house, where warm light spilled through windows that had never been protected by the kind of security measures that law enforcement officers typically installed in their homes.

He'd been watching from the concealment of a side street for over an hour, positioned where he could observe the front porch and driveway without being visible to anyone inside the house or to anyone driving by who might notice an unfamiliar vehicle.

The sight of Sheriff Callahan kissing her deputy on the front porch had triggered something unexpected in Tommy's chest. Not jealousy exactly, but something darker and more possessive. He'd witnessed the intimate moment through military surplus binoculars, had seen the way she'd stepped forward with deliberate intent and kissed Trevor Bolton with the kind of passion that transformed professional partnership into something far more personal and vulnerable.

The image bothered him in ways he hadn't anticipated, creating an ugly knot of emotion that went beyond simple tactical concern. It wasn't that he felt romantic attraction toward the sheriff. His capacity for human attachment had been burned away along with his childhood security blanket. But she represented something more significant than just another law enforcement officer who needed to be eliminated as part of his psychological completion.

Sheriff Callahan belonged to him in the same way that prey belonged to predators, in the way that victims belonged to the forces that would eventually destroy them. She was his to hunt and stalk and ultimately kill, and the introduction of a romantic attachment created variables that threatened to complicate the ritual that had been building since the night he'd planted his first red flag.

The possessive feeling that twisted in his chest wasn't love or desire. It was ownership, the same emotion that a child might feel when another kid tried to play with a toy that had been reserved for destruction. Sheriff Callahan would belong to him until the moment they came face-to-face for their final confrontation, and after that, she would belong to no one except the flames that would consume whatever remained of their deadly game.

But Deputy Bolton's involvement changed the tactical landscape in ways that required careful consideration and possibly modification of plans that had been developing for weeks in the underground sanctuary where Tommy had learned to exist like some human mole creature. The deputy was skilled and alert, had probably received the same training that made the sheriff such a formidable adversary, and his protective instincts would make him an additional obstacle to overcome during whatever climactic violence would end their extended dance of predator and prey.

More importantly, the romantic attachment between them created an opportunity for psychological warfare that went beyond simple murder into the realm of emotional destruction that could be far more satisfying than physical violence. If Tommy could force the sheriff to choose between her survival and the life of someone she loved, the resulting trauma might prove more devastating than any wound he could inflict with conventional weapons.

The rain continued to drum against his windshield while he sat in the darkness and planned modifications to strategies that had been evolving since his release from the hospital, where doctors had convinced themselves that medication and therapy could repair damage that went deeper than conscious thought into the primitive structures of brain and soul that governed survival and violence.

Soon, he would make his move. Soon, the sheriff would understand that love was just another weakness that predators could exploit, another form of red fabric that could be burned away when the flames grew hot enough to consume everything that victims held sacred and safe.

Chapter Fourteen

Shea spent most of the following day hunched over her desk in the sheriff's office, surrounded by stacks of yellowed paperwork and rolled topographical maps that represented decades of record-keeping for one of Arkansas's most remote wilderness areas. Her eyes burned from hours of cross-referencing old park maintenance logs with current property maps, searching for discrepancies that might reveal locations where someone could hide without detection by routine patrols or casual hikers.

The maintenance logs told a story of gradual budget cuts and deferred upkeep that had left portions of the park system abandoned, while property maps showed structures that no longer appeared on current documentation due to administrative oversight or deliberate omission. Somewhere in the gaps between official records and ground truth lay the answer to where Tommy LaCrosse had established his base of operations.

Meanwhile, Trevor worked across the table, methodically digging through incident reports, insurance claims, and personnel files tied to the LaCrosse brothers' time in the foster care system. His computer screen displayed a timeline of their childhood that painted a picture of two boys bouncing between temporary homes and institutional placements. At the same time, the system struggled to find permanent solutions for children whose trauma exceeded the resources available to help them heal.

The FBI agents had commandeered the conference room for their research efforts, their laptops and communication equipment transforming the space into a temporary command center that buzzed with electronic activity but had yet to produce actionable intelligence. Despite their federal resources and behavioral analysis expertise, they seemed no closer to predicting Tommy's next move than local law enforcement had been weeks earlier.

By lunchtime, Trevor had found something that made him sit up straighter in his chair and beckon Shea over to examine his discovery. "Look at this entry from twelve years ago." He drew her attention to a maintenance report buried in the digital archives. "Ranger Station number three was officially decommissioned due to foundation instability and structural damage that made it unsafe for continued use. All public access was restricted, and the building was supposed to be padlocked pending eventual demolition."

Shea frowned as she studied the document, noting details that raised more questions than they answered. "The report mentions padlocking the facility, but there's no follow-up documentation about demolition or final disposition."

She grabbed her collection of current park maps and spread them across the table, comparing the maintenance report's location coordinates with documentation that visitors and rangers used to navigate the wilderness areas around Misty Lake. "It's not marked on any of the recent maps. Not even listed in the database of decommissioned structures, which means no tourists, no routine ranger patrols, no maintenance crews or researchers would have any reason to stumble across it."

The oversight was perfect for someone who wanted to be isolated from the kind of human traffic that might lead to accidental discovery. An abandoned ranger station would provide shelter from the weather while offering storage space for equipment and supplies, all while remaining invisible to the comprehensive search efforts that had been sweeping the more obvious hiding places.

Trevor grinned. "It's the perfect place to hide." Trevor reached for his jacket and service weapon. "Remote enough for complete privacy, substantial enough to provide long-term shelter, and abandoned long enough that nobody remembers it exists."

"Let's go pay it a visit." They were finally closing in on their quarry after weeks of chasing shadows through the mountains.

The drive took them deep into the western sections of Misty Lake's sprawling forest system, following dirt roads that grew progressively narrower and more overgrown as they moved away from areas that received regular maintenance or visitor traffic. Ancient pines and hardwood trees leaned overhead like cathedral arches, their branches so thick they blocked most of the afternoon sunlight and created a tunnel of green shadows that seemed to press in from all sides.

By the time they located the abandoned ranger

station, the sun had begun its descent toward the mountain ridges. The building appeared through the trees like something from a horror movie—a squat, rotting structure that seemed to be melting back into the forest floor from which it had risen.

The roof sagged dangerously in the middle, suggesting structural damage that went far beyond the cosmetic decay visible on the exterior walls. Windows had been boarded up with plywood that was now warped and discolored by years of weather exposure, while the front porch listed at an angle that made the entire structure look like it was slowly capsizing.

"Place feels like it's been waiting for us." Trevor peered through the windshield.

The air around the ranger station carried scents that spoke to abandonment and decay—damp earth, decomposing pine needles, and something metallic that might have been rust from corroded fixtures or something more sinister that Shea didn't want to contemplate on until they'd completed their investigation.

They both snapped on latex gloves before approaching the building. Their flashlights cut through the gathering darkness as they stepped carefully across rotting floorboards that groaned ominously under their weight.

The main room contained nothing but the detritus of long abandonment—a metal desk missing two of its drawers, a topographical map of the lake area that had curled away from the wall where moisture had dissolved whatever adhesive had once held it in place, and broken glass scattered across warped flooring that crunched underfoot.

But Shea's examination of the space revealed something that made her pulse quicken with the recognition of deliberate concealment rather than natural decay. Her flashlight beam caught a faint gap in the wall paneling along the back of the room, a seam so subtle that it would have been invisible to anyone not specifically looking for signs of hidden construction.

When she ran her gloved hand along the edge of the gap, her fingers found a small metal latch that had been painted to match the surrounding wood. The mechanism clicked when she pulled it, and a narrow door swung inward with the tortured groan of hinges that hadn't been oiled in years.

Stale air rushed out of the hidden space, carrying odors of mildew, dust, and something organic that suggested long-term human habitation in a confined area. The combination created an olfactory signature that spoke to secrets that had been festering in darkness for far too long.

"Found something," she called to Trevor, who immediately moved to join her at the concealed entrance while keeping his service weapon ready for whatever might emerge from the shadows beyond.

The room, perhaps eight feet by ten feet, had been transformed into something that went far beyond a simple hiding place. This was a shrine to obsession, a carefully curated exhibition of psychological damage that had been accumulating for years in the darkness where normal people would never think to look.

Wooden shelves lined one wall, and they were stacked with dozens of red nylon camping flags arranged with military precision. Each flag was identical to the ones they'd found at crime scenes, creating a visual impact that suggested months or years of preparation for the killing spree that had terrorized their community.

But it was the opposite wall that truly revealed the scope of Tommy's psychological deterioration. Photographs had been pinned to the wooden surface in overlapping layers that created a mosaic of surveillance and stalking that represented countless hours of watching potential victims without their knowledge.

Some images were blurry long shots taken from concealment in the forest, showing campsites from distances that would have required telephoto lenses or binoculars to capture. Others were disturbingly intimate, shot from close enough range to show sleeping faces through tent walls or couples cooking over campfires while completely unaware that predatory eyes were documenting their most vulnerable moments.

The photographic collection represented more than evidence gathering. It was a way for someone whose own childhood had been destroyed to feed off the safety and happiness that normal families took for granted during their wilderness adventures.

In the far corner of the hidden room, positioned on a child-sized chair that looked like it had been salvaged from an elementary school classroom, sat an arrangement of toys that made Shea's stomach clench.

A bright red fire truck sat prominently in the center of the display, its paint faded but still recognizable as the kind of toy that young boys used to act out fantasies of heroism and rescue. Beside it was a stuffed rabbit missing one ear, the fabric worn smooth by years of handling that suggested it had once been someone's beloved companion during times when comfort was desperately needed.

A small wooden top completed the arrangement, its surface scratched and scarred by decades of use but still perfectly balanced on its metal point. All three objects were covered with dust that spoke to long abandonment, but they had been positioned with deliberate care to face the door as if they were waiting for visitors who would never come.

"This isn't just trophy collection," Shea said, her voice barely above a whisper. "This is his entire emotional life condensed into one room. Everything he lost, everything he remembers, everything that made him what he is today."

She moved closer to the photograph wall, her heart hammering against her ribs as she began recognizing locations and victims from their investigation. At least three of the images showed campsites where people had later been found murdered, captured during the stalking phase that preceded their violent deaths.

"Look at this." Trevor directed his flashlight toward a lower shelf where something had been partially concealed beneath a mason jar filled with rusty nails.

He carefully moved the jar aside and extracted a school photograph that showed two young boys posed against the kind of artificial background that elementary schools used for their annual picture days. Both children looked uncomfortable in their dress shirts and combed hair, but it was their eyes that told the real story. One boy's gaze held the wariness of someone who'd learned not to trust adults with cameras, while the other showed the hollow emptiness that marked children who'd already seen too much violence.

Trevor turned the photograph over and read the words that had been scrawled on the back in a child's careful handwriting: "Thomas and Daniel LaCrosse—1988." The date placed the image sometime after the fire that had claimed their parents, but before the system had separated them into different foster placements.

"This must be one of the last pictures taken of them together." Shea studied the faces of two boys who'd shared the same trauma but had processed it in different ways. "Before Tommy's behavioral problems became severe enough to require institutional placement."

She pulled an evidence bag from her jacket pocket and held it open for Trevor to deposit the photograph, along with any other potential evidence they might discover in this hidden sanctuary. "It doesn't look like he lives here full-time. More like he uses it as a storage facility for things that are important to him."

The distinction was crucial for understanding their adversary's operational patterns. If Tommy maintained a separate living space elsewhere, it suggested a level of organizational sophistication that went beyond the simple cave-dwelling existence they'd been imagining based on his brother's descriptions.

"I'll get a larger evidence bag from the patrol car," Trevor said, already moving toward the door.

The moment he stepped outside, Shea felt exposed and vulnerable in ways that had nothing to do with being alone in a dark room with disturbing contents. The hair on the back of her neck rose as survival instincts screamed warnings about unseen eyes watching her every movement from concealment in the forest that surrounded the abandoned building.

The sensation was so intense that she found herself turning in slow circles, playing her flashlight beam across the walls and corners of the hidden room as if expecting to find someone crouched in the shadows with a knife or gun trained on her position. But the space was too small to conceal a human presence, and the feeling of being observed seemed to come from outside the building rather than within the room itself.

When Trevor returned with larger evidence bags and additional lighting equipment, they worked quickly to document and remove the camping flags, children's toys, and selected photographs that might provide more insight into Tommy. Every minute they spent in the hidden room felt like an eternity, and Shea was relieved when they could finally seal the evidence bags and retreat to their patrol car.

The drive back to town passed in relative silence. They'd found Tommy's secret shrine, but the discovery raised as many questions as it answered about how someone could maintain such elaborate preparations while remaining invisible to law enforcement efforts that had been searching for him for weeks.

~

Tommy knew something was wrong the moment he approached the old ranger station through the forest paths that had become as familiar to him as the hallways of the psychiatric hospital where he'd spent seven years learning to hide his true nature from doctors and social workers who thought they could repair damage that went deeper than conscious thought.

The building looked the same from the outside—still the rotting, abandoned structure that had provided perfect camouflage for his activities over the past months. But subtle signs visible only to someone who'd learned to read the environment for traces of human intrusion told him that his sanctuary had been violated by people who had no right to disturb the careful arrangements he'd created.

Footprints in the dust outside the front entrance showed boot treads that didn't match his worn boots. The door was slightly ajar in a way that suggested it had been opened and hastily closed rather than settling naturally into its usual position. Even the air seemed different, carrying trace scents of unfamiliar cologne and cleaning products that marked the passage of law enforcement officers who'd learned to maintain professional hygiene standards even in the worst environments.

He stepped inside the main room and froze at the sight that confirmed his worst fears. The hidden door to his private space stood open, revealing the violation of the only place in the world where he'd been able to preserve the fragments of his childhood that the system hadn't managed to steal or destroy.

With a curse that echoed off the rotting walls like the cry of a wounded animal, he rushed into the secret room to find empty shelves where his collection of red flags had been stored with military precision. The toys that had anchored his connection to the innocent child he'd once been before fire and violence had transformed him into something else entirely were gone, leaving only dust outlines on the wooden chair where they'd waited patiently for his return. Two sets of footprints disturbed the dust that had accumulated on the floor.

She'd been here. Sheriff Callahan and her deputy had invaded his private space and stolen everything he had left of the life that had ended in flames when he was eight years old. They'd taken the photographs that documented months of careful observation, the camping flags that represented his connection to the violence that had become his only form of prayer, and most devastating of all, the toys that reminded him of a time when red fabric had meant safety rather than triggering homicidal rage.

The violation went beyond simple theft of physical objects. They'd contaminated his sanctuary with their presence. They transformed it from a shrine to lost innocence into just another crime scene to be processed by people who would never understand the significance of what they'd destroyed.

Rage boiled up from the depths of his psyche. The emotion was pure and clean and terrible, unmarked by the medication-induced numbness that had characterized his emotional responses during his time in institutional care.

He would make them both pay for their presumption in violating the only space in the world where he could remember being something other than a monster. Sheriff Callahan would learn that some lines couldn't be crossed without consequences.

The deputy would discover that protecting someone you loved from a predator who'd learned to hunt in the spaces between civilization's rules was a task that exceeded the capabilities of training, weapons, and professional procedures.

Both of them would understand, before he was finished with them, that some forms of theft couldn't be forgiven or forgotten or resolved through arrests, trials, and imprisonment. Some violations demanded payment in blood and fire and the kind of suffering that echoed across decades of accumulated trauma.

They'd taken his past. Now he would take their future.

~

Shea and Trevor grabbed hamburgers and fries from Lucy's Diner before returning to the sheriff's office, their appetite dampened by their discovery. But their bodies required fuel for what promised to be a long night of evidence processing and tactical planning. The familiar comfort food felt strange in their mouths after spending hours in a room that had been dedicated to obsession and violence, but they forced themselves to eat while reviewing what they'd learned from Tommy's hidden sanctuary.

They carried their meals into the conference room where FBI Agents Snowe and Larson hunched over laptop keyboards, their screens displaying behavioral analysis software and communication monitoring equipment that represented the federal government's latest technological approaches to hunting serial killers. Shea couldn't help but wonder if the agents ever did anything other than stare at computer screens, because Tommy LaCrosse certainly wouldn't be caught by people who preferred digital investigation to pounding the pavement and following leads through the wilderness where he'd chosen to make his stand.

She handed each agent a paper bag containing their dinner orders, noting their distracted acknowledgment as they continued typing and monitoring whatever electronic systems they'd established to track their elusive quarry. "Any progress on the communication intercepts or geographic profiling?" .

"Still processing data from the cell tower analysis," Agent Snowe replied without looking up from his screen. "But we're confident that he's operating from somewhere within a five-mile radius of the lake, probably using multiple communication devices to avoid detection by our monitoring equipment."

Her cell phone rang before she could respond. A quick glance at the screen showed "Unknown Caller," which immediately triggered her investigative instincts and made her reach for the recording equipment they'd set up to capture any direct communication from their suspect.

"Sheriff Callahan," she answered, her voice carrying the professional calm that law enforcement officers learned to maintain even when their hearts were racing with anticipation.

"Those things you took from my place," a male voice said without preamble, the words carrying the flat affect of someone who'd learned to suppress emotion in favor of tactical calculation. "They belong to me."

She snapped her fingers to get the attention of Trevor and the federal agents, then activated the speakerphone so everyone in the room could hear both sides of the conversation while the agents worked to trace the call's origin through whatever technological magic they'd brought to bear on their investigation.

"What things are you referring to, Tommy?"

"Don't play games with me, Sheriff," the voice took

on an edge that suggested barely controlled rage simmering beneath the surface calm. "You're more intelligent than that, and we both know exactly what you removed from my private space."

Trevor leaned closer to the speakerphone and hissed instructions to the federal agents: "Ping the call location. Find out where he's transmitting from so we can coordinate a response team."

"Why don't we arrange a meeting place, Tommy? It's time we had a face-to-face conversation about how this situation can be resolved."

"Stop saying my name. You're not fooling me by using therapeutic communication techniques. That's the same approach they used during my years in the hospital, and I learned to see through it long before the doctors decided I was ready for release back into society."

The accusation stung because it was partially accurate. She had been using techniques learned during crisis negotiation training, though her motivation was tactical rather than therapeutic. "My apologies, Tommy. It wasn't intended as manipulation, just a habit developed during years of police work."

"This is a burner phone, Sheriff. Your federal friends won't be able to trace my location. Not until I decide the time is right for our final meeting."

He paused, and she could hear something that might have been wind through trees or traffic on a distant highway, but nothing that provided valuable intelligence about his current position or immediate plans.

"Watch your back." His voice dropped to barely above a whisper that somehow carried more menace than any shouted threat could have conveyed. "I'm coming for you, and when I do, you'll understand that some things are too sacred to be stolen by people who don't comprehend their significance."

The line went dead, leaving nothing but electronic silence and the sound of her heartbeat hammering against her ribs as she processed the implications of receiving direct threats from someone who'd already demonstrated his willingness and ability to kill law enforcement officers.

"I guess I'm packing an overnight bag and sleeping in your guest room. Again." Trevor unwrapped his hamburger. "I don't want you going anywhere alone until LaCrosse is either behind bars or in the ground."

She didn't argue with his protective instincts, knowing that an objection would be both futile and unwise given that their adversary had just promised to escalate his violence toward personal targets. The professional part of her mind recognized that accepting Trevor's protection was a necessity, while the personal part of her felt grateful for his willingness to put himself at risk for someone he cared about.

"Were you able to determine his transmission location?" she asked Agent Snowe, who was studying readouts from the communication monitoring equipment with the frustrated expression of someone whose expensive technology had failed to produce the results that federal budgets had promised.

The agent shook his head with obvious disappointment. "All we could determine is that he's somewhere on Misty Mountain, probably using a device with signal boosting capability to extend his range beyond what normal cell phones could achieve. He terminated the call before our triangulation software could narrow down his position to anything more specific than a several-square-mile area."

Shea popped a french fry into her mouth. The specific location didn't matter as much as the certainty that Tommy was coming for her, probably sooner rather than later given the rage she'd heard in his voice when he'd talked about the violation of his secret shrine.

When he made his move, she would be ready to end their deadly game once and for all, regardless of what federal protocols or legal procedures might suggest about the proper way to handle armed and dangerous suspects who'd demonstrated their willingness to kill anyone who stood between them and their chosen targets.

Chapter Fifteen

Shea crouched behind a massive fallen pine log that had been weathered smooth by decades of mountain storms, her position chosen to provide cover while maintaining clear sightlines to the decoy campsite they'd constructed fifty yards away. The dead tree trunk still carried the scent of resin and forest decay, mixing with the night air that had grown thick with humidity as midnight approached without bringing the confrontation they'd been anticipating. She took a puff of her inhaler to stop the wheezing from the pine.

Two undercover officers laughed over their constructed campfire with the forced casualness of people trying too hard to appear relaxed, their conversation carrying just far enough to be heard by anyone watching from concealment in the surrounding forest. A string of red LED lights had been hung from the portable gazebo they'd erected, creating the kind of visual trigger that had attracted Tommy LaCrosse to his previous victims.

The entire scene was a masterpiece of psychological manipulation designed by FBI behavioral analysts. Red camping equipment was positioned with strategic visibility, the campfire burned at precisely the right intensity to create appealing shadows, and the officers' conversation included references to their planned departure the following morning—information that should have motivated an immediate attack if their psychological profile was accurate.

But as Shea glanced at her watch and saw the numbers approaching midnight, doubt began creeping in. They'd been maintaining their positions for over four hours, long enough for muscle cramps to develop and attention to waver despite the high stakes of their operation. Where was Tommy? Had their elaborate trap been too obvious, too carefully staged to fool someone who'd learned to recognize law enforcement tactics during his years of institutional confinement?

The peaceful sounds of evening in the Arkansas wilderness provided a deceptively calm soundtrack to their tense vigil. Lake water lapped gently against the shoreline. An occasional pop from the campfire mixed with the steady chorus of crickets and night birds that filled the forest with life even during the darkest hours.

"Thermal imaging is showing nothing moving in the tree line," Trevor's voice came through her earpiece in a barely audible whisper. "He's either not here, or he's watching from a position that our equipment can't detect."

Instead of responding immediately to Trevor's report, Shea continued scanning the darkness beyond the warm glow of the campfire, her trained eyes searching for any hint of movement or unnatural shadow that might indicate human presence in terrain that should have been empty of everything except wildlife and vegetation. The wind shifted direction, bringing with it the faint scent of wet wood and smoke that seemed different from the controlled burn of their decoy campfire.

A faint flicker appeared on the lake's surface, barely visible at first but growing steadily brighter as it reflected something that was generating far more heat and light than any campfire should produce. The orange glow expanded across the water like spilled paint, and suddenly she understood with sickening clarity that their carefully planned trap had been turned against them.

A thunderous whoosh split the night air as the undercover officers' tent erupted into flames. The undercover offices scrambled backward from their positions near the campfire as burning fabric and superheated air created a miniature inferno that sent embers swirling into the darkness like malevolent fireflies.

"All units move in!" Trevor's voice cracked over the radio.

Shea rushed toward the burning campsite, her eyes already searching for the source of the incendiary device that had transformed their trap into Tommy's latest demonstration of psychological warfare. That's when she spotted the arrow embedded in the bark of a nearby oak tree, its wooden shaft vibrating slightly from the force of impact that had driven the steel point deep into living wood.

She yanked the projectile free and unfolded the piece of paper that had been wrapped around its shaft, her hands trembling as she read the message.

"You can't stop what's already burned," the note read in the same block lettering they'd seen before, but this time the words carried additional weight because they'd been delivered through an attack that proved Tommy could strike at their operations at any time.

Before she could share the message with the other officers who worked frantically to contain the fire and secure the crime scene, her radio earpiece erupted with loud static that made her flinch away from the painful electronic shriek. The interference resolved into something far more disturbing—the sound of a woman crying, her voice distorted by fear and the poor audio quality of what appeared to be a recording made under extreme duress.

The crying gave way to barely audible whispers as the woman begged for her life. The audio had the tinny quality of old recordings, suggesting it had been captured on inferior equipment and stored for later use.

"That's audio from the first victim's cell phone," Trevor said, appearing at her side with his own radio crackling with the same horrific broadcast. "Forensics recovered it from the crime scene, but we never released it to the media or included it in any public statements about the investigation."

The implications hit Shea like a physical blow as she realized that Tommy had somehow obtained evidence from their investigation and was now using it to torment them during what should have been their moment of tactical advantage. The woman's whispering grew more distorted as the transmission continued, the desperation in her voice building to a crescendo before cutting off abruptly.

She scanned the dark shoreline with a growing understanding that whoever was broadcasting the recording had to be close enough to tap into the park service's radio network, which meant Tommy watched their response to his latest attack. The knowledge that he could observe their confusion and frustration while remaining invisible to their surveillance equipment added another layer of violation to an evening that had already gone catastrophically wrong.

The undercover officers worked with members of the volunteer fire department to extinguish what remained of their tent and prevent the flames from spreading to the surrounding forest, their faces blackened with soot.

"This wasn't a failed trap." Shea clenched her hands into fists. "He turned our operation into his own game, used our bait to create another opportunity for him to demonstrate his superiority over law enforcement."

Trevor nodded as he studied the arrow and note that represented Tommy's latest taunt. "He was watching us the entire time, could have been positioned right behind one of us."

The campfire popped loudly in the sudden silence that followed the end of the radio broadcast, the sharp sound causing Shea to jerk involuntarily. Tommy grew bolder with each day.

The two FBI agents who'd been coordinating surveillance from positions along the lake's perimeter approached with the defeated expressions of federal specialists whose expensive equipment and behavioral analysis had proven inadequate for tracking a target who seemed to exist in the gaps between their technological capabilities. After a brief, whispered conversation near the water's edge, they headed toward their black SUV with the purposeful stride of people who'd decided to abandon a tactical approach that had failed.

Agent Snowe paused at Shea's position long enough to deliver a professional assessment that confirmed her growing suspicions about the fundamental flaws in their operational planning. "Too many personnel on site tonight," he said. "Too many radio transmissions, too much equipment, too many variables that could have alerted the subject to our presence."

The criticism stung because it was accurate. Their elaborate trap had been compromised by the very federal resources that were supposed to provide tactical advantages over local law enforcement capabilities. Tommy had recognized their operation for what it was. He had turned it into another opportunity to demonstrate his psychological dominance over people who thought they could hunt him using conventional methods.

As the federal agents drove away into the darkness, leaving local law enforcement to clean up the mess and process whatever evidence might be salvaged from another failed operation, Shea felt the weight of command settling on her shoulders like a funeral shroud. The next trap would have to be different—simpler, more personal, designed to appeal to Tommy's growing obsession with making her his final victim.

The next trap would involve only her, alone and apparently vulnerable, in a location where Tommy would feel confident enough to abandon his hit-and-run tactics in favor of the kind of direct confrontation that would allow one of them to finish their deadly game permanently.

~

Tommy allowed himself a moment of genuine satisfaction as he watched the chaos unfold around the burning tent, the orange flames reflecting off the lake's surface like scattered coins while law enforcement officers scrambled to contain damage that had already served its purpose. From his concealed position on a shallow rise where he'd beached a stolen kayak among the tall reeds that bordered this section of the shoreline, he had an unobstructed view of the entire disaster that his enemies had created for themselves.

His grin carried the pure joy of someone who'd learned to find pleasure in other people's pain and confusion. This emotional response had been cultivated during years of institutional living where small victories over authority figures provided the only available form of entertainment.

Playing with Sheriff Callahan was proving to be almost as satisfying as killing random campers and setting fires that consumed evidence along with human lives.

He'd stolen the kayak as soon as he'd discovered Shea and her goons setting up the camp earlier that day. She had to know he watched her every move. So, why be surprised when he let them know he knew of their tactics?

He'd spotted the undercover officers immediately upon arriving at their elaborately staged deception, their posture too rigid and their conversation too deliberately casual to fool anyone. The woman's laugh had been particularly unconvincing, carrying the forced quality that marked people who were performing rather than genuinely enjoying themselves.

Even a child would have been able to recognize them as law enforcement personnel attempting to create an attractive target for a predator who'd already demonstrated his preference for campers displaying red equipment in isolated locations. The entire operation had been so obviously artificial that Tommy had briefly considered the possibility that it was an intentional double deception, designed to make him think it was a trap while providing a genuine opportunity for him to claim additional victims.

But careful observation had revealed the truth. This was nothing more than incompetent police work. Instead of falling into their clumsy snare, he'd decided to use their trap as an opportunity to demonstrate his superiority over people who'd never learned to think like true predators. The flaming arrow that had ignited their tent represented not just an attack on their operation but a message about the futility of trying to cage something that had learned to live in the spaces between civilization's rules.

He'd been tempted to notch another arrow into the compound bow he'd acquired through theft from a sporting goods store two counties away, to send additional projectiles into the cluster of officers who were working frantically to prevent their controlled burn from becoming a forest fire. But discretion had proven more valuable than immediate gratification, and he'd contented himself with watching them scurry like ants whose hill had been kicked by a cruel child.

The radio he'd used to broadcast the recording of his first victim's final moments represented another trophy from his growing collection.

The recording itself was one of several he'd made during his attacks, carefully preserved on multiple devices to serve as both entertainment during lonely nights and ammunition for warfare against people who thought they could track him. The woman's pleas for mercy provided a soundtrack that helped him sleep, her voice joining the chorus of victims who would never escape the dark spaces where he kept their final moments.

He slid the radio back into his waterproof gear bag and prepared to withdraw from his observation post before the expanded law enforcement response could threaten his escape route. The kayak would carry him back to the hidden dock where he'd transfer to a stolen pickup truck for the overland journey to whatever temporary shelter he'd chosen for the remainder of the night.

But first, he allowed himself another few minutes to savor the sight of Sheriff Callahan's frustration as she examined the arrow and note he'd left for her to find. Even from his concealed position fifty yards away, he could read the tension in her body language, could see how it ate away at the professional confidence that had made her such an attractive target.

The campfire popped again with a sound like distant gunfire, and he watched her jerk involuntarily at the unexpected noise. Soon, she would make the decision that he'd been working to provoke since the beginning of their deadly game. Soon, she would face him alone, without backup or sophisticated equipment or the comfortable illusion that civilization's rules could protect her from something that had learned to hunt in the darkness between human settlements.

When that moment came, he would be ready to complete the ritual that had been building since the night an eight-year-old boy had learned that sometimes the only way to stop being a victim was to become something that victims feared more than their original tormentors.

~

Shea's voice crackled over the radio with the sharp authority of someone whose patience with failed tactics had reached its breaking point. "Unit six, begin immediate sweep of the waterline. I want patrol boats in the water within five minutes, and I want every dock, boat slip, and potential hiding place checked thoroughly."

The response was immediate as officers who'd been positioned around the lake's perimeter moved to execute a comprehensive search of areas that should have been secured during the initial phase of their operation. Boat engines roared to life in the distance, their sounds echoing off the water.

"He came in from the water," Trevor muttered. "We focused all our surveillance on the forest approaches and never considered that he might use watercraft to reach the target area."

Shea handed him the note she'd retrieved from the embedded arrow. "He's conducting a master class in how to dismantle law enforcement operations while making the people involved look like incompetent amateurs."

Once the lake had been declared clear by patrol boats equipped with searchlights, the volunteer fire crew packed their equipment with the efficient movements of people who'd responded to enough emergencies to recognize when their services were no longer needed. Across the dark water, a loon's cry drifted through the night air with the mournful quality that made the sound both beautiful and unsettling in the context of their failed operation.

Shea stared at the lake's black surface. He was out

there somewhere, probably watching their cleanup efforts and taking satisfaction from another successful demonstration of his ability to strike at law enforcement targets without suffering meaningful retaliation.

"We almost had him tonight," Trevor said, though his tone suggested he was trying to convince himself as much as reassure his partner about their chances of eventual success.

"No. He had us from the moment we started planning this operation. We walked into his trap thinking we were setting one for him."

She turned away from the water and headed back toward their patrol car. This failure felt different from the usual setbacks that marked any complex investigation. It represented a fundamental misunderstanding of their adversary's capabilities and motivations.

It was nearly two o'clock in the morning by the time they returned to the sheriff's office, the building quiet except for the night shift dispatcher and the eternal hum of fluorescent lights that never slept. Shea tossed her jacket over the back of her desk chair and placed the evidence bag containing Tommy's latest note in the growing collection of taunts and threats that documented his campaign against law enforcement.

Trevor joined her a few minutes later, carrying two steaming cups of coffee from the break room. "Thought you could use this," he said, handing her one of the cups while noting the exhaustion that was beginning to show through her professional composure.

She accepted the coffee with a small nod of thanks, then carried her cup into the conference room. The photographs of victims stared down at them with the accusing eyes of people who'd died while law enforcement chased shadows and processed evidence that led nowhere.

Trevor settled into one of the chairs with a weary sigh that spoke to the accumulated stress of weeks spent hunting someone. "The reeds along the shoreline are tall enough to conceal someone in a kayak. He would have had to position himself close enough to the target area to ensure accuracy with his archery, which means he was probably within fifty yards of our perimeter during the entire operation."

His expression darkened. "He's getting to you, isn't he? The psychological pressure, the constant threats, the feeling that he's always one step ahead...you can't let him into your head, Shea."

"He's getting to all of us." She locked gazes with Trevor's concerned expression. "Every failed operation, every successful attack, every demonstration that he can strike at our people without consequences—it's all part of a larger strategy to make us doubt our abilities and second-guess our decisions."

Trevor leaned forward. "I'm not going to let him hurt you."

"That might be a promise you can't keep." The knowledge that Tommy had already demonstrated his willingness to target law enforcement personnel turned every personal relationship into a potential weapon that could be used against them.

It was cases like this one, investigations where the killer might target people she cared about as part of his psychological warfare, that had motivated her decision to keep emotional distance from colleagues and maintain the kind of professional isolation that protected others from becoming collateral damage in her war against human predators.

The choice to accept a sheriff's position in a small mountain town had been partially motivated by her desire to stay far away from college friends and family members who might become targets.

Like he so often seemed to do, Trevor read her thoughts. "He won't get to me. We've come through bad situations before, Shea. We always get our suspect in the end, one way or another."

Yes, they'd always succeeded before. But there was always a first time for failure, and the stakes of this case were too high to allow for the kind of learning experience that might cost innocent lives or destroy the careers of good officers who'd made tactical errors while facing an unprecedented threat.

As they sat in the conference room surrounded by evidence of their failure to stop a predator who'd been terrorizing their community for weeks, Shea found herself wondering whether their luck was finally running out, and whether Tommy LaCrosse would prove to be the case that ended their winning streak in the most permanent way possible.

Chapter Sixteen

The neighborhood garage sale in the quiet residential community where the LaCrosse brothers had spent their final months together before the system separated them beckoned to Shea. She cut a quick glance toward where Trevor questioned a former neighbor about memories of two traumatized boys who'd arrived at their foster placement already damaged by experiences that would shape the rest of their lives.

The sale sprawled across the front yard of a modest ranch house that had seen better decades, its collection of mismatched items creating the kind of archaeological display that spoke to multiple generations of accumulated possessions being purged by people who'd grown tired of storing memories that belonged to other families. Shea rummaged through the odd assortment of household goods, children's toys, and forgotten keepsakes that all looked as if they'd been through at least three previous owners before landing on this particular lawn.

She wasn't searching for anything specific, but the mindless task of examining other people's discarded belongings helped her process the information that had been whirling through her brain. Sometimes the best insights came when the conscious mind was occupied with routine activities that allowed the subconscious to make connections that might otherwise remain hidden.

Her attention was caught by something wedged between a pile of old board games with torn boxes and a stack of water-warped paperback novels that had been rescued from some basement flood. A cracked wooden frame contained what appeared to be a child's drawing, the kind of artwork that elementary school teachers displayed on classroom walls to encourage creative expression in their young students.

The paper had yellowed with age and exposure to sunlight, but the image remained clearly visible despite the passage of years. Drawn in thick crayon lines with the clumsy precision that marked childhood artwork was a man wearing a long red cloak, his head turned slightly to reveal a profile that seemed both familiar and deeply unsettling.

Fire curled behind the cloaked figure in jagged orange arcs that suggested violence rather than warmth, while smoke or steam rose in angry spirals that filled the upper portion of the drawing with chaotic energy. But it was the man's features that made Shea's skin crawl with recognition—black circles for eyes that seemed to stare directly at the viewer, and hands that were drawn too large and too claw-like to belong to any normal human being.

She flipped the frame over with trembling fingers and found what she'd been hoping to discover written on the backing in faded pencil: "Tommy, Age 8." Below that, in different handwriting that probably belonged to a teacher or social worker, was an address that she recognized as belonging to the Henson family, the last foster placement that Tommy had lived in.

The discovery sent chills racing down her spine as she realized she was holding a window into Tommy's psychological state during the crucial period when his traumatic experiences would eventually drive him to become a serial killer. This picture had once meant something significant to a frightened eight-year-old boy who was trying to process experiences that no child should ever have to endure.

"What can you tell me about this drawing?" she asked the middle-aged woman who was managing the garage sale from a folding chair positioned near the cash box.

The woman shrugged. "Not much to tell, really. I found it on a shelf in my aunt's garage when I was cleaning out her stuff after she moved. She fostered a lot of kids over the years and never threw anything away—kept boxes and boxes of their school projects and artwork like she was running some kind of museum."

Shea's pulse quickened. "Where is your aunt now? Would it be possible to speak with her about the children she cared for?"

"She moved to Oklahoma about two years ago to live with my cousin's family," the woman replied, consulting a small address book she pulled from her purse. "I can give you her contact information if you think it might be helpful, though I should warn you that her memory isn't what it used to be."

Shea thanked the woman, paid a dollar for the framed drawing, and headed to where Trevor was concluding his interview with the elderly neighbor who'd watched the

LaCrosse brothers during their turbulent stay with the Henson family.

"Found something interesting." She showed him the drawing while explaining the circumstances of its discovery. "The address on the back matches our records for Tommy's last foster placement. This picture was created during the period when his behavioral problems were becoming severe enough to require removal from family-based care."

Trevor studied the image. "The red cloak, the fire imagery, the demonic facial features…this isn't the kind of artwork that normal eight-year-old children produce. This is someone trying to make sense of violence and fear."

The address was only two streets away from their current location, close enough to walk if they'd wanted to stretch their legs but far enough to justify driving given the investigative urgency that had been building throughout their visit to Tommy's childhood neighborhood. "Let's take a look at the foster home." Shea was already moving toward their patrol car while her mind raced through possibilities about what they might discover.

The house that had once provided temporary shelter for two traumatized boys stood empty and abandoned, its appearance suggesting that no one had lived there for months or possibly years. Paint peeled from the siding in long strips that fluttered in the mountain breeze, while the front porch sagged under the weight of structural damage that had never been repaired.

No smoke rose from the crooked chimney that dominated the roofline, and several windows were covered with plywood sheets that had been nailed in place to prevent vandalism or unauthorized entry. The overall effect was of a house that had died along with whatever family warmth it had once contained.

But it was the smell that hit them as soon as they approached the front door—a sweet, cloying odor that Shea had learned to recognize with sickening certainty. The metallic tang of decomposing blood mixed with other biological processes marked the presence of death in an enclosed space.

Shea withdrew her service weapon before pushing open the front door, which hung slightly ajar despite the abandoned appearance of the property. The hinges groaned with the sound of metal that hadn't been oiled in years, and stale air rushed out to greet them along with intensified traces of the smell that had drawn their attention from outside.

"Someone's been here recently." Trevor pointed out fresh footprints in the dust that covered the entryway floor. "Multiple sets of tracks, including what looks like evidence that heavy objects were dragged across the threshold."

They followed the stench through a hallway lined with family photographs that had been left behind when the house was abandoned, their frames now coated with dus. The smell grew stronger as they approached the living room, where the source of their growing dread waited to be discovered.

Two shapes lay beneath mismatched quilts on a sagging sofa. Flies buzzed lazily in the warm air that circulated through broken windows, their presence confirming what Shea's experience had already told her about the condition of whatever lay beneath those covering fabrics.

She pulled back the first quilt. An elderly woman lay beneath the fabric, her face waxy and sunken in the way that marked several days of decomposition in a warm environment.

The second quilt covered an elderly man in a similar state of decay, though his remains showed additional evidence of violence in the form of bruising along his jawline that suggested he'd been struck with considerable force before his death. Both bodies were positioned with a care that spoke to deliberate arrangement rather than the casual disposal that characterized most murders.

"I think we found Tommy's former foster parents," Shea said.

Trevor cleared his throat and moved closer to examine the bodies without disturbing the crime scene more than necessary for their preliminary assessment. "They've been here for several days, based on the decomposition and insect activity. But these people were supposed to be living in Oklahoma, according to our background research."

"Looks like Tommy brought them back here. This wasn't a random attack. It was something he'd been thinking about for a long time."

She called the county crime scene team while backing out of the house as quickly as professional procedures would allow, her mind already racing through the implications of discovering that Tommy had escalated from killing strangers to targeting people from his past .

The question that bothered her most was why Tommy would choose to kill the Henson couple, who, according to his foster care records, had been among the few adults who'd shown him genuine kindness during his chaotic childhood. Their treatment notes described them as patient and understanding caregivers who'd worked hard to help both LaCrosse brothers adjust to family life despite their behavioral problems.

That evening, after spending hours coordinating with crime scene technicians and federal agents who were analyzing the latest escalation in Tommy's pattern of violence, Shea made a decision that went against every protocol and safety procedure that governed law enforcement operations during active manhunts.

She slowly opened her bedroom window, taking care not to make any sound that might alert Trevor to her intentions, and whispered for Heidi to stay behind and watch over her partner. The German Shepherd whined softly, her canine instincts apparently sensing that something was wrong with this departure from normal routine, but she obeyed the command and settled into position where she could monitor Trevor's safety.

Shea slipped into the night with the stealth of someone who'd learned to move quietly during years of tactical operations, her heart hammering against her ribs as she drove through dark mountain roads toward a secluded lakeside clearing that offered the perfect combination of isolation and visibility for what she had planned.

She parked her personal vehicle in a concealed position and began setting up the most dangerous trap she'd ever constructed. One that used herself as bait.

A single-person tent was erected in the center of the clearing, positioned to be visible from multiple approach routes while offering minimal cover for anyone who might be watching from the surrounding forest. She placed a bright red camping cooler outside the tent entrance as ba beacon for someone whose damaged psyche had been conditioned to respond to that particular stimulus.

A battery-powered lantern provided just enough illumination inside the tent to cast her silhouette against the nylon walls, creating the illusion of a vulnerable camper settling in for the night without any awareness of the predator who'd been stalking law enforcement personnel for weeks.

Under her dark clothing, she wore a bulletproof vest that would provide some protection against knife attacks but wouldn't be sufficient if Tommy had acquired firearms during his escalating campaign of violence. Her service weapon was positioned within easy reach, while a backup knife was strapped to her lower leg.

She was as ready as anyone could be for a confrontation that would likely determine whether Tommy LaCrosse continued his killing spree or finally paid the price for terrorizing innocent people who'd made the mistake of camping with red equipment in his hunting territory.

The waiting was the hardest part, sitting in artificial light while her nervous system remained hyperalert for any sound or movement that might indicate an approaching threat. Every rustle of leaves in the mountain breeze could be footsteps, every crack of settling wood could be someone moving through the forest with homicidal intent.

The first sound was almost nothing—just the slow, deliberate press of a boot into pine needles, so quiet that it might have been imagined by someone whose imagination had been primed by weeks of hunting an invisible predator. But then came movement, the shift of shadows that spoke to human presence rather than wildlife, followed by the rush of a figure charging toward her position with the kind of violent intent that made survival instincts scream warnings.

The tent flap burst inward with explosive force as Tommy launched himself into what he believed was a space containing a helpless victim, his blade already raised and aimed for what should have been a killing strike to her chest. The lantern light caught the steel of his weapon.

Shea rolled sideways with reflexes honed by countless hours of tactical training, drawing her knife as the attacker's momentum carried him past her original position. His blade caught nothing but nylon tent floor, the fabric parting with a whisper that spoke to the sharpness of whatever weapon he'd chosen for this assault.

She drove upward with her shoulder aimed at his midsection, feeling the solid wall of muscle and bone. The tent filled with the sounds of their struggle—ragged breathing, the creak of stressed fabric, and the scuff of boots fighting for purchase on ground that had been turned treacherous by their violent dance.

Tommy slammed her against the side of the tent with enough force to bow the aluminum support poles, the frame threatening to collapse under the impact of two adult bodies fighting for their lives. His knife arced toward her again, this time aimed low where her vest wouldn't provide protection against a blade seeking soft tissue and vital organs.

She trapped his wrist with both hands and twisted with the kind of leverage that martial arts training had taught her to use when facing stronger opponents, feeling the tendons in his forearm shift under her fingers as bones and joints were stressed beyond their normal range of motion. The technique should have been enough to disarm most attackers, but Tommy's grip remained firm despite what must have been considerable pain.

His free hand came up toward her face, fingers spread to claw at her eyes or crush her windpipe, and she was forced to release his weapon hand to defend against the new threat. Her head snapped back under the impact of his palm strike, stars exploding across her vision as her brain processed the blow.

Instead of fighting against his momentum, she went limp and allowed his forward motion to carry him past her defensive position. Kicking out with all the force she could muster, she caught him behind the knee in a strike that targeted the joint most vulnerable to lateral pressure.

He stumbled forward, his balance compromised by the unexpected attack, giving her time to pull the backup knife that was strapped to her ankle. Without hesitation, she drove the blade upward into the space between his ribs.

The knife went in, but not deep enough to cause the kind of immediately incapacitating damage that would end their fight. The choked sound he made told her that she'd done some meaningful damage. Still, experience had taught her that wounded predators were often more dangerous than healthy ones because pain could override the self-preservation instincts that normally limited human violence.

Tommy stumbled backward, his hood slipping enough to reveal features that had been scarred by fire. His eyes still held the flat emptiness that marked someone whose capacity for normal human emotion had been burned away along with his childhood innocence.

"Hello, Tommy."

Surprise registered on his scarred features, quickly replaced by a smile that held no warmth or humor—just the predatory satisfaction of someone who'd found exactly what he'd been looking for. Before she could attempt another knife strike, he withdrew from the tent and melted back into the forest darkness, his laughter echoing off the surrounding mountains.

She didn't lower her weapon until she'd reached her patrol car, her nervous system still flooded with adrenaline. The sight of Trevor's vehicle parked nearby allowed her to exhale fully for the first time since Tommy had burst into her improvised trap.

"Shea." Trevor closed the distance between them in three quick strides, his voice carrying the mixture of relief and anger that marked someone who'd discovered that a partner had taken unnecessary risks without backup or coordination. "You're bleeding."

"It's not my blood," she replied, noting the dark stains on her knife that confirmed she'd managed to wound their adversary despite his escape. "I got Tommy between the ribs, but he managed to get away before I could finish what we started."

Trevor's voice shook with the kind of fury that came from caring about someone who'd deliberately put themselves in mortal danger. "What possessed you to sneak out and face him alone? You could have been killed, and we never would have known what happened until we found your body."

"I'm fine." She climbed into her truck while her mind had already began processing the lessons learned from their first direct confrontation. "How did you know to come here?"

"Heidi woke me. I traced your phone." Trevor's expression suggested that he understood exactly how the dog's behavior had alerted him to Shea's unauthorized departure. "Smart animal. She knew something was wrong when you left without taking her along."

Shea nodded, recognizing that part of her might have wanted Trevor to follow her despite the risks that his presence would create during a confrontation with someone who'd already proven his willingness to target law enforcement officers. Maybe she'd needed to know that backup was available, just in case something went wrong with her dangerous gamble.

The space between them seemed to narrow as unspoken words hung in the night air, filled with emotions that had no place during active investigations but couldn't be completely suppressed when facing the possibility of permanent loss. For a moment, she thought he might say something about the feelings that had been building between them.

Instead, Trevor took a deep breath and stepped back. "Let's get you home." His voice carried resigned acceptance of her methods even as his protective instincts rebelled against the risks she'd taken. "I'd tell you not to do something like this again, but we both know you're probably the only person who can stop LaCrosse before he kills more innocent people. I'll follow your lead without complaint. Just don't die on me."

~

Clever girl. Tommy's breath came in wet rasps while he stumbled through the forest darkness, one arm pressed tightly against his side where Sheriff Callahan's blade had slipped between his ribs. Every step sent sharp, hot pulses of pain through his torso, but the sensation was something he both hated and savored because it proved that their game had finally escalated to the level of personal violence he'd been craving.

When he reached a shallow ravine where a seasonal creek had carved a depression in the mountainside, he stopped and leaned against the smooth bark of a paper birch tree, gasping for air. At the same time, his damaged lung tried to process oxygen despite whatever internal bleeding might be complicating his respiratory function.

She'd seen him—actually looked directly into his scarred face without flinching at the disfigurement that had marked him since childhood. The lantern light had caught the edges of his burn scars and revealed features that most people found disturbing, but Sheriff Callahan hadn't shown the instinctive revulsion that he'd learned to expect from normal humans who'd never been forced to look at the aftermath of violence.

Instead, she'd tried to kill him with the same clinical efficiency that he used when dispatching his own victims, driving her knife toward vital organs. The realization that she was capable of matching his own capacity for violence filled him with something that might have been respect if he'd retained the ability to feel normal human emotions.

It was no longer about the color red or childhood trauma or even the ritualistic aspects of violence that had initially motivated his killing spree. Now it was about her. The one person who'd proven capable of seeing him clearly and responding with appropriate force rather than the hesitation and moral qualms that had protected him during previous encounters with law enforcement.

He waited for the tremors to stop, then used his knife to cut a strip from his shirt tail, fashioning a crude bandage that would help control the bleeding until he could reach whatever medical supplies he'd accumulated in his various hiding places. The makeshift dressing wouldn't provide professional-quality treatment, but it would keep him functional long enough to plan the final phase of their deadly game.

In his mind, he replayed the moment when her blade had penetrated his defenses, the sound of surprise that had escaped her lips when she'd realized that her strike had found its target. But it wasn't fear he'd seen in her eyes during those crucial seconds. It was the heat of someone who'd finally found a worthy opponent and was prepared to fight to the death rather than submit to becoming another victim.

Good. She understood now that their confrontation wouldn't end with arrests or trials or the comfortable illusion that civilization's rules could resolve conflicts between predators who'd learned to exist outside the boundaries of normal human society.

He'd call her tomorrow and tell her where their final meeting would take place. It was time to end their extended dance of hunter and hunted. Time to discover which of them possessed the stronger will to survive when all tactical advantages and professional procedures had been stripped away.

The game that had begun with camping flags and psychological warfare would conclude with fire and blood and the kind of violence that marked the end of one story and the beginning of another, darker tale that would be told around campfires for generations to come.

Chapter Seventeen

It was nearly midnight when Shea's phone buzzed with the insistent vibration that cut through the silence of the sheriff's office like an electric shock. She'd managed to convince Trevor to take a much-needed nap in the break room after hours of continuous work, his exhausted form stretched across the worn couch where countless officers had grabbed moments of rest during long investigations. The building settled around them with the familiar creaks and sighs of aging timber, while outside the mountain wind carried the promise of another autumn storm.

She almost ignored the call, her attention focused on the stack of incident reports and evidence summaries that represented the aftermath of weeks spent hunting a killer who'd terrorized their community. Every muscle in her body ached from the previous night's confrontation, and nothing sounded more appealing than finishing her paperwork and finding a few hours of uninterrupted sleep before the federal agents arrived for their morning briefing.

But the possibility that someone might need emergency assistance overrode her personal exhaustion, and she reached for the phone with the weary resignation of someone whose job never truly ended. "Sheriff Callahan."

"You've been waving your little flag, Sheriff." Tommy's voice came through the speaker with the conversational tone of someone discussing the weather rather than murder. "I see you out there, trying so hard to catch me. Do you see me yet?"

Her chest tightened as she recognized the predatory satisfaction in his voice, the sound of someone who'd been watching and planning while she thought she was hunting him. "I see you, Tommy." She kept her voice steady despite the adrenaline that was already flooding her system.

"You can't stop what's already burned," he continued. "I've told you this before, but you haven't been listening carefully enough."

The line filled with static, then resolved into the horrific recording that had haunted her dreams since the investigation began. The final moments of his first victim, her voice growing weaker as she begged for a mercy that would never come. The audio played for thirty seconds that felt like hours, each whispered plea serving as a reminder of everyone they hadn't been able to save.

When the recording ended, Tommy's voice returned with directions to an abandoned boathouse on the north shore of Misty Lake, a location that had been closed to public access for years due to structural damage but would provide the privacy he required for their final meeting.

"Come alone," he said, though his tone suggested he already knew she would ignore that instruction. "It's time to finish what we started."

The line went dead. She grabbed her service weapon and quickly scribbled a note for Trevor, explaining where she was going and requesting backup despite Tommy's demand for a solo confrontation. Whatever happened at the boathouse, she wanted someone to know where to look for her body if things went wrong.

The drive through winding mountain roads felt like a journey into some other dimension where normal rules didn't apply and violence could erupt without warning. Heavy clouds hung over the peaks like a gray shroud, promising another seasonal storm that would wash away evidence and complicate whatever crime scene might result from their encounter.

Nothing moved in the darkness except the faint ripple of lake water disturbed by night breezes as Shea approached the abandoned boathouse through overgrown trails that hadn't seen maintenance in years. The structure loomed against the sky like a skeletal reminder of better times when families had used this location for peaceful recreation rather than as a battleground between predator and prey.

She barely registered the crunch of branches breaking under heavy footsteps before Tommy crashed into her from the side with the explosive violence of a wild animal that had been waiting in ambush. The impact drove the breath from her lungs and sent her tumbling across ground that was still soft from recent rains, her flashlight spinning away into tall grass where its beam created crazy patterns of light and shadow.

Tommy moved with the feral speed of someone whose survival had depended on violence since childhood, his knife already raised and reflecting moonlight that turned the steel blade into a slice of captured fire. She rolled to avoid the downward strike, feeling the tip of his weapon graze her ribs and tear through fabric that provided no protection against sharpened metal.

Pain exploded along her left arm as the blade sliced through her sleeve and opened a gash that began bleeding, the warm flow serving as a reminder that she was only one mistake away from joining the growing list of Tommy's victims. The wound wasn't deep enough to be immediately incapacitating, but blood loss would become a factor if their fight continued much longer.

"Not like this," she gritted through clenched teeth, twisting her body and shoving upward with every ounce of strength she could muster from muscles that were already beginning to fatigue under the stress of life-or-death combat.

They tumbled together across wet soil that made footing treacherous and turned their struggle into a desperate scramble for position and advantage. Their bodies slid toward the lake's edge where murky water waited to claim whoever lost the battle being fought just yards from its shores.

Tommy might have been stronger, but his movements were increasingly fueled by frenzy rather than tactical thinking. Shea was smarter, more disciplined, and she drove her elbow into his ribs with enough force to produce a satisfying crack that suggested damage to bone or cartilage.

Tommy growled like an injured animal and shoved her face into mud that filled her mouth and nose with the taste of decomposing vegetation and mineral-rich earth. Her chest seized as panic clawed at her lungs, and for a terrifying moment, she was transported back to childhood asthma attacks that had left her gasping for air while her body betrayed its most basic function.

But she'd survived worse situations than this, had learned to control panic responses that could prove fatal during violent encounters. Jerking her head sideways, she managed to take in a huge, gasping breath that filled her lungs with precious oxygen, then bit down on Tommy's wrist with enough force to draw blood and elicit a howl of pain and surprise.

He loosened his grip enough for her to scramble free and regain some advantage, but the respite was temporary as he lunged again with his knife gleaming in the pale moonlight. She grabbed his weapon arm, muscles straining against his superior strength, while their faces came within inches of each other.

His eyes burned with the madness that had been building since childhood, but beneath the surface fury, she could see something else—the terror of a frightened boy who'd never learned healthy ways to process trauma and fear. For just a moment, looking into those damaged eyes, she almost pitied him for what his father's cruelty had created.

That split second of hesitation cost her the advantage she'd been fighting to maintain. Tommy twisted with desperate strength, forcing the knife closer toward her chest while her arms quaked under pressure that threatened to overwhelm her ability to resist. The steel blade inched steadily closer to vital organs as her muscles began to fail under the sustained effort.

"Shea!" Trevor's distant voice ripped through the

night air like a lifeline thrown to someone who was drowning in violence, and she felt a surge of hope mixed with terror at the knowledge that someone she cared about was approaching a situation that could easily claim multiple lives.

"He's next," Tommy whispered with a smile that held no warmth or sanity. His words confirmed her worst fears about his intentions toward anyone who tried to interfere with their deadly game.

The threat to Trevor triggered something primal in Shea, a protective instinct that gave her access to reserves of strength she hadn't known she possessed. Locking her jaw with determination that went beyond mere survival, she summoned everything she had left. She shifted her weight in a movement that years of combat training had burned into her muscle memory.

With a raw cry that came from the deepest parts of her being, she pivoted her hips. She redirected the knife's trajectory, turning Tommy's momentum against him as the blade that had been intended for her heart found its way into his torso instead.

The steel sank deep between his ribs, penetrating tissue and organs with the wet sound of metal parting flesh. His body stiffened as his nervous system processed the catastrophic damage, and for a moment, the fury disappeared from his eyes to be replaced by a look of almost relief.

He stared at her with lips that trembled from shock and blood loss, and when he spoke again, his voice carried the innocent quality of the child he'd been before fire and violence had twisted him into something monstrous. "It's still burning," he whispered, his words barely audible above the gentle lapping of lake water against the shore.

Blood spilled across Shea's hands as Tommy's grip on his weapon finally loosened, and he collapsed backward into the shallow water, where gentle waves began carrying away the evidence of their struggle. Threads of crimson spread across the surface like scarlet ribbons, creating abstract patterns that would dissolve and disappear long before crime scene technicians arrived to document what had taken place.

She fell to her knees in mud and blood that smeared across her uniform, her heart hammering against her ribs with the irregular rhythm that marked the aftermath of extreme physical stress. For just a moment, looking down at Tommy's still form, she felt genuine grief for the frightened boy he'd been before trauma had transformed him into the predator who'd terrorized their community.

It was over. The killing spree that had claimed multiple innocent lives and pushed law enforcement to their limits had finally ended in the shallows of the same lake where it had begun. But the victory felt hollow, tainted by the knowledge of what childhood abuse could do to developing minds and the recognition that some forms of damage couldn't be repaired through conventional means.

She fell back onto the wet ground near the lake's shore as Trevor emerged from the tree line, his face reflecting the mixture of relief and horror that marked someone who'd arrived just moments too late to prevent violence but in time to witness its aftermath.

~

Trevor's heart nearly stopped at the sight of Shea

lying motionless on the muddy ground, her uniform dark with blood that could have been hers or Tommy's or both. Ten feet away, the killer's body lay sprawled in the shallow water where gentle waves were already beginning to wash away the evidence of their final confrontation.

For several seconds that felt like hours, he couldn't force his body to move, couldn't process the scene before him or determine whether the woman he loved was alive or dead. Relief and horror collided in his chest as he saw her stir, saw her eyes track his movement as he approached with the careful steps of someone who feared that sudden movements might shatter whatever fragile reality had allowed her to survive.

He dropped to his knees beside her and grabbed her arm, half afraid she might disappear if he didn't maintain physical contact that proved she was real and alive and still breathing despite the violence that had nearly claimed her life. "Tell me you're okay," he said, his voice hoarse with emotions he hadn't known he was capable of feeling. "Please, Shea, tell me you're going to be all right."

She managed a small nod, but her eyes remained fixed on Tommy's body with the glassy stare of someone who couldn't quite believe that the nightmare was finally over. Blood loss and adrenaline crash were making her movements sluggish, while emotional shock began to set in as her mind tried to process what she'd been forced to do.

Rage bubbled up inside Trevor. Not just at the killer who'd forced this confrontation, but at himself for not being there when she'd needed him most. He'd been sleeping while she faced death alone, had failed in his most basic duty to protect someone whose safety mattered more to him than his own life.

He pulled her into his arms with more force than was probably appropriate, holding her against his chest while blood from her wounds soaked into his clothing. His throat burned with words he wanted to say, emotions he needed to express, but he didn't trust his voice to remain steady enough for coherent speech.

Instead, he pressed his forehead against hers in a gesture that grounded them both in the present moment. In her trembling, he felt the strength that had carried her through the worst kind of violence. In her silence, he heard the unspoken truth that they would face whatever came next together.

As backup sirens echoed faintly across the woods, growing steadily louder as other officers responded to the emergency call he'd placed while running through the forest, Trevor tightened his grip on her hand and spoke the words that had been building in his chest since the moment he'd realized she was in danger.

"It's over, sweetheart," he said, his voice carrying all the love and relief and protective fury that he'd been suppressing during weeks of professional investigation. "The nightmare is finished, and you're safe now."

He rocked her gently in his arms until the paramedics arrived with their equipment and professional efficiency, but even then, he didn't let go of her hand, couldn't bring himself to break the physical connection that proved she was alive and whole and still fighting despite everything Tommy LaCrosse had put her through.

The killing was over, but their story would continue.

Dear Reader,

Thank you for reading Banner of Death. If you enjoyed the latest installment of Shea and Trevor's story, please leave a review or rating on Amazon. They mean so much to an author.

God Bless.
Cynthia

www.cynthiahickey.com

Cynthia Hickey is a multi-published and best-selling author of cozy mysteries and romantic suspense/thrillers. She has taught writing at many conferences and small writing retreats. She and her husband run the publishing press, Winged Publications. They live in Arizona and Arkansas, becoming snowbirds with three dogs. They have ten grandchildren who keep them busy and tell everyone they know that "Nana is a writer."

Connect with me on FaceBook
Twitter
Sign up for my newsletter and receive a free short story
www.cynthiahickey.com

Follow me on Amazon
And Bookbub

Shop my bookstore on my website for better prices and autographed books.

Enjoy other books by Cynthia Hickey

The Sheriff of Misty Hollow
<u>Girls' Weekend Survival</u>
<u>The Threat</u>
<u>Evil Returns</u>
<u>Drowned in Silence</u>

Cowboys of Misty Hollow
<u>Cowboy Jeopardy</u>
<u>Cowboy Peril</u>
<u>Cowboy Hazard</u>
<u>Cowgirl Blaze</u>
<u>Cowboy Uncertainty</u>
<u>Cowboy Christmas Crisis</u>
<u>Cowboy Pitfall</u>

Misty Hollow
<u>Secrets of Misty Hollow</u>
<u>Deceptive Peace</u>
<u>Calm Surface</u>
<u>Lightning Never Strikes Twice</u>
<u>Lethal Inheritance</u>
<u>Bitter Isolation</u>

<u>Say I Don't</u>
<u>Christmas Stalker</u>
<u>Bridge to Safety</u>
<u>When Night Falls</u>
<u>A Place to Hide</u>
<u>Mountain Refuge</u>

Stay in Misty Hollow for a while. Get the entire series <u>here</u>!

The Seven Deadly Sins series
<u>Deadly Pride</u>
<u>Deadly Covet</u>
<u>Deadly Lust</u>
<u>Deadly Glutton</u>
<u>Deadly Envy</u>
<u>Deadly Sloth</u>
<u>Deadly Anger</u>

The Tail Waggin' Mysteries
<u>Cat-Eyed Witness</u>
<u>The Dog Who Found a Body</u>
<u>Troublesome Twosome</u>
<u>Four-Legged Suspect</u>
<u>Unwanted Christmas Guest</u>
<u>Wedding Day Cat Burglar</u>

Brothers Steele
<u>Sharp as Steele</u>

<u>Carved in Steele</u>
<u>Forged in Steele</u>
<u>Brothers Steele</u> (All three in one)

The Brothers of Copper Pass
<u>Wyatt's Warrant</u>
<u>Dirk's Defense</u>
<u>Stetson's Secret</u>
<u>Houston's Hope</u>
<u>Dallas's Dare</u>
<u>Seth's Sacrifice</u>
<u>Malcolm's Misunderstanding</u>
<u>The Brothers of Copper Pass Boxed Set</u>

Time Travel
<u>The Portal</u>

Tiny House Mysteries
<u>No Small Caper</u>
<u>Caper Goes Missing</u>
<u>Caper Finds a Clue</u>
<u>Caper's Dark Adventure</u>
<u>A Strange Game for Caper</u>
<u>Caper Steals Christmas</u>
<u>Caper Finds a Treasure</u>
<u>Tiny House Mysteries boxed set</u>

Wife for Hire – Private Investigators

<u>Saving Sarah</u>
<u>Lesson for Lacey</u>
<u>Mission for Meghan</u>
<u>Long Way for Lainie</u>
<u>Aimed at Amy</u>
<u>Wife for Hire</u> (all five in one)

A Hollywood Murder
<u>Killer Pose, book 1</u>
<u>Killer Snapshot, book 2</u>
<u>Shoot to Kill, book 3</u>
<u>Kodak Kill Shot, book 4</u>
<u>To Snap a Killer</u>
<u>Hollywood Murder Mysteries</u>

Shady Acres Mysteries
<u>Beware the Orchids, book 1</u>
<u>Path to Nowhere</u>
<u>Poison Foliage</u>
<u>Poinsettia Madness</u>
<u>Deadly Greenhouse Gases</u>
<u>Vine Entrapment</u>
<u>Shady Acres Boxed Set</u>

CLEAN BUT GRITTY Romantic Suspense

Highland Springs

<u>Murder Live</u>

<u>Say Bye to Mommy</u>
<u>To Breathe Again</u>
<u>Highland Springs Murders</u> (all 3 in one)

Colors of Evil Series

<u>Shades of Crimson</u>
<u>Coral Shadows</u>

The Pretty Must Die Series

<u>Ripped in Red, book 1</u>
<u>Pierced in Pink, book 2</u>
<u>Wounded in White, book 3</u>
<u>Worthy, The Complete Story</u>

Lisa Paxton Mystery Series

<u>Eenie Meenie Miny Mo</u>
<u>Jack Be Nimble</u>
<u>Hickory Dickory Dock</u>
<u>Boxed Set</u>

Hearts of Courage
<u>A Heart of Valor</u>
<u>The Game</u>
<u>Suspicious Minds</u>
<u>After the Storm</u>
<u>Local Betrayal</u>

<u>Hearts of Courage Boxed Set</u>

<u>Overcoming Evil series</u>
<u>Mistaken Assassin</u>
<u>Captured Innocence</u>
<u>Mountain of Fear</u>
<u>Exposure at Sea</u>
<u>A Secret to Die for</u>
<u>Collision Course</u>
<u>Romantic Suspense of 5 books in 1</u>

INSPIRATIONAL

Nosy Neighbor Series
<u>Anything For A Mystery</u>, Book 1
<u>A Killer Plot</u>, Book 2
<u>Skin Care Can Be Murder</u>, Book 3
<u>Death By Baking</u>, Book 4
<u>Jogging Is Bad For Your Health</u>, Book 5
<u>Poison Bubbles</u>, Book 6
<u>A Good Party Can Kill You</u>, Book 7
<u>Nosy Neighbor collection</u>

<u>Christmas with Stormi Nelson</u>

The Summer Meadows Series
<u>Fudge-Laced Felonies</u>, Book 1
<u>Candy-Coated Secrets</u>, Book 2

Chocolate-Covered Crime, Book 3
Maui Macadamia Madness, Book 4
All four novels in one collection

The River Valley Mystery Series
Deadly Neighbors, Book 1
Advance Notice, Book 2
The Librarian's Last Chapter, Book 3
All three novels in one collection

Historical cozy
Hazel's Quest

Historical Romances
Runaway Sue
Taming the Sheriff
Sweet Apple Blossom
A Doctor's Agreement
A Lady Maid's Honor
A Touch of Sugar
Love Over Par
Heart of the Emerald
A Sketch of Gold
Her Lonely Heart

Finding Love the Harvey Girl Way
Cooking With Love

Guiding With Love
Serving With Love
Warring With Love
All 4 in 1

Finding Love in Disaster
The Rancher's Dilemma
The Teacher's Rescue
The Soldier's Redemption

Woman of courage Series

A Love For Delicious
Ruth's Redemption
Charity's Gold Rush
Mountain Redemption
They Call Her Mrs. Sheriff
Woman of Courage series

Short Story Westerns
Flowers of the Desert

Contemporary

Romance in Paradise
Maui Magic
Sunset Kisses
Deep Sea Love

<u>3 in 1</u>

<u>Finding a Way Home</u>
<u>Service of Love</u>
<u>Hillbilly Cinderella</u>
<u>Unraveling Love</u>
<u>I'd Rather Kiss My Horse</u>

Christmas
<u>Dear Jillian</u>
<u>Romancing the Fabulous Cooper Brothers</u>
<u>Handcarved Christmas</u>
<u>The Payback Bride</u>
<u>Curtain Calls and Christmas Wishes</u>
<u>Christmas Gold</u>
<u>A Christmas Stamp</u>
<u>Snowflake Kisses</u>
<u>Merry's Secret Santa</u>
<u>A Christmas Deception</u>

The Red Hat's Club (Contemporary novellas)

<u>Finally</u>
<u>Suddenly</u>
<u>Surprisingly</u>
<u>The</u> Red Hat's Club 3 – in 1

<u>Short Story</u>

<u>One Hour (A short story thriller)</u>
<u>Whisper Sweet Nothings (a Valentine short romance)</u>